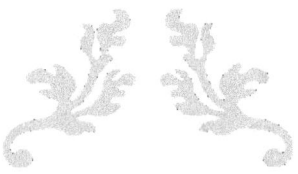

ANGUS

La Patron Series by Sydney Addae

Angus

Several years ago, Angus Blackwolf appeared at the site of a lab Silas, La Patron, was taking down. At the time Silas had no idea of the identity of the wolf watching from the shadows. That was then, fast forward several years later, as Beta to La Patron, Angus' commitment to his Alpha is absolute. So when he is sent out of the country with instructions to tell no one, not even Silas, Angus balks. It's only when he learns the fate of his mate is in his hands that he abides by the rules and walks away from everything he's come to love.

Thanks to all my Den-mates and admins, Michelle and Vicky, you are all the best at keeping me laughing with new creative ideas. I heart you much.

A special shout out to Vicky Z., Sally R., Karen M., and Kelly, I could not have presented this story without your help.

Thanks

Sydney

CHAPTER 1

Shyla Mason walked through her quiet dining room into the large oak paneled den. Opening the glass double doors, she looked out into the lush garden beyond and took a deep breath. Nature's finest bouquet teased and enchanted her. Stepping onto the colorfully paved patio, she wrapped her arms around her waist, threw her head back and hummed a song she'd heard earlier today in the mall. Cool air tickled her arms as she lifted them high in the air and twirled. The heavy fabric of her denim skirt curled around her legs when she stopped to lean against the tall column which separated the patio and gardens. As the automatic night lights brightened the foliage she glanced at the arch still in place from her friend, Vanessa's, wedding.

Sighing, she stepped off the covered porch. Her fingertips skimmed the green leaves as she moved toward the dais in the middle of the garden. A month ago, her co-worker and best friend, Vanessa had been a beautiful bride, her love for her mate plain for everyone to see. And Ethan. Shyla smiled in remembrance of his ridiculously large grin during the entire festivities.

Glad her friend had found love and was happy, Shyla wished, as she had so many times before, she had someone to share her life with. Over the past two centuries, she had been the "Mengistia" or keeper of secrets, a timekeeping group who served the Goddess. Duties were passed down through the females in her line. One day she'd prepare her daughter for the job. Looking around at the manicured garden and lawn, a sense of peace rested on her shoulders. This place always calmed her.

"Hopefully, one day soon, you'll welcome a new Mistress to these grounds. Treat her as graciously as you've treated me."

Smiling, she walked slowly into the house and picked up the employee contract from the new school principal. Should she return to the school the following semester? She'd been head librarian for many years, and had a lot of good times, but it wouldn't be the same without Vanessa. Maybe it was time to shake things up, do something different, take a trip, a cruise. She cringed at the idea of going alone. She tossed it on the table and headed to the kitchen.

Or she could travel the state, check out events in person rather than pull them offline for recording. It might be more fun, plus, she'd get to meet more people, maybe bump into her mate like Vanessa did. "Stop it," she muttered as she picked up her lone plate from dinner and washed it.

"Everything happens in its own time." She finished rinsing the glass and fork, and set them in the dish rack to dry. "You've been perfectly content, don't waste time on things you can't change." Content? Her mind battled with her flesh over the truth. She was a long way from content. How pathetic had she become that she'd memorized several platitudes to beat back the loneliness and give herself a pass for being alone?

"Shyla?"

Glad to change the direction of her thoughts, she smiled and took a seat in the den. *"Mom, how are you? It's been a while since we talked. How's dad? Where are you and papa this time? Still in Florida or have you moved on?"* She inhaled and waited. Her mom wasn't much for socializing or chit-chat, but she got an A for effort, hence the long stretches between conversations.

"It's worse than I thought."

Shyla frowned. *"Huh? What's worse?"* She had no idea what her mom was talking about.

"I knew when your best friend got married it would be hard for you, but I didn't think it would be this bad. I told Harvey it would be bad, but you know your father, he thinks you're the made of granite."

"Granite?" Shyla chuckled to hide the groan her mother's words caused. *"I'm not that bad."*

"No, you're not." Her mom paused. *"Are you okay? Do we need to cut our trip short and come spend time with you?"*

Shyla heard the grimace in her mom's voice and swallowed her laugh. No one would give Rosaria Mason the Mother of the Year award, the woman had little patience for frivolous things or feelings. She would return to the house she'd lived in for 200 years, but everyone, including Shyla, would be miserable.

"No, I'm good, but thank you for the offer. I know how you detest coming here." Shyla covered her mouth with her fingertips to keep back a giggle.

"Detest is a strong word but I guess it'll do. Being Mengistia is stifling work, you're stuck in that house, guarding secrets. I know you love the smell of old pages and books, I did too, at first. Now it just smells musky, bad, old."

"I get it. You detest the place." Shyla laughed, glad to hear her mom's voice. *"They're my friends, I know and trust them. Knowledge is power they say."* She'd always had a thirst for knowledge. The books and scrolls in this chamber fed that need and then some. She'd spend hours absorbing new languages, revisiting bygone eras, and taking glimpses into the lives of men and women. It was heaven.

"Get flesh and blood friends, share some knowledge, stop being cooped up in that house, it'll suffocate you."

Shyla looked at the tall paneled walls and architectural details from centuries ago and smiled. *"I have a job. I don't stay in the house all the time. Why not agree to disagree?"* It was best to stop her mom before she got all steamed up and invited her to spend time with them.

"All right, all right, so stubborn, like your sire. Why not come spend some time with us at the beach? It'll be a nice vacation, do some sight-seeing."

"Beach?" Not a chance. *"That's an idea. I'll let you know."* She tried to sound sincere, but when her mom responded she knew she'd failed.

Laughter came through their link. *"You forget I birthed and raised you. I know what that tone of voice means, so I'll back off graciously and leave you to your days and nights in your castle. Harvey's still in the bathroom, you want to wait?"*

"No. Just tell dad I send my love and I'll talk to him next time. Enjoy the beach, have fun." Shyla stood and stretched. A nice long soak, a glass of wine, and some light jazz would be lovely.

"If I didn't worry about you so much, I could." Her mom released a long sigh. Years ago, that sound had made Shyla feel guilty, now she recognized it for what it was, a weapon for manipulation.

"When I was your age I was training you for your duties. It's not right. I mean, you're not supposed to do that job alone, not to mention being local pack historian and working at that school. How're you going to meet anybody?" her mom asked.

"Rosaria Mason, you are not to worry about me," Shyla said, adding a little steel in her voice. *"I will meet my mate when the Goddess decrees it. She knows my duties and responsibilities better than anyone. Just enjoy your vacation, have fun. That's what I want more than anything."*

Her mom snorted. *"More than anything? That's the problem. You should want your mate, your daughter, more than anything."*

Shyla rolled her eyes as she punched in the security code to lock down the house. It had been a long day and she planned to work on the garden tomorrow. Plus, there was a play being put on by the community college in town she'd like to see. Alone? That sucked. Maybe she'd call a few pack mates to see if anyone was interested in seeing 'Annie' on stage. Better than staying home watching TV.

A flash of light caught her attention and she re-entered the code. *"Yes, you're right. I misspoke. I want all those things. Take care and tell Dad I love him."* She stepped onto the patio and picked up the scroll lying on the table. Looking around, she wondered who'd been on her property without her knowledge.

Her mom laughed. *"Okay, okay, I get the hint. I'll talk with you next week before we leave on our cruise. Stay in touch."*

"Will do. Have fun, don't worry about me. You know the house has me on lock down."

"Unfortunately, I do. Talk to you later."

Shyla rubbed the paper. It wasn't old, not as old as some she'd seen, but it wasn't anything you could buy from an office supply store, either. *"Sounds good, talk to you later."* She disconnected, reset the alarm, and did a quick scan of the security cameras located in the hall bookcase. Seeing and scenting no one, she looked at the scroll again and noticed her title, Mengistia, on a small label at the top.

Groaning, she headed to her bedroom to shower. The glass of wine and jazz could wait, but she'd get comfortable before heading downstairs into the safe. Inside her room, she tossed the scroll on the bed and walked to the shower.

Ten minutes later, dressed in comfortable sweats, socks, and old leather ankle boots, she took the scroll down into the secured chambers. As she approached, lights turned on, a soft breeze grazed her cheeks in welcome, and the stones lit in a haphazard pattern which was never the same. Heat rose from the stones, which was why she always wore socks and boots when she came down here. The first time she'd seen the lights on the floor, her mom had explained it was a part of the security system and if someone wasn't authorized to enter the chamber, the floor would fry them like eggs. She'd thought the imagery funny at the time until a pack mate ventured down the steps and into this private hall. The full-blood's heart had exploded from the jolts of energy.

Over the years, they'd beefed up security to make it harder for intruders to enter the hall, but the house protected its secrets better than she or anyone else could.

Shyla stood in front of the entry for a few seconds. Cool air swept up and down her body. She breathed in and released it slowly. Her mom said this was the chamber's way of positively identifying her and making sure she didn't enter the room under duress because her thoughts would be released when she exhaled.

The door opened inward and after she stepped through, it closed behind her. She headed toward the high table in the middle of the room. At first glance, one couldn't see what made this library, or chamber as her mom insisted she call it, so different. The house didn't give up its secrets easily. She sat in the high-backed chair, lights turned on above her, and slowly the glow brightened the room. Rows upon rows of shelves filled the four, ten-foot walls. Each laden with books, scrolls, like the one she planned to catalog, with tablets and chests on the floor beneath the last shelves. A sense of peace engulfed her as she looked around.

She placed her palm flat on the desk. A soft whirring sound broke the quiet as it opened and a large monitor rose, blinking on.

"What do you have for us today?" the computer asked.

Shyla's dad had revamped the computerized system to make it more interactive and easier to log any new information as well as cross-reference older items. It saved time and she appreciated it.

"Don't know yet, someone left this scroll for me on the patio." She looked at it again and unrolled the paper. There weren't a lot of words on the long sheet. Shyla understood several languages, many of them dead, but they were important to complete her duties as Mengistia. She was not familiar with this one.

"On-Le-she-La-KO-Nee-DA," she tried sounding out and then reading the words again.

A bright light exploded in the room. She sensed her body move without her will as she was sucked through the light before slamming into something hard.

CHAPTER 2

Angus, KnightForce captain and brother to La Patron, waved Oklahoma KnightForce agent Nathaniel forward. "I think this is the last of them. According to Thorne, these four just started recruiting in this area. At any rate, there's no sign they've been successful convincing others to join or retaliate against La Patron." He strode behind Nathaniel, who led two cuffed full-bloods to the truck.

Thorne claimed the rebels used his mate as leverage to compel him to work for them as a spy. Thorne was the younger brother of Rose and Lilly. Rose was mate to Tyrone. Lilly was mate to Cameron. Since Tyrone was the son of Jasmine, and Cameron was the godson of Silas and West Virginia Alpha, he had access to La Patron's compound and some secrets. His role in helping the rebels complicated matters to the point Angus was certain the young pup would die by Silas' hand. Instead, Silas had rifled through Thorne's memories, took pertinent information regarding the rebels, and relayed it to Angus. Thorne, his mate and their pups were serving a long sentence in Texas under Alpha Theron.

"Yes, Sir. I'll take them to Alpha Chan's for processing and trial. The fact they chose his territory pissed him off, he took it personally. I doubt they'll ever make that mistake again."

Remembering the dark look on the Alpha's face when he learned of the rebels recruiting just outside Tulsa, Angus agreed with Nathaniel. If these two and the others already locked up wanted to see daylight, they'd need to appeal to the merciless Alpha's good side. To date, Angus hadn't seen it and doubted it existed.

Silas and Chan had a long history. Much of what went on in the past between them Angus wasn't privy to, but he wasn't too fond of the Alpha. The man's comments bordered on narcissistic. In the end, all that mattered is La Patron trusted the Alpha, and Angus served La Patron.

"You did a great job. As your captain, I'm proud." He slapped the tall man on his back after locking up the two full-bloods.

Nathaniel beamed. "Thank you, Sir. If it wasn't for that tip you gave, I wouldn't have known where to look."

Angus rubbed his chin, recently he'd started growing a goatee and was still unaccustomed to such a small patch of hair on his face. "That's my job. Making life easier and better for pack. As soon as we get rid of the bastards, the better and safer our people will be."

"Don't know what made them decide to go west, from Maryland to Oklahoma," Angus said as he slid into the front seat. "They stood out here, the pack had no problem turning them in." He looked at Nathaniel as they pulled onto the road. "Let's hope that becomes the norm." Pack hadn't taken kindly to strangers speaking against half-breeds, especially the females. They were fast becoming the pack's fiercest advocates.

Nathaniel nodded. "La Patroness' new group helped a lot. It's hard to believe we've never harnessed the collective sleuthing power of our bitches before. They've been proactive in alerting my office whenever someone enters our territory, and if humans act suspicious, we know about it within hours instead of days or weeks. La Patroness is brilliant, we are blessed by the Goddess with her."

Angus chuckled. Jasmine, wife of his brother, and La Patroness, couldn't understand how human women with breeding capabilities continued playing the same tricks on unsuspecting male full-bloods. Some breeders enslaved both human and full-blood males to do their bidding. It had happened twice, which was two times too many for Jasmine. Since these breeders had no power over females, she'd created a watcher's group consisting of Alpha and KnightForce mates, and any other females of her choosing, across the country to organize within their areas to report anything suspicious. So far the plan had worked better than anyone had hoped or expected.

"Yes, she's one of a kind, which is a good thing for La Patron." Jasmine's new group needed office space which meant offices in the compound had to be expanded for new computers, software, staffing. It was amazing how fast and smooth everything went. All Jasmine did was smile and point, deadlines disappeared, inventory came off back orders, and pack tripped over themselves for the honor of working for La Patroness. Jasmine had that effect on people, they wanted to serve and be around her, which both pleased and bothered her mate. Angus loved to tease Silas about being housebroken, whipped. His brother took it in all in stride and warned him it would happen to him one day. Unable to envision any female impacting his life the way Jasmine had changed Silas, he'd just shake his head and laugh it off.

Nathaniel grinned. "We are blessed by the Goddess with the pair of them. I cannot imagine pack without my Alpha." He looked at the La Patron tattoo on one arm and the KnightForce tattoo on the other. The remainder of the ride was in silence as Angus thought of his return to the compound in the morning. Unless Silas had something special for him to do, Angus would work in his lab on some of the old equipment from The Liege.

In several of the past raids, Silas had confiscated a lot of weapons from the Liege, one item was a collar used on full-bloods to subvert their will. Angus tinkered with the collars to see if they could be modified or disabled by a remote he'd created to free the full-bloods who had been forced into servitude. Last week, he'd added crystals to the mix to see if they would offer additional energy. So far nothing worked, but he sensed he was close to a breakthrough. He would ask Hawke to go over what he'd done so far, see what he'd missed.

When they arrived at Chan's compound, Angus assisted Nathaniel by taking the prisoners to the underground cages. It took a few minutes to get them registered, identify their packs, and settle them inside the cages.

Nathaniel shook his head as he followed Angus outside. "Those last two have been at this for a while."

Angus looked over his shoulder at the man. "Yeah? What'd you find out?"

"The older one, Bitman, started some trouble in Pennsylvania. Alpha Samuel wants him returned for dispatchment. He's sending Blue for him. The rest don't have warrants or records. Alpha Chan will deal with them," Nathaniel said as they moved away from the building.

Crescent Blue had been another superior KnightForce trainee. From everything Angus heard, Samuel was more than pleased to have the agent on his team. "That's good. We can't save them all, some refuse to reform."

Thankful Chan was in another part of the state and he didn't need to play politics, Angus followed. He was tired and ready to return to the compound in West Virginia. He had no opinions on how the Alphas handled their jobs as long as they obeyed Silas.

"Dinner?" Nathaniel asked.

"No, go home to your mate and enjoy the evening. I'll head to the hotel, grab a bite in town, and call it an early night. I'm flying out first thing." He stopped, faced the young pup, and placed his hand on his shoulder. "Like I said before, you're doing a great job, La Patron and I are both pleased how you took down the rebels without bloodshed. You have done us both proud." He embraced the pup and stepped back.

"Thank you, Sir. This has been a great experience, hunting with you. I've learned much and appreciate your patience and training. If you ever need me, I am at your disposal." He nodded and walked toward his vehicle. Angus headed toward his truck. *"Silas?"*

"Chan has contacted me with the good news. Samuel is glad Bitman, one who's escaped him for many years, will return for justice. All in all, you did a good job," Silas said.

"Nathaniel took the information given and tracked all four rebels, today he brought in the last two. I remained in the shadows watching, just as I'm sure you did." Angus pulled out of the parking lot and headed toward town.

"Actually, I didn't watch this time. Adam was involved in a football game at school and I cheered him from the sidelines. You'll need to see his next game in two days, he's a natural athlete."

Angus laughed. *"What was it? Some kind of little league? And is it fair for La Patron to cheer his son and not the others? What did Jasmine say?"* He imagined Silas watching his pup on the field. No doubt he tried and failed to tamp down his pride and enthusiasm.

Silas snorted, the sound snaked through their connection. *"Yes, just teams from within the school playing each other. I didn't plan to go but Adam asked. Jasmine said we'd discuss how to handle it later because me watching caused problems."*

Angus frowned. *Problems? How?"* He turned into the parking lot of the hotel and parked near the front.

"As you said, is it fair for the Alpha to cheer only his son? Other little ones cried, some played so hard they were hurt. Adam made a mess of things trying to show off after he saw me. You'll need to go and watch for me since I've been banned for now."

Angus laughed at Silas' sad tone. *"Banned? Has Jasmine approved my attendance?"* He headed toward the lobby and then to the elevators.

"Yes, she suggested you go. Somehow she believes you'll behave better than me and the twins."

Angus laughed again. *"Reese and Rone were at the game? A little league game? Bless the Goddess. Please tell me Adam's team won or that he scored in some way or did something worthy of my sweet sister's wrath?"*

"According to my Sweet Bitch, it's not about winning."

Angus snorted. *"It's always about winning, otherwise why bother to play?"*

"Exactly. But she says it's not about winning, which was the answer given to the losing team," Silas said.

"Ouch. Adam's team lost?" He unlocked his room door and went inside.

17

"Yeah. But he had so much fun losing, I had to cheer him on." Silas laughed.

Of all four pups, Adam was the easiest-going. He loved playing games, sports, hanging outside, and pulling pranks. Whereas the other three had seriously high IQs, Adam was smart, just not as smart as his den-mates and that didn't seem to bother him in the least.

"I can see that. What did the others say of the game? Did they watch?" He could see Renee, his artsy niece, and Jackie, his serious strategist, either cheering Adam on or sitting with an electronic tablet in the stands.

"They were there, I'm not sure how much they saw. Jackie and Renee played on their tablets, David and Sarita watched and talked mostly. None of them cheered, which made me and the twins so noticeable." Silas laughed. *"It was all good fun. If Adam or any of the others participate in sports or anything in the future, I don't want to miss it because I'm La Patron. I'm their father too. If they need me, I'll be there, and everyone will need to adjust."*

Angus smiled as he propped his feet on the sofa. *"Of course, pack wouldn't have it any other way."*

"The plane will be there in a few hours, you'll be home in the morning." It was a statement, but Angus answered anyway.

"Yes, I'm hungry and tired. After I eat, I plan to get some rest, get an early start. Should see you a little after breakfast."

"Good, good. Everything okay? You and Chan get along alright?"

"Yeah, only saw him once, last week when I got here, no problems. He stayed out of Nathaniel's way, let him do his job." Angus knew Silas was more concerned about him and the arrogant Alpha bumping heads, but that would never happen. At least Angus wouldn't start anything.

"Appreciate that," Silas said, sounding relieved. *"Eat, get some sleep, and get on the plane. See you in the morning."*

18

"Sounds good, talk to you later." They disconnected. Angus ordered two medium rare steak dinners and a bottle of red wine. He hopped in the shower before the food arrived, and was drying his hair when room service knocked on the door.

Inhaling the tantalizing scent of the half-cooked meat teased his nostrils. His stomach growled in anticipation. After the server left, Angus attacked the food with the zeal of a starving man. Minutes later, two large T-bones littered the plate. He tossed back the red wine as if it were water. Hunger sated, he pulled back the cover on the king-sized bed and lay face down. His thoughts settled on the collars in his lab, the necessary adjustments to the remote, and Adam's football game. With a smile, he fell asleep.

"Wake up. Angus, I have need of you," the deep voice said as it peeled layers from the sleep-induced fog surrounding Angus' thoughts.

Rolling onto his side, Angus tried to return to the dark comfort only a deep sleep provided. Something sharp pierced his side. Snarling, he sprung up, prepared to fight, and looked around. When he saw nothing, he gazed at the red dot on his abdomen that pulsed with pain. Inhaling, he sought the culprit as he turned around the room.

"Who's there?" he asked when he couldn't identify any scent.

"I have need of you."

"Who are you? Show yourself," Angus said, looking up at the ceiling and then around the small space.

A large black wolf emerged from what appeared to be a cloud in the middle of the room. The huge beast, with glowing emerald green eyes made brighter in the dark, walked slowly toward him. When he closed the distance to an arm's length, he stopped, giving Angus time to focus on what had to be the most realistic dream ever.

"I have need of you." The words didn't come from the black wolf's mouth, nor was it a private mental transmission like Angus had with Silas and other pack members.

"Who are you?" Angus suspected this creature had appeared for decades in his dreams but wanted to be sure.

The wolf shook his large head and a second later, a tall, muscular male with long white hair and close-cropped beard stood in front of him. Dressed in a long burgundy robe, his visitor crossed over to the lone sofa in the room and sat. "You know who I am. You call me Grandfather. Now sit and listen." He waved imperiously to the desk chair. His luminous green eyes watched Angus until his butt met the fabric of the seat.

Sitting here, watching, seeing the wolf from his dreams was quite unbelievable, shocking really. His mind reeled as he took in the relaxed demeanor, the long hair, and inscrutable face. Unable to comprehend, he looked at the rumpled bed and half-empty glass of water from dinner. He pinched his thigh and looked back to see if he was still there. He was.

"Grandfather?"

The older man nodded. "As I said, I have need of you." He shook his head and looked up at the ceiling as if gathering his thoughts.

Fascinated, and unable to utter a word, Angus stared at the legend come to life. Should he ask about his lost Alpha? The full-blood had walked off one day and never returned. Or was Ulric supposed to be the Alpha of his old pack all along? He'd always wondered if he was supposed to challenge the wolf for the Alpha position, but his heart was never in it. Had he failed his heritage in some way by not stepping up for the Black Wolf? Why hadn't grandfather ever reached out to Silas? More importantly, what did he want with Angus now?

"There has been a breach," Grandfather said slowly.

Immediately Angus thought of his research and then the crystals he used in his chameleon bracelets which allowed the wearer to assume the identity of another, search memories or determine the composition of objects. Silas' greatest concern was the bracelet falling into the wrong hand. Since Angus was the sole creator of the chameleon he incorporated several safety measures into the bracelet but nothing was 100% full-proof. "Breach?" He needed more information before he said anything.

"Yes."

Angus didn't know what to think but refused to say another word until he knew more. Seconds ticked and neither spoke. He looked at the empty wine bottle and plates on the table before turning back to his uninvited guest. Grandfather's eyes glowed an eerie green as they met his. "Tomorrow you will return to the place of your birth, there is something you must do there."

"My birth?" Angus frowned. Plias was the last place he would willingly visit.

"Yes." The older man stood and looked down at him. "Tomorrow. You must arrive before the next morning or it could be too late."

Standing, Angus peered into eyes so like his own. "Has my Alpha approved this journey?" If Grandfather was a full-blood patriarch, he understood Angus couldn't just fly off without permission from Silas, and that hadn't happened.

"No, and he cannot know." Grandfather held up his hands. "You must trust me on this."

The man asked the impossible. Angus crossed his arms. "No."

"If you do not do exactly as I say, your mate will die."

The steely words slammed into Angus with the force of his grandfather swinging a baseball bat into his body. Air escaped as he tried to speak around the block of shock lodged in his throat. "Mate?"

"Yes. It's important that you return to your pack lands and travel to a place I will show you. Unfortunately, you cannot tell anyone of this, and your link with your Alpha will cease once you leave this country."

Mate? Die? How could this be? Surely the Goddess would have told Silas. His Alpha would know something "How do I know you're telling the truth?" Angus asked to stall for time. He needed to think. How could he leave the country without telling his brother?

"Have I ever lied to you before?"

"Not that I recall. But I don't know you, not really. You come to me in my dreams and talk to me. Now you tell me to abandon my Alpha, go to a place I swore never to return, and save someone my beast and I have no idea actually exists," Angus said.

"True. In time Silas will know, but not now. I do not have time to prove the truth of my words, you will either believe me or not. But if you wish to save her, you'll meet me at the old training grounds in 24 hours. A flight has been booked for you, but you must leave now to catch it." He paused and the light dimmed in his eyes. "If you tell your Alpha that I have come to you with these instructions, you forfeit the right and ability to rescue your mate. When I tell you I cannot say more, it's because I cannot. Even this visit may be misconstrued as interference."

Interference? What was going on, he thought. "How do you know this is my mate? I've never met or had an inkling of her." He still couldn't wrap his mind around traveling across the world to rescue someone he didn't know without his Alpha's permission. His wolf leapt at the idea of their mate being in danger and urged him to follow the Black Wolf's advice immediately.

"Just as I know your pain over the loss of your parents centuries ago, and then the loneliness you experienced for decades because of Ulric, I know your mate. She will die if you do not move quickly and catch the plane tonight."

"I cannot leave and not tell my Alpha." He recalled the pain Silas felt when Angus had been unconscious months ago and refused to put him through that again.

Grandfather sighed. "Tell him you must leave but cannot tell him of the emergency, tell him your connection will be lost once you enter certain locations, tell him you will contact him when you are done. That is all. You cannot discuss me, your mate, or anything else I have told you."

"That's easy, you haven't told me anything," Angus grumbled as he threw his clothes into his luggage.

Grandfather returned to his wolf form and sat on the floor with his head on his paws watching Angus pack. When he finished, Angus met the canny old wolf's stare. "I'm ready. Did you call me a cab as well?"

"No. You have to return your rental car anyway. Get a move on." And with those parting words, Grandfather disappeared.

CHAPTER 3

"Ow," Shyla said, placing her palm on the side of her head as she tried to see through the dim, dusty fog. As she spoke, the blood stopped flowing while the wound on the side of her head healed.

"What just happened?" No one answered. "Anybody here?" She placed her hands on the floor and pushed up. Shaky, it took a moment to realize wherever she was, it didn't accommodate her five foot, ten inches. As the dust settled, she saw more of what appeared to be a ballroom or library, she wasn't immediately certain which.

Musty odors tickled her memories. "Library," she muttered as her fingertips grazed cool, smooth stone with writing engraved down one side. She leaned in to see the letters and gasped at the beautiful craftsmanship. Long, gracefully curving letters created by a master to stand the test of time, held her speechless.

"Beautiful," she whispered in awe. Holding onto the column, she tried to see what lay behind her. The moment her hand reached forward, a light flicked on, highlighting a row of books. Looking down she assumed the walls stood around 20 feet tall and she stood behind the rails of the highest row. Although the rest of the room was still dim, she assumed she'd fallen into a master library or something similar to what she kept at home.

Home.

Her home didn't allow intruders into her chambers, but someone or something had broken through centuries of protection. But why? Better yet, who? *Think. Think*, what happened before the light? The scroll, she was reading the information. Was it the scroll? Stomach quivering, she placed her hands on her hips as she spoke. "Okay, I'm here, what now?"

Nothing.

Shyla stepped to the side, entered small alcove and stretched. Arms raised, her fingertips brushed against something and it fell. Dust rose and billowed around the small object, surprising her because everything looked so clean. Stooping, she picked up the thin, deep red leather-bound book, and flipped it over.

She swiped the cover with her palm, and tried to read the title. The words seemed familiar, but she couldn't quite grasp what they meant. Opening the book, she stared at the same wording as the title. Normally she'd love to unravel the mystery of the book, but the urgency of her situation made her unsettled. A ladder was lodged a few feet from the alcove where she stood.

Scenting the air, she allowed her beast to come closer to the surface and tried to contact her mother. When there was no answer, she tried her local pack leader, and then Alpha Jayden, through their mental link.

There was nothing. No link. No connection. No communication. Shyla's heart raced with the knowledge she was utterly alone without family or pack to help. Mouth dry, she was desperate for some solution to this odd, maddening situation.

"Goddess, please help me. I don't know what to do, or where I am. I need your help to get home." Silence met her request. As her eyes adjusted to the fog she made out more of the cavernous room. Unlike the chamber at home, the atmosphere had a malevolent feel.

Apprehensive, she looked over the railing to gauge the distance if she fell, and didn't like the odds. Just because she would heal fast didn't mean she appreciated getting hurt, especially when there were ways to prevent it. Grateful for her boots and socks, she stepped carefully toward the ladder. Upon reaching it, she realized she still held the book and decided to leave it. She placed it next to the ladder hook and stepped on the first rung. Pitiful sounds from her beast slipped through her lips, startling her to the point she almost fell.

Holding the ladder with both hands, she closed her eyes, offered a prayer of thanksgiving to the Goddess, and glanced at the book. "Take it? Is that what you want? I don't understand it." She grabbed the book and stuck it beneath her shirt into the waistband of her jogging pants. With each step downward, hairs on the back of her neck stood. Her heart raced even though it made no sense. She was alone in a library, she should have been ecstatic instead of swallowing buckets of dread. When she reached the first floor, something brushed against her. Fear spoke to her in its seedy voice, telling her legs to go weak, her stomach to lurch, and her heart to jump.

She screamed and missed a couple steps, but didn't hit the floor. Where was her attacker? She saw and scented nothing. A low growl rose from her lips as her beast rose. Sharp, stinging pain ripped across her back. Shyla screamed again but hugged the ladder close as burning pain raced through her body. "Climb," she told her shaky legs. "Go up."

This time she heard the subtle sound of the wind as it brushed against her back. Again, she screamed. Pieces of her shirt and skin flew from her body as if someone had used a potato peeler. Tears ran down her cheeks as she forced herself up the stairs, praying to the Goddess that whatever it was that attacked her remained below, otherwise, she would die. Her stomach heaved. Intense heat radiated from her back as sweat poured down her face. Dizzy, she saw another alcove almost to the top and released a sigh. Thankfully, whatever attacked her remained on the lower floors and not high in the stacks. She gulped air and arched in pain as her skin re-knitted. Several moments passed before she could leave the ladder for the narrow wooden ledge leading to the alcove.

Breathing hurt. Her heart raced. All she wanted was to curl up into a ball and wait for pack. But no one would come, no one had answered her call. With small, careful steps, she made it to her destination, sat on the bench in the niche, and stared into the dimly lit room below. Okay, now she knew she wasn't alone. *What the hell was that?* She dropped her face into her palm and tried to figure how her night had gone so terribly wrong. This place wasn't normal. Whatever attacked her wasn't normal. Leaving her chamber at home wasn't normal. So what was going on?

Frustrated, she tilted her head back and yelled. "Hello! Can anybody hear me? Where the hell am I? How do I get the hell out of

Oz without that thing killing me? I didn't even get to drink my glass of wine!" She dropped back against the wall. One hand rested on her stomach as she took a deep breath to think. Her fingertips outlined the book she had stuffed in her pants. Pulling it out, she looked at the cover. "I've seen this before." She tucked her feet beneath her and opened the book. Soon she recognized the old language and read the first ten pages. None of it made sense and she sat the book aside.

Her beast whined.

"What are we going to do?" she whispered. "Whatever that was down there won't let me near the door. I don't see any windows. We're stuck." Fear took hold and she wondered if she'd die sitting in a dusty library.

Shyla laughed but it held no humor. "Library kills Librarian. That's crazy." Gut wrenching anxiety gripped her. She picked up the book and continued reading even though she had no idea what anything meant. When she finished, she sat the book aside and leaned back.

"That's weird," she said to her beast. "Felt like I just ate something." The whole idea was preposterous, but she couldn't put her finger on what was so off about that book. She pulled out another book from the shelf and started reading. By the time her eyes grew heavy, several books were stacked on the floor beside her. Unable to hold her head up further, she slipped into a deep sleep.

CHAPTER 4

Silas strode down the hall toward his private quarters hoping to catch his mate before she started her day. He glanced at his watch. She should have returned from walking the pups to school.

"Jasmine?"

"Yes?"

"I need a few minutes of your time. Are you in our rooms?"

"Yes. I can tell by the tone of your voice something has happened." She paused. *"Is our family okay?"*

"I'm almost there." He didn't want to start now because she'd just have more questions which he wouldn't be able to answer. His deepest hope was that she'd have some perspective on Angus' situation that he hadn't been able to see or understand. His wolf wasn't okay with the way things had happened, but he didn't know what to do. He turned the corner, Jasmine stood in the opened doorway watching him approach. Dressed in a peach and cream tailored dress, she looked every inch the sexy, business executive she'd become. His chest swelled with pride over her organizing the bitches all over the nation into a powerful Intel unit. He read the concern in her eyes, reached for her and held her close as he closed the door behind them.

"It's Angus."

She stiffened but didn't stop or interrupt. He didn't say anything else until they sat on the sofa and she faced him.

"He's headed back to Plias, where we were born."

She frowned and nodded slowly. "Why?" She shook her head. "Why now? Does this have to do with Elyria? Her burial? Is something wrong?"

Silas had forgotten that his daughter, a child he never knew existed, had been buried in Plias. Discovering his seed had turned into a murderous, psychopath who'd kidnapped Asia and Hawke's daughter, Sarita, out of anger, had scorched his relationship with his mate. Things had been tense and difficult for a couple months after, but they had weathered that storm and he had no intention of ever crossing that bridge again.

"No. That's what's so strange. Ten minutes ago, he contacted me from the airport. Instead of telling me his ETA for here, he said something came up and he has to go to Plias, but wouldn't tell me what was so important, or how long he'd be gone. He apologized for not being able to tell me more right now."

Jasmine frowned. "That doesn't sound like him." She paused and sat back on the cushions watching him. "What do you think is going on?"

"That's just it, I don't know. We talked about the case he was working on, I told him about Little League, we laughed and he said he'd be on the plane this morning. But he was supposed to come here, not head to New York."

"He contacted you from New York?"

Silas nodded. It bothered him that Angus had waited until he was about to board to let him know about all of this. It caught Silas by surprise.

"Like I said, it's not like him," she said, her light brown eyes filled with concern. "But, despite what happened months ago, Angus can take care of himself. You know that."

Silas wasn't so sure. Two humans shot Angus with a drugged dart and almost drained his blood to sell to drug dealers. It still rankled him to know Angus had come close to death that way.

Jasmine leaned into him. "Admit it. Angus can take care of himself." She took his much larger hand into her smaller one and rubbed her finger across his palm. "We'll miss him, but he needs to be free to do what he has to do. And for him to leave me and the kids without saying good-bye, it must be extremely important and beyond his control. So, we need to support him and not make things tougher for him." She kissed the back of his hand, easing his beast. "Okay?"

"I support him," Silas said, and then pulled her close for a long, hot kiss. When they broke apart, she had that dazed look in the depth of her eyes that made his chest expand with masculine pride. No one else did that to her, just him. He tapped the end of her nose. "But I'm going to ask the Goddess if he's in trouble or not."

"Hopefully she'll answer you." Jasmine moved and sat astride his lap. She placed her arms around his neck and pulled him close. "That kiss wasn't very satisfactory."

He chuckled at the mischief in her gaze.

"No?"

She curled her lips and shook her head. "Nope." Her fingers played with the strands of his black hair as she stole glances at him.

His dick hardened as he waited to see where this was headed. "My apologies. Let me attempt to make it right." He leaned forward, pulled her closer to him and captured her mouth. His lips captured the sweetness of hers.

Her breath hitched as his thick fingers rubbed against her wet panties. "You're wet."

She opened her legs further.

"Exquisite," he said against her lips. With one hand, he reached beneath her dress and ripped off her panties.

Her brow rose but she didn't speak. His fingertip traced an invisible line down her throat, circled her breast and pinched her pointed nipples.

Heat rushed between her legs. Need spiraled, fogging her mind. The tight bow of craving snapped. She placed both hands on the side of his face, pulled him in and kissed him for several moments like he was the air feeding her existence. His kiss was brutal, his tongue unapologetic. That was fine with her.

Gasping, they broke apart. Chest heaving, she saw the mask of need on his face and knew he was right there on the edge with her. His large palm covered her breast and pushed gently. Understanding immediately, she lay on the sofa with one leg on the floor as he shoved her dress out of the way. He palmed her breast. Sitting up, she pulled the dress over her head and tossed her bra aside, not wanting anything to come between them.

His predatory gaze on her body sent an expectant thrill through her. He flicked her nipple before suckling the hard peak while his fingertips explored the rest of her on its downward journey. Her flesh quivered under the onslaught. The string of pleasure between her breast and pussy tightened, ratcheting her need, leaving her panting, wanting more. Without thought, her legs widened to allow his questing fingers have their way. His mouth moved to the other breast as his finger penetrated her.

A moan of bliss escaped her parted lips, while her head thrashed from side to side. An incredible itch, deep inside her core seethed and writhed, the only way to describe the feeling, needed scratching. She lifted her hips and moved in tandem with his thrusting fingers.

Silas pushed deeper, faster.

She met him thrust for thrust. Sweat rolled off her forehead as she bucked upward to reach her goal. Then it hit, spiral after spiral of ecstasy so strong her entire body shook. Her back arched taut as waves of ecstasy rolled over her. Tremors shot through her, rippling her core.

Temporarily sated, she stretched and watched him lick his fingers.

"I need you." His raspy voice filled her with hope.

"Inside me." She leaned back and gazed at his lust-filled face. "I want you inside me."

She absorbed the shudder that went through him. His tongue flicked her pebbled nipple. "Yes," she whispered in awe as his large member sprang free as he pushed down his pants. It stood magnificently during her inspection. Pale, long and thick with a wide mushroomed cap, his cock bounced against his stomach as he maneuvered them on the large sofa.

His hand stroked down her arm, and he placed her hand on his cock. "Feel what you do to me, Sweet Bitch. I'm hard as nails for you," he whispered against her throat. "You do this to me. I want you so bad, I hurt." His hand rolled hers over the head, spreading the pre-cum over the mushroomed tip before guiding her down the wide column to the base.

"Is this for me?"

His breath hitched. "Yeah."

"Then give it to me, I want it." Her hand stroked the thick pulsing rod slowly. His thighs trembled as his hand grabbed hers.

Rising, he thrust forward and slid inside her tight sheath. Her back arched as she took all of him. She rolled her hips.

"Shit, you're so hot, so tight. Give me a minute. I need—"

Ignoring his plea, she rolled her hips again, enjoying the friction. "You feel so good." He remained motionless above her, teeth gritted as she fucked him from beneath. Panting and grunting as pleasure twirled in her belly, she sensed it building again.

Leaning forward, he kissed her sweaty brow. "Let me help." He slammed forward into her, his balls slapping between her thighs. Her body caught fire. The muscles of his lower abdomen flexed and bunched, contracting hard with every plunge.

Incoherent words competing with grunts and moans flew from Jasmine's mouth as she crested. Colors flew across her lids. A tightening in her belly burst free, hard enough that her vision blurred and her ears felt as though they're going to explode. Her toes curled as she panted for breath. "Soooo good," she whispered when she could talk.

Slowly her eyes opened. Silas leaned over her, sweat dripped from his face onto hers, their fast breaths filled the room.

"Ready?" he whispered with a smug grin.

She nodded. Damn if he hadn't earned that grin.

Silas moved slowly within her again. Her pussy had been made for him, it fit tight, greeting him on every thrust in homecoming. He planned to up the ante with new and better memories of their couplings. This was his woman and he loved the look of sweet bliss on her face as she came. His ego demanded he put it there again and again. He wanted her to equate him with her pleasure.

Stoking the embers of her release, he bit down lightly on her ear, just hard enough to hurt a little. Her moan of contentment pushed him over the edge, he groaned as he pumped furiously into her tightness.

Intoxicated by the cries filling the room, Silas intensified their rhythm. Goddess, he was blessed having her. Her passion fueled his. They passed their unquenchable need for one another back and forth between them in a loop.

Her hands on his ass, cries for more, humbled and spurred him on. His heart expanded as he received her most treasured gift, her trust. Every part of him merged with her during this taking. His arms tightened as he filled her, recommitting his heart, and life.

With a loud growl, his body spasmed through the last of his release.

He'd never felt so alive as he did when they made love.

"You're addicting," Jasmine said softly as she reached out, touching his silky hair, stroking it in wonder. "And distracting. Now I'm late for work."

Silas lifted her and walked toward their bedroom. "Don't worry, I'll give you a note to give to your boss."

This wasn't the first time Silas remained on his knees hoping and waiting for the Goddess to appear. When he'd first arrived in America to carry out the Goddess' instructions for the new world, they'd communicated daily. Things were so wild, rough and unpredictable. That was when he learned the Goddess was not omniscient, especially when it came to the humans full-bloods co-existed with.

Because the Goddess didn't know how certain things would turn out, she gave him a few rules and after the first two years told him to trust his judgment. At the time, he had been upset she'd disappeared, leaving him in hostile territory. Those early years, he'd fought more Alpha challenges than he cared to remember. He and his growing pack were constantly on the move, finding others, taking care of those weaker, and defeating everyone who didn't accept his leadership.

If his sweet bitch had seen him then, barely human, she would have run fast and far. Would he have gone after her then? He didn't think so, even knowing she was his mate, he would have denied a human mate. It took over 300 years for him to be in the right head space to accept humans, even though he'd fought their initial attraction every step. Focus, he chastised himself.

"Goddess, I need a word with you, please." Despite the churning in his gut over Angus, Silas kept his request simple. Ten minutes had passed since he'd done the ceremonial cleaning and initial request. Within the next few minutes, she would either grant his request or not. What happened with Angus? Silas' gut said something big was going on. It would be big for Angus not to share the information. But what? He couldn't imagine anything that would cause Angus to act the way he did.

Seconds later, the room brightened. He lowered his face to the floor and waited. Heat raced up and down his spine as the seconds ticked. Would she allow him to speak? To answer his questions?

"Your overwhelming concern for your brother is unnecessary. All is as it should be. Change is the one thing we can all predict, it always happens. It's the trajectory or path change travels that remains in the shadows."

"How does this change affect Angus? Will it impact my den? My pack?" The last time she'd mentioned change in that placid tone, he'd just learned humans could give birth to half-breed pups. If something of this magnitude was happening again he wanted to know.

"What is happening will happen, you are prepared. Be strong my wolf and don't fear. All is how it should be." The room darkened at her leaving.

Silas closed his eyes as he went over her words in his mind. "All is as it should be? Does that mean Angus is supposed to be heading to Africa?"

"What's wrong?" Jasmine asked.

He sat back on his heels and scooted out of his prayer circle. *"Just talked to the Goddess."*

"I'm on my way up."

Silas exhaled and leaned against the wall with his arms on his knees. No matter how he re-hashed her words, he still sensed something was wrong. Angus was in trouble. He couldn't shake that feeling.

The door opened. Jasmine walked inside, washed her hands, removed her shoes, and sat on the floor in front of him. "What did she say?"

Silas repeated the conversation with the Goddess, watching Jasmine's reaction.

"That's it?"

He nodded, feeling a little vindicated for his reaction by her incredulous tone.

She picked up his hand and rubbed the back. "Sounds like Angus has to walk his own path for a little while. That she appeared to calm you means Angus had to go, he may not have had a choice. Especially if it had to do with his old pack."

"I'm his Alpha. It should've gone through me first," he said. "Only the Goddess can override the connection between Alpha and pack."

"Isn't that what she did? I mean she knows about this, that pack protocol's been violated, but she didn't mention that."

Silas thought about her words for a few minutes. "Good point. What did she mean about change?" He met her gaze.

"Change is absolute. Nothing ever remains the same forever."

"She told me something once," he said searching his memory. "The one thing that is definite is change. It's coming with a time of testing. Your obedience and service to me have not gone unnoticed.

You will be rewarded, although it may not seem so at the time. Be vigilant, you'll need your eyes to see. Be faithful, you'll need your ears to ferret out the truth. Be merciful, your nose will lead you to understanding. Be courageous, your heart will suffer but will guide you to the truth. Taste the truth and embrace it, reject the lies and you will ride the wave of change. Your wolves need your direction now more than ever." His gaze met hers as he finished repeating the Goddess' words.

"That's deep. Still obscure if you want specifics, but that's how she talks." Jasmine shrugged and he wondered if her mind was on the matter at hand.

"Something is changing and it has to do with my brother. Does he know?" Silas watched her.

"Let's be honest. Angus is no fool or chump. He knows something but he didn't share. I think that's what's bothering you." She pointed at him. "Once he gets there and has a free moment, he'll contact you. Give him some space to handle whatever it is he feels he needs to do."

Silas bit back the growl rumbling in his throat. "That's not how it works. I'm his Alpha. I don't get the information later, he asks first, we can discuss it and then I approve. It's how pack operates. If someone asked or told my Beta to run an errand without going through me, it shows disrespect."

"Angus wouldn't do that." She patted his hand.

"Yet, that's what he did. My second in command left the country and I have no idea why. He's my brother, Jasmine. Something is going on, he could be walking into some kind of trap or worse, and I cannot contact him."

She moved, sat on his lap, and placed her palms on the side of his face. "What do you mean you cannot contact him? Your mental link is gone?" The concern in her eyes placated him a bit. Finally, she was taking this whole thing more seriously.

"Yes. There's this dark void inside. He's not there." He tapped his chest.

She placed a kiss on his lips and laid her head on his chest. "He's not dead, Silas. The Goddess would've told you. Maybe he's doing an assignment for her or something on that level and she didn't want to tell you. That would explain a lot."

Silas nodded slowly. "Yes. She said things were as they should be. And she's the only person, other than me, who could cancel our mental links." He squeezed her tight and placed a kiss on her forehead as he thought it over. "Thanks, that scenario makes more sense now. She probably told him not to tell anyone, that's why he refused to say more." Silas nodded. "I can see him obeying her. That's different." His beast settled somewhat as they sat on the floor in silence.

"I love you," he said, rubbing his palm down the side of her face and onto her shoulders. "You're good for me. I need your wisdom and steadiness. Thanks for loving me."

Jasmine snuggled closer into Silas's chest, feeling the vibrations as he spoke. "Love you too, Wolfie." Her thoughts raced ahead to the meeting she'd just left Rose and Asia in charge of when she sensed Silas' turmoil. No matter what anyone said or thought, she knew better than most her mate was more beast than man with a thin, polished human veneer. It never benefited anyone for him to remain agitated too long. His beast saw things in black and white, she'd spent years working with him to venture into gray areas, but it was not his default way of thinking.

"We will be short-staffed," he said.

"Hmm?"

"Angus. Who will handle his job? Asia and Reese can't take it on right now." He didn't add staffing and outfitting her new project left them with few people he'd allow in the compound. It would need to be someone he'd already vetted.

"What about Damian? There are three KnightForce agents in Florida, he could work here until Angus comes back," she said.

"He could, but Gem is overseeing the new hospital and can't leave. Even though they aren't bonded, the separation will be difficult for them both. I'd rather not split them apart. It's best she's able to focus on the research and patients right now."

Jasmine agreed. "Ethan? He just got married, they could stay here until Angus gets back. I'd love to spend more time with Vanessa. Plus, I'd be interested in her thoughts on our outreach." Not only that, but Jasmine sensed Vanessa was a powder keg of untapped energy. Silas would prefer to have Ethan's mate close.

"That might work. I'll see if Jayden can spare him and what we can set up." He rubbed her back and placed another kiss on her forehead. "What were you doing before you came here?"

"Weekly meeting. We'd just started, Rose and Asia are handling it." She moved to stand. Silas held onto her hips until she stood straight, and then he stood.

"I've got a meeting in ten minutes. Have lunch with me." He placed a kiss on her forehead.

She looked into his emerald green eyes, touched the tips of his jet-black hair brushing against his chin, leaned forward and grazed her lips against his. "What time?" She whispered against his lips.

"Two hours?" He wrapped his arms around her waist, pulling her close.

"Okay. I'll order lunch and meet you in the bedroom in two hours."

Silas chuckled and smacked her hips as she pushed away.

"Hey, stop that Wolfie or lunch will be in the kitchen." She grinned as she walked away.

"Makes no difference where I eat, as long as you understand you're on the menu."

The dark promise in his voice shot to her core. Ridiculous how this man still got to her after all this time and probably always would.

"You're my mate, Sweet Bitch, I'm supposed to make you hot from now until eternity."

Jasmine looked over her shoulder at him standing so tall, so utterly handsome and sexy in the middle of the room. "No arguments from me on that, especially since I do the same to you." With a smile, she strode out the door.

CHAPTER 5

Uneasy over the swiftness of his decision to change course, Angus stepped off the plane onto the soil of his birth. Buried feelings from decades past rose swift and strong as he inhaled the air. Shifters and humans moved about the small airport, yet he barely saw them. His thoughts lingered on the urgent mission he'd been compelled to accept. During the entire flight, between wondering about his mate, who was she? What was she like, did she want pups, and what Silas would think of this life or death mission he'd embarked on. What advice would Silas give him? Jasmine? He wished he could speak with them, but just as Grandfather said, their mental links were disconnected.

Angus couldn't shake the idea of walking into a storm, an unsettling situation when dealing with too many unknowns. The silence, no, absence, of his Alpha slammed into him but didn't hinder his steps. Now that he'd made the decision to follow grandfather's instructions, he'd see them through. A quick glance at his bracelet added a layer of confidence. No one could remove it, and even if they cut it from his arm, the chameleon would not work for anyone else.

Outside, a cloud covered the sun, giving a brief respite from its brutal glare. Once again the irony of being alone, unable to count on anyone else in his birthplace, hit hard. When Alpha Ulric, his former Alpha, suggested he leave Plias and the pack, Angus' heart had bled. Turned out of a pack, set aside like yesterday's trash, crippled him for years. Rather than leave the continent, he'd worked with other groups, away from his homeland, to defeat their enemies. It was only when the Liege threatened the Black Wolf pack specifically, that Ulric asked for his help and even then, didn't truly want him around. The two had a stormy history. Angus doubted they'd ever truly trust each other. He hoped the Alpha had no knowledge of his arrival and that he could fulfill this quest without setting eyes on the full-blood.

"Angus."

The voice of his former Alpha, his nemesis, washed over him. The last time they'd spoken had been more congenial than any time in the past two decades, but it wasn't the best. With a perfected mask of calm and competence, Angus squared his shoulders and reminded himself he was La Patron's Beta. No longer alone, he commanded respect and even now could call out to several Alphas in this country to assist him on behalf of La Patron.

Wariness filled Ulric's eyes as their gazes clashed.

"You're alone?" Angus strove to be as nonchalant on the inside as he projected on the outside. Seeing Ulric alone brought back memories of the Alpha taunting him, trying to instigate a challenge to fill their missing Alpha's position. Angus had wanted no part of taking over the pack and Ulric branded him a coward for refusing the fight. Old wounds rose and festered as they watched each other.

"Of course. I was told this is had to be handled quietly." Ulric looked around and then back at him. "Are you expecting trouble?"

Unsure what Ulric knew of his visit, but unwilling to ask questions, Angus shook his head and walked toward the parking lot. Ulric walked beside him in silence and veered off to a black jeep parked near the back. Inhaling, Angus sensed no trouble or deceit, and slid in the front seat of Ulric's vehicle.

When Ulric didn't immediately start the jeep, Angus prepared to battle.

"I was told we needed to fix the problems between us before I take you to the drop point," Ulric said.

"What?" Angus hadn't expected that. Grandfather claimed time was of the essence and it would take a lot longer for him and Ulric to clear the air of decades of abuse and problems.

To his credit, Ulric sounded pained and didn't look at him. "Grandfather said we both made mistakes through the years, but I totally fucked up because of my jealousy and fear that you'd be a better leader than me."

"What?" Never in a million years did he expect to hear Ulric admit things Angus always suspected were at the root of their problems.

"When your parents died during the hunt, you and your brothers kept to yourselves for a while. Then Silas left the three of you behind. Alpha kept the three of you close, he said it was because your sire and mam died for the pack."

Angus swallowed hard at memories of his sire and mam during the hunt. The pack was after a herd of antelope and somehow ran too close to a cub. The huge bear came charging, his sire distracted it from the rest of the pack and his mam helped. Both died that day.

"I'm not proud, but that always bothered me, the way he preferred your den. When Declan and Merle never returned from their last hunt —"

"Did you have something to do with that?" Angus snapped, prepared to kill the bastard right then.

"What? No. How could you think such a thing?" Ulric appeared affronted.

"You were supposed to go with them, remember? Alpha sent six of you, four came back," Angus reminded him.

"We told everyone what happened. Declan and Merle said they wanted to check something and never returned. We waited and then looked for them, but their tracks had disappeared," Ulric said.

Angus remembered that day he became an orphan in truth. Alpha moved him to his den, treated him as a son and made sure he was taken care of. After living with Silas and Jasmine, Angus realized how lucky he'd been to have Alpha take notice of him, but it wasn't the same as your own den. The strong bond between him and Silas superseded all others, for him at least. He'd give his life for his brother without thought. Within the compound, Angus'd had pack and family, both equally important.

Ulric was still talking. "You stayed behind with the pack and I… well not just me, a lot of us, didn't really treat you fairly. It wasn't that you didn't fit in, you did your part in the hunt and everything. It was just…"

This attack or peeling back layers from years ago had been so swift Angus hadn't had time to prepare his internal I-don't-give-a-damn defense. Inside, where he kept his feelings locked tight, the lonely wolf was still scared that someday he would lose the few people in his life who truly mattered. Those who were the rocks of his center, allowing him to stand alone and not be lonely. He'd spent the past few years solidifying his new persona, and liked the wolf he'd become. But that hadn't always been the case. Grandfather and Ulric knew it, damn them both for picking the scab of his past hurts and fears.

"Just what?" Angus didn't bother hiding his irritation. Obviously, Ulric wouldn't take him to Grandfather, who was the only person who knew the next step in this macabre play.

"Different. You were so damn different." He held up his hand. "Not that it's any excuse, but you wanted to wait for Alpha to return from the dead."

"We didn't know he was dead." Even hearing his often-repeated defense not to allow Ulric, or anyone else, take over the Alpha's spot, sounded lame.

"We did. You didn't accept it. And wouldn't accept anyone else, including me. When you didn't accept the Alpha challenge, I realized you didn't want the position. You really believed he would return."

"That's what I told you all along," Angus snapped.

"It was foolishness to expect a pack not to have an Alpha."

Angus opened his mouth and then snapped it shut. Silas had told him the same thing. "For that, you tossed me out of the pack?" Memories and echoes of the pain of isolation resonated through him. During that time, he'd lived alone in the nearby caves. There were days he'd thought he'd go mad without social interaction. It was only his books and work that saved him.

"No. Fear. I was afraid you'd sway the pack from the vision I had for us. Even though you gave your loyalty to me, I never believed you wanted me as Alpha. That uncertainty grew to hate I'm embarrassed to say, because you'd done nothing wrong. I simply didn't like you and no longer could tolerate your presence."

The comments were so unexpected, so brutally honest, Angus just stared at him. He couldn't think past the notion that his Alpha hated him for no real reason. All these years he'd suspected the man didn't like him, they'd argued, didn't get along, but he never thought an Alpha could hate a pack member. He was wrong.

When Angus didn't say anything, Ulric continued. "That's the reason I suggested you find another pack. Then when the pups started disappearing, I sent someone for you and heard you were working with another group." He paused.

Angus didn't bother explaining how his team had infiltrated the Liege using the chameleon bracelet. Ulric was aware of some things that happened, but not all, and he'd never know if Angus had to be the one to tell him.

"Then I heard you'd reconnected with your den mate, La Patron."

His jaw tightened at the way Ulric made the last comment sound as if Angus had received an invitation from Silas and had a huge fucking den reunion. Silas had no idea Angus existed and that cut deeper than anything Ulric had ever done. To think your den-mate left to find a better life was one thing, but to learn he had no idea he had a family was a blow Angus never wanted to experience again. They'd just discovered recently the Goddess had wiped Silas' memory so he could do her bidding.

Flipping through the pages of his personal history was a waste of time. Nothing changed. He looked at Ulric. "What is rehashing all of this supposed to do?"

"How should I know?" Ulric yelled, slammed the steering wheel and then calmed. "I was told to apologize for being an ass all those years, to make things right. I assumed if I told you what was going on with me it would help. Other than that, I don't know what else to do."

Angus played with the idea of just accepting Ulric's explanation and dropping the matter. He couldn't. Not without telling his side. "Pack was all I had, my sire, mam, and brothers were gone. You kicked me out because you didn't like me. Imagine being a lone wolf, without anyone to talk or hunt with. Was it your intention to hunt me down and kill me after I went mad?"

Silence was his answer.

"I'm Blackwolf." Angus slapped his chest, drawing Ulric's attention. "Beta to La Patron, the Goddess' chosen. Brother to La Patroness and protector of the Wolf Nation. Your jealous insecurities didn't kill me, they made me stronger. There is no love in my heart for you, but there is no anger or hatred either. You don't matter to me."

Ulric's jaw tightened but he didn't speak.

"An Alpha who holds hate for a pack member without cause will be judged, not by the one he hates, but by the ones least expected. As far as I'm concerned, this matter is finished. I've moved on and your conscience should now be clear."

"Thanks," Ulric said after a few moments, and then started the car. They drove out of the city and into the jungle without speaking.

Angus wondered where they were headed and what the next portion of his journey would reveal. So far he didn't sense the urgency Grandfather spoke of. As far as he was concerned, they'd just misused time talking at the airport.

The car stopped.

Angus didn't speak as he stepped out and looked around.

"This is where he told me to bring you," Ulric said.

"Thanks, I appreciate it." Angus stretched out his hand.

Ulric took it and nodded. "If you need me, call. I think our links still work."

Angus nodded but didn't respond. Instead, he turned and started walking further into the trees. Moments later, he heard the jeep drive off.

He stopped, inhaled, and placed his hand on the bark of a tree. It had been too long since he'd touched a tree for the simple pleasure of enjoying the roughness beneath his fingertips. Eager to run, his beast swatted against his belly.

"Not now, we must find Grandfather before the 24 hours." He continued deeper into the forest, reveling in the natural scents of nature. The sky vanished almost completely beneath the thick canopy of leaves, only a few fragments of blue could be seen like a large patchwork blanket. Air rich with the fragrance of leaves and loam filled his chest. Trees thick and old with twisted roots and strong. The occasional bird in a tree or a squirrel dashing up a nearby trunk were the only signs of life he saw. An hour later, he came to a fast-moving stream, the sound had a hypnotic quality. Looking around, he knelt and drank some of the cool water from his cupped palm. Standing, he sensed someone behind him.

"Come with me."

Angus turned and watched the large black wolf who'd visited him in his hotel room lope deeper into the dense foliage. Growing up, Angus spent a lot of time in these woods, but the area Grandfather descended had an ancient, other-worldly feel to it. How had Angus missed this section before? The air chilled as they walked down an incline and turned right onto a rock laden hill. Scents and sounds intensified as they continued through an untouched section of nature. At any minute, he expected to see an extinct animal or something equally as bizarre. Instinctively, Angus sought Silas to share the beauty and met silence.

As they crossed a bubbling stream, the air changed. It seemed charged with something. His beast rose as the hairs on the back of his neck tingled. The entire landscape flipped. Every apocalyptic movie he'd seen could have been filmed here. Everything looked dead or dying. It was as if they'd walked into a combat zone. Had the stream been a dividing line between life and death? Angus looked over his shoulder and saw nothing but decay.

"Here."

Silence pressed in on him, all he could hear was the constant thump of his own heart as he stared into the darkness below. It was as if the Goddess had turned the dial and amped up the colors of the night. Everything seemed bathed in shiny shades of gray. From the dying leaves on the bent-over limbs, to large rocks that looked as if they'd been repainted by moonlight. The path, if he could call the rocky landscape that, disappeared into a dark canopy of trees. The still air seemed to suck every sound for miles around, nothing moved or could be heard. Even the insects seemed subdued, as if tensed for what was to come.

"Here what?" Angus asked, watching the wolf.

"Now you see the urgency."

"I don't see what you see." Angus turned to look at the rocks that seem to go down a long hilly ravine.

"Your mate is down there. She's being held prisoner. You must save her." He turned to face Angus. "Saving her will cost you. Her life will come at a high price. A time will come when you'll need to make a decision, my hope is it will be the right one."

Angus thought about it for a moment. He'd lived over 300 years, done most things he'd dreamed of and lived to share the tale. "If saving my mate costs my life, so be it. Where do I find her?"

"Shift, allow your beast to lead you. He's the only one who can at this point. It's up to you, I can help no further." Grandfather sat back on his haunches, watching.

Rather than utter the sarcastic remarks bubbling beneath the surface, Angus nodded. "Thank you, Grandfather. I appreciate your assistance." He flowed into his beast and inhaled.

"Find your mate, Angus. Time is of the essence," the old wolf called.

Angus picked his way down the rocky trail a few feet and looked back. Grandfather had gone. On a rocky path headed to nowhere, uncertainty grabbed him by the throat. He sought Silas and came up empty. Just as he convinced himself he'd been sent on a fool's errand, his beast growled.

"Mate!"

CHAPTER 6

"Mistress, we have a report of human breeders in Texas," Asia said, walking into Jasmine's office and sitting in the chair next to the desk.

Jasmine placed her pen aside and looked up at her close friend. For Asia to personally bring it to her, it must have some sort of merit. "Tell me about them."

"A message came from the Alpha's mate, Shelby. One of the women who work in their grocery store noticed a human woman with a full-blood. The man acted strangely so she called it in. Shelby was working in the area and went to check them out. When she entered the store, the full-blood ignored her direct command to stop. Being the Alpha's mate, things took a nasty turn when the full-blood tried to leave. They have both the female and the full-blood in their office for questioning."

"What's going on in Texas?" Jasmine asked, wondering about the incident.

Asia shook her head. "Not sure yet, want me to go down and question them?"

"No, we're already short Angus. KnightForce needs at least two captains available. When are Ethan and Vanessa arriving?" Jasmine asked.

"Later tonight. I'm looking forward to spending a little more time with Vanessa. She and I talked a bit at her wedding reception. Her energy is strong, bright and refreshing. Do you plan to have her work here with you?"

Jasmine hadn't thought about Ethan or Vanessa, but the idea had merit. "She can. Do you need help in your office?"

"Maybe, I'll let you know. Shelby is waiting for your instructions," Asia said.

"Have KnightForce, no that's right, no men," Jasmine said as she sat back in her chair. "Let me talk to Shelby." She pushed the school reports aside and turned to face her monitor. Asia set up the call and a few moments later, Shelby was on the screen.

"La Patroness, thank you for getting back to me so quickly. The female's name is Doria, I mean Daria. Daria Williams. She lives in Miami Beach and claims to be on her way to California. I think she's a breeder, although I can't be sure. The full-blood servant is under her control although she claims he's her boyfriend. When I told her to release him, she said she couldn't. Theron is with him now."

Jasmine wasn't sure what to make of this. "Is she alone? Part of a group? What's she doing in Texas so far from US 10?"

"She gives the appearance of cooperating, but I sense she's not. One thing is certain, she knows of our nation, protocols, breeders, everything. Never argued or put up a fight, nothing," Shelby said, looking at her notes.

"Do you think she was surprised by how quickly we handled things?" Asia asked.

"Yeah, maybe she's done this before with no problems," Jasmine said.

"Could be. I'll ask Marisa, the cashier who called it in," Shelby said, and paused.

"*Mistress, are you sure you don't want me to go and see check this one out. I could try to read her thoughts, find out if there's some kind of plot going on,*" Asia said.

"*Angus said some breeders couldn't be read,*" Jasmine countered, although she was tempted to allow Asia to go.

"*He's a man. What if that barrier doesn't work with females? It's good information to know either way. I could leave in an hour or two, question the breeder, and return before nightfall, barring any emergencies.*" Asia continued, looking at Jasmine.

"La Patroness, Marisa said the breeder did look surprised when she asked her a question, something like if this was her first time in the area. Daria stuttered and said no, she'd been through before.

50

Marisa said the breeder didn't talk anymore and gathered her supplies quickly after that."

"What did she buy?" Jasmine wondered what the breeder wanted from the pack's grocery store.

"We make private label snacks that can only be purchased here, she had ten packs of high energy bars, chips, and a 12-pack of cola."

"Make sure the breeder and the full-blood are scanned for bombs and anything that could harm the pack before placing them both in isolation. Asia will be there in a couple of hours to interview Daria and the full-blood. We'll decide what to do afterward." Jasmine watched Asia stand, no doubt telling her mate of this trip and giving instructions for him and Sarita, their daughter, for later.

Jasmine disconnected the call and pointed at Asia. "Do a thorough scan and disable her. Also, get what you can from the full-blood, places they've been, people he's talked to on her behalf, let's get as much information as possible so I can pass a complete report on to Silas."

"Yes, Ma'am." Asia turned to go.

"Be back here tonight. No heroics, no getting hurt, no emergencies. I agree we need to know what's going on and your methods of using the bracelet to gather that information is the fastest, but that's all I want you to do. Alpha Theron, Shelby, and KnightForce will handle things after we submit a report." Jasmine held the other woman's gaze until a smile crept up Asia's face.

"I won't kill anyone, Mistress."

"Good, our watcher's group is too new to become vigilantes. Just remove or disable her ability to enslave our men and let her go."

"Yes, Ma'am." Asia left, leaving Jasmine sitting at her desk in silence.

"Please don't let this Daria be a real problem," she muttered and glanced at the clock. Three hours before the children would be home and she'd be done working today. Her fingertips grazed the documents she needed to approve for the school's new project and a few other things. But her thoughts remained on the breeder in Texas.

"Silas?"

"Yes?"

"We have a breeder in Texas, Shelby called it in." She spent the next few minutes updating him on what she discovered and ended with Asia on her way to disarm the woman.

"Disarm? What do you mean?"

"She'll scramble or disconnect the woman's ability to enslave our men."

"Can that be done without killing the female? I thought it was something built into the fabric or DNA of the breeder," he said.

"Why did you think that?" she asked, curious. *"You've lived with a breeder for a while now, you're something of an expert on how we work."*

Silas snorted. *"No one knows much about how breeders work, only that some are stronger than others and that you have innate defenses to protect you."*

"We can handle a wolf, sexually that is. We heal relatively fast and don't age as fast, either. Unmated breeders can call wolves when they are in heat. Some of us are loving, loyal, and lusty wenches, perfect mates for full-bloods." She chuckled.

"What you say is true, Sweet Bitch. But there is always a flip side. Good to bad, dark to light, empty to full. That's the challenge we have with these breeders. We don't know how dark or empty or bad they can be. If there is a counterpart to your goodness, we are in trouble."

"Perhaps. But we will deal with that when the time comes."

"Indeed."

"To answer your question, I don't know if Asia can short-circuit the breeder's capabilities. I do know she will try. That's all we can hope for."

"Good job. By the way, Ethan and Vanessa will be here within the hour. They were cleaning out Vanessa's storage unit near her old home when he got the message. They're on the way."

Jasmine's heart lifted. *"That's great, invite them to dinner, I'll have some rooms prepared for them. Do you think I should have Vanessa work on the Outlook project along with Rose and Asia, or help out in KnightForce offices?"*

"Either would be good." Silas paused. *"Or you could turn over those school project proposals to her and let her advise you on them."*

Jasmine looked at the stacks of paper and grinned. *"I love you, Wolfie. That's a perfect idea, she's a great teacher and should be able to bring a different perspective. You have just saved me hours of work."* She pushed away from her desk and stood. *"I'm headed out to oversee the room preparations and dinner. The kids will join us, send Cameron a message."*

"I will, but you should also give Lilly a personal invitation, just as you'll tell Rose and your mom."

"You're right, I'll do that right now. I'm excited. Vanessa's funny and I really enjoyed talking to her at her wedding."

Silas chuckled. *"Behave, Sweet Bitch, don't scare Ethan's mate tonight, wait until tomorrow."*

"Bye." Jasmine disconnected and headed to the elevator. Rose and Tyrone walked toward her.

"Hey, Mom," Tyrone, her son, said, leaning forward and brushing a kiss against her cheek.

"Morning, Mom," Rose said, kissing Jasmine's other cheek.

"Hello, you two, you headed to work?" Rose, her daughter-in-law worked as Silas' administrative assistant and Tyrone's office was down the hall from Silas'.

"Yes, Ma'am," Tyrone said. "Just finished lunch. Where are you headed?"

"Upstairs to make sure the rooms are ready for Vanessa and Ethan. Oh, dinner tonight, six o'clock at our place, bring my grandsons."

"Yes, Ma'am," Rose said as she and Tyrone continued down the hall holding hands.

"Where's Rese? Danielle?" Jasmine asked as she waited for the elevator.

"I'm here," Tyrese, Tyrone's twin, said, sticking his head out of a doorway down the hall.

"Dinner at our place tonight at six," Jasmine yelled as she stepped into the elevator.

CHAPTER 7

In the darkness of dreams, Shyla's mind conjured magical beasts with jaws honed with razor sharp teeth, large fire breathing dragons, fairies and other magical folk. Troubled dreams were nothing new to Shyla, she was Mengistia and had read thousands of books detailing countless secrets, some pleasant, most not.

But this dream had a strange flavor to it. She lay on a steel table in the middle of a dark room, even with her beast's assistance she couldn't see her chest or feet. The air was heavy as if it held a thousand moans in check, with one long sigh slipping through every few seconds. A peculiar mix of jasmine and mint teased her nostrils.

Nothing tangible held her on the table but she couldn't rise or move no matter how hard she tried. Sounds of crickets from the forest danced in the air.

Shyla tried to call out, but instead of words, she whistled. Confused, she continued trying to ask for help and wound up doing nothing more than what amounted to bird calls.

Coldness seeped into her skin, within minutes her muscles shook and teeth rattled. Cool breezes flowed over her skin, sending jolts of pain through her body. Gasping for her next breath, she opened her eyes and wrapped her arms around her stomach to remain steady. Nausea gripped her as she ducked her head, praying for several minutes not to be sick. As her belly calmed, she realized she stood in darkness. A dull spotlight shone down on her, highlighting her sweat suit and ankle boots. Good, they hadn't touched her, well, she wasn't naked. But she couldn't move.

Fear grabbed her. The hair on the back of her head rose as she tried to look around. Horrified by the vast stretch of emptiness, her stomach clenched and water filled her eyes.

No matter how hard she tried, just as in her dream, her gaze could not penetrate the darkness beyond the dim light, regardless which way she looked. Inexplicable gloom with a sense of menace laced the air. This depth of dark wasn't good or normal.

Shyla concentrated on her faith in the Goddess, La Patron, and her Alpha. She replayed memories over and over, taking comfort in pack to beat back fear. In the distance, muffled voices from her left and from behind her arose. Invisible bonds loosened and she could turn in a circle, but not leave it. Desperate for answers, she called out, releasing a series of whistles instead of asking where she was and the purpose of her being held.

Waves of condemnation and rejection swept through her like the steady stream of a waterfall. What was going on? Why was she here? She'd done nothing wrong.

"Is this the Mengistia you spoke of?" a voice said in the darkness. Shyla tried in vain to see who spoke.

"Yes. She has taken the book, we've looked everywhere and cannot find it."

"What book?" Shyla wondered.

"Leave us, I will deal with her."

A cold sweat left her shaking and wide-eyed, a prisoner of her nightmare as she waited for her jailer. Whoever it was stood outside the small circle of light, she couldn't tell if it was a man or woman.

"Why did you take the book? Where is it? Did you read it?"

Shyla tried to swallow and couldn't. "What book?" she whispered. Pleased she could speak, she had a few questions of her own. "Where am I? Why am I here?"

"It was a small red book in the stacks. Security says you broke in and took the book, that's a crime punishable by death."

Shyla tried to quell the loud hammering in her chest. "What? I was at home and was sucked in here somehow. I saw a red book but I don't have it, and I've been here the entire time. It's probably still there." She tried to leave but couldn't.

"Sucked here? Explain."

Shyla repeated what happened at home and ended with her now standing in front of the entity.

"What was on the scroll, do you recall?"

"I had a hard time pronouncing the words, I tried a few different variations and then poof."

Neither spoke for a few moments. "It seems there is trouble afoot. Did you read the book?"

Unsure if there was a good or bad answer, Shyla hedged. "I read four or five books earlier, I'm not sure which one —"

"Cease with the games, you know I speak of the small red one. Did you read it?"

"I think so. I was tired and falling asleep, I can't be sure."

"It has been opened. That is why I am here. Because someone opened the Red Tabloid."

Shyla's stomach dropped and she couldn't, wouldn't, dig the hole deeper for herself. Reading calmed her better than anything. Whenever she got nervous, she read. This time it may have cost her life.

"Were you seeking it?"

"What? No. I was home, in Maryland, minding my business and entering a scroll into the database. I didn't ask or try to come here, wherever this is." She looked left and then right, but saw nothing.

A long sigh split the air. "This is madness."

"Yes, it is and I'd like to go home now." Shyla strove to sound confident, with a little righteous indignation thrown in.

"Unfortunately, the clock has started ticking, the die cast, and even though you are an unwilling participant in all this, you must remain until the outcome is revealed."

"What? You don't understand. I'm the Mengistia of the Eastern United States under La Patron's protection, a member of his pack. You can't just keep me here without contacting my Alpha," Shyla said, using bravado to combat the fear coalescing around her chest.

"Yes, I am aware and for that, I'm sorry. The book you read cannot be unread. Its secrets cannot be removed from you. That is the danger of the Red Tabloid. Only three people in the past three centuries have ever read it."

"If I read the book, I have no idea what it said or meant." Despite wanting to know what happened to the others who'd read the tabloid, fear locked her in a choke-hold, preventing her from uttering the question.

"Matters not. The mere fact it allowed you to read it means it was meant to be and you're a part of all this."

"All what?" Shyla snapped now that it appeared she wasn't about to die.

"The penalty of reading the sacred Red Tabloid without permission is death. But not your death, not immediately anyway. It's the death of the one you hold dearest."

"My parents? Why the hell would you go after my parents?" Shyla struggled to break free but couldn't.

"No, it's not your parents. It's your mate. Your mate will die if you don't do exactly what I say."

Shyla's breath left her body as if a hybrid full-blood had punched her in the gut. In a way, that would have been better. She tried to breathe in and out, but oxygen wouldn't enter her lungs. Hungry for air, her heart raced so fast she thought she'd pass out. But no, she couldn't lose track of this conversation. Her mate, someone she had no idea existed, was in danger. Hairs on the nape of her neck bristled and a rash of goosebumps crisscrossed her body as she tried to form her question.

"What mate?" Her voice sounded like a scratchy whisper.

"Surely you know you have a mate even if you've never met him. Haven't you been preparing for him?"

"What? No. I mean I want a mate, we all do, but I haven't been doing anything different," Shyla said, trying to understand what was happening and concerned about this mysterious mate that had her beast rising.

"When was the last time you went on a date? Spent time with a man? Had sex?"

"That's none of your damn business," Shyla yelled as heat rose to her cheeks.

"It's been years and the reason is because you wanted your mate, not anyone else. Which is a good thing because mates are jealous, territorial, and will do anything, even give their lives, to protect their mates. You'll lose yours before you ever see him if you don't follow my instructions. And if you don't think I can do this, then try to leave, try to contact someone, anyone through your link."

Rage rose swift and scorched her mind. The idea of a mate filled her both with joy and anguish. How could this be happening? "This is all wrong. I serve my pack, my nation. Why am I being treated like this?" It took everything within her to speak calmly without releasing every vile curse bubbling just beneath the surface.

"It's… it's because things have happened that never should've. You shouldn't be here and even though it's not your fault, you're now a part of something bigger than both of us. As humans say, the cards have been dealt, we now have to play the hand."

"Look," Shyla's tongue slid out to moisten her dry lips. "None of this is my fault, how can I pay a penalty for something I didn't do? It's not fair." She knew she sounded like a desperate whiner, which she was, but it didn't matter. Knowing she could cause the death of her mate tipped the scales. If she needed to beg, sound like a crazy person, or scream until her lungs collapsed, that's what she'd do to get out of this bizarre nightmare.

"Fair is a luxury for those without access to knowledge. Just think, you hold secrets of our world in your mind even though you don't recognize them. Who knows when they'll surface? Will you treat them kindly or bend them to a dark end? How can we take a chance without, well, without doing what is required? Your mate has been informed of your imminent demise and is on his way to save you." The voice chuckled. "Both of you rushing to save the other, total strangers willing to give their lives for the other. Ah, the Goddess is good at what she does, that's for sure."

Hope rose at hearing the Goddess' name. "Does she know what you're doing?"

"Probably, if not now, she will soon." Another sigh, and then a strong wind whipped through the room.

Shyla closed her eyes to protect them from the breeze. Her thoughts tumbled over the other. Her mate was on his way? Who was he? Could he save her without getting killed? That was still hazy. She didn't understand how he'd die by saving her unless he had to fight that wispy thing that attacked her earlier. Was he a fighter? All full-bloods knew how to fight. What if he was human like Vanessa? Her stomach dropped again and she was sure she'd be sick.

"In the end, what will be will be. Rest now."

The words bounced around Shyla's head with the force of a hammer hitting every surface. She cried out in pain as her limbs grew weak and she dropped to the floor. The small pool of light vanished, along with rationale thought.

CHAPTER 8

Each time Angus thought he'd found his mate's scent, it changed, as if there was a huge merry-go-round hidden beneath the rocks where he couldn't see. His chest tightened with the need to find and see her. To deliver her from whatever or whoever took her from him. The possessive thought started slow but picked up steam in his mind. No one came between a full-blood and his mate.

No one and nothing.

Determination flowed through his body. He'd never give up until he found her and then he'd teach the assholes a lesson they'd never forget. Tossing back his head, he released a long, rallying howl to whoever challenged him by touching her. He waited a moment and howled again before picking through rocks, boulders, and fallen trees to find her.

A half mile or so later, Angus veered to the left and looked up. A dragon blood tree stood fifty feet from him, its mushroomed head invisible in the hazy mist hovering above.

What the hell is that doing here? He wondered as he loped toward it for a better look. He had never seen one this wide around the base, but the peeks of green on the umbrella-shaped top verified his guess. Trotting around, he saw a few others dotting the rocky hillside. These trees grew on the Indian Ocean island of Socorro, near the horn of Africa, hundreds of miles from here.

Searching for clues, he inhaled and smelled nothing, not even the blood-like resin from the tree. Disappointment changed to excitement as he shifted to his hybrid, activated the chameleon, and merged with the tree. Immediately, he fell forward and landed on a hard, dusty slab.

Angus rolled to the side just in time to prevent his chest from being smashed by a large, sumo wrestler-like guard. He jumped up to avoid the double-ham fist of another guard. Unfortunately, he landed in the path of the first guard, the punch in his gut winded him.

With no time to recover, Angus evaded blows by moving faster than his opponents, wearing them down. Thoughts that these two assholes had touched his mate, brought her to this place, sent fire racing through his body. Adrenaline spiked, Angus punched one guard in the belly, the force of his anger sending him flying against the wall with a loud boom. Blood streaks on the pale white surface marked the end of that servant.

The other guard growled, stomped his feet as if he were a bull about to charge while glaring at Angus. Unimpressed with the theatrics, he waited for the anticipated charge, and stepped to the side, prepared to give the guard a solid uppercut beneath the chin. But the guard changed directions and slammed into Angus. Both of them tumbled to the floor.

With beefy hands wrapped around his neck, Angus struggled to breathe. Looking into the vicious eyes of his attacker, Angus placed his hands on top of his opponent's hands, and with sheer force, pulled the fingers from around his neck. No matter how hard the guard grunted or the veins rose on his forehead, Angus surpassed him in strength. With the hands removed, Angus closed his fist, crushing bones without releasing his quarry. No matter how hard the guard tried to get away, he was truly captured.

Amid screams of pain, the sound of breaking bones, the scent of fear rose. The guard probably wished his demise had been as swift as his companion. But thinking of his mate, Angus refused to be generous as he activated the chameleon and ravaged his opponent's mind for clues regarding his mate.

She was here. Somewhere in this underground maze. This one didn't have any particulars, but someone named Chancellor did. Elated to have more information and yet weary of the delay this attack caused, Angus released the man and broke his neck before leaving the room to search for the Chancellor.

He morphed to human as he moved down a long dirt corridor. The light dimmed and the air cooled the further he walked. Eventually, the corridor narrowed so that only one person could travel at a time. Then it stopped at a large black wall. Angus had seen these in a few old castles he'd visited through the years. Placing his fingertips against the surface, he allowed his beast to rise. Together they listened to the almost inaudible clicks as he placed his fingers in the correct sequence to disengage the door. After what seemed like hours, but was just several minutes, the door slid open.

Terracotta floor tiles, green and cream printed wallpaper, and several niches filled with small statues or art lined the hall. As the door closed behind him, Angus fiddled with the idea of searching for his mate in his hybrid form. He didn't sense her, but he'd bet everything he owned she was somewhere in this place. Instead of seeking his mate, he sought the Chancellor, the keeper of secrets. He'd heard of the position but had never met one before because they didn't answer to Alphas. They were set apart and protected by the Goddess.

When he came to the first set of closed doors, he placed his hand on the door and initiated his bracelet. Merging with the wood, he discovered this was an entertainment room, a possible decoy in his mind. He released the connection and continued his search. Further down the hall, there was a small door that blended so well into the wall he almost missed it, probably would have if his beast hadn't noticed.

Since no one accosted him, plus he couldn't pick up a heartbeat, and the total absence of any odor, not even decay, he was probably being watched. Those big ass guards saw him coming and were at the door, which meant someone else knew he was here. Looking up and down the hall, he placed his hand against the door as if he were simply leaning to get his bearings. After engaging the chameleon, he sensed humming, like a machine behind the door.

He remained in that position a few moments trying to unlock it and couldn't. The door was a combination of wood and steel. In his largest form, he may be able to break it down but once again, the ceilings were too low to shift. Angus didn't want to guess what kind of materials were behind the ceiling holding the dirt and rocks from aboveground from caving in on this place. Rather than bury them all beneath the surface, he continued his search down the hall.

Three doors. One hidden. Two weren't.

Angus returned to the first door, the one he dubbed the entertainment room, and walked inside. Opening his senses, he searched for pockets of air that would indicate hidden entrances or staircases. To the right, he noticed several upholstered chairs, different colors and styles, arranged in a weird pattern. Two had their backs turned to the others. One had been moved so that it touched a faux, wallpapered window that depicted a colorful view of the ocean. He stared at the window for a few moments and touched it lightly with his fingertips.

Nothing.

Two other chairs faced in opposite directions, but the truly strange thing was they sat on a dark, dingy rectangular rug which clashed with everything else in the room. His gaze swung between the chairs, then at the rest of the space. His beast growled at his indecision but Angus was certain, well almost certain, that the chairs meant something. What? He wasn't sure. After studying them several more minutes, he gave up and left the room.

He had been wandering around for almost an hour and with the exception of the hidden door, hadn't discovered anything. Grandfather said time was of the essence, your mate is down there being held prisoner. You must save her. Saving her will cost you. Her life will come at a high price." Angus clearly recalled their conversation. What was he doing wrong? It came to him. Grandfather had said something else. "Shift, allow your beast to lead you. He's the only one who can at this point. It's up to you, I can help you no further."

"Damn," Angus muttered as he flowed into his beast and returned to the room with the chairs again. This time he filtered everything, searching for the tiniest clue. He bumped each chair, moving them about, looking beneath them, pawing the rug to move it out of the way.

He sat on his haunches and stared at the wallpapered window. The calming, vibrant blues of the ocean, the fluffy clouds on a nice summer day called out to him. His beast whimpered and touched the picture in several places.

A small panel in the middle of the ocean opened. Angus crawled through and slid forward a few feet until he hit a tile floor. Traveling in one direction, he took the stairs and entered what had to be a huge library or the Chancellor's chamber. He sensed movement before he felt something brush against him.

Gretchens. Airborne creatures that protected the secrets. As long as he didn't have anything belonging to the chamber on him he was safe, otherwise, they'd rip him apart to keep him from leaving or stealing anything in the room. Once they brushed against him, he walked around the room and stopped.

His heart slammed in his chest as his beast growled. His mate had been here. Angus looked up and around the cavernous room. Was she still here? In this place?

He couldn't be sure but didn't think so. The scent wasn't fresh but it lingered. A wave of relief washed over him with this proof he wasn't chasing his tail. Nothing happened in a Chancellor's chamber that she wasn't aware of, which meant somehow this Goddess-protected servant was involved with hiding his mate.

A low growl erupted from his chest as he hunted the Chancellor. He morphed to human when he reached the door she'd escaped through. Angus inhaled, morphed to hybrid, and kicked open the door. It flew forward like a missile, catching another guard in the chest and pinning him to the wall.

Chest heaving, Angus strode into the room. A female dressed in a long beige robe stood to the back of the room behind three men or hybrids, Angus wasn't sure what they were but it didn't matter. He assumed she was the Chancellor and pinned her with his gaze.

"Where is my mate?" he asked, ignoring her soldiers.

"You have violated the Goddess' orders by storming in here. You cannot —"

"Did the Goddess tell you to take my mate?" Angus asked, knowing the answer.

Even though she was covered from head to feet, her face, the only thing he could see, turned red. "There are things you don't understand." Her voice sounded sad.

"You have taken my mate, which means you've disobeyed pack law. Either bring her to me now or face the consequences," Angus said, eying the grunting beasts who moved slowly toward him.

"As I said, there are things you don't understand. My hands —"

"Are covered in blood because of your betrayal of your oath," Angus yelled as he raced forward, grabbing an opponent and smashing him, face down, onto the hard floor and then slamming his foot on his back. The loud crunch of bones breaking froze the other two for a second as they stared at their comrade on the ground.

Rather than waste time, Angus ran toward the next two, grabbed them, one in each hand, and slammed them together like booming cymbals. Dropping one to the ground, with a quick twist, he broke its neck, did the same to the other and tossed them aside. His gaze landed on the Chancellor, who watched him steadily.

"Where is my mate? I won't ask this nicely again," Angus said, taking long strides to reach her.

"Listen to me. There's a lot at stake."

Angus reached forward and hit an energy field. If he hadn't worked with energy and crystals for over a hundred years, the smug smile she wore would be warranted. But he had. Reaching forward he touched the shield and identified the spell she used and countered it.

"Now we can negotiate," she said, unaware that he was breaking down the wall between them. "She read a book, one that no one in this generation has been able to read. It chose her for some reason, which is why she's trapped here."

Angus' brow rose as he morphed to his human form and continued breaking down the barrier between them. The chameleon tingled, ready for use. He'd need to be quick, catch her off guard before she threw up a mental shield.

"Good, at least you're reasonable."

He watched her and wondered at her age. Not that it was important but it kept him focused on unraveling the shield. Done. His hand shot out and grabbed her around the neck. Immediately he activated the chameleon bracelet and searched her mind for his mate, for more information on what was going on.

His surprise attack gave him a few moments to steal information she never would have uttered. Looks of horror, then shame, and finally anger, crossed her face as she locked him out of her mind.

"How dare you?" she hissed.

"No. How dare you betray the Goddess and your people in this way," he countered now that he knew his mate was safe, sleeping in another room. His beast didn't want to talk, he wanted to find their mate, but Angus tamped down his need in lieu of gaining knowledge. Something was happening here that involved both him and his mate.

She jerked back as if he had slapped her and touched the side of her head. Fear flashed in her eyes. "What... what did you see?"

Angus played with the idea of not telling her, but Grandfather said time was of the essence. "You allowed someone into your chamber who never should have been there. That person tricked you, learned something he shouldn't have, and that's what started all of this." Her eyes filled and she turned away. He sensed her shame and regret. "What's going on?" Thinking to make things easier for her, he spoke as if he were talking to one of the pups in the nursery.

Her head whipped up and her eyes flashed as she pointed at him. "Don't you dare pity me."

Angus stiffened as he narrowed his gaze. "What the fuck's going on, tell me now," he ordered.

She wrapped her arms around her waist and looked at the far wall for a few moments. Chuckling, she shook her head. "I've been Chancellor for several centuries. Perhaps it's time for someone to take over my duties, we have several Mengistia scattered on every continent. Maybe the Goddess will choose one of them." She glanced at him with a rueful grin. "Maybe even your mate. She's Mengistia, a very good one from what I've heard."

"So why is she being punished?" Angus couldn't think about his great fortune, not now. Later he'd thank the Goddess for blessing him with someone who shared his passion for history, books, and had a healthy thirst for knowledge.

"No one is punishing her. It looks like that, but it's not the case." Straightening her shoulders, she turned and met his gaze. "This is a lonely job. There, I admit it. I was lonely and took the bait. I actually believed he cared for me. It wasn't until he left and didn't return my messages that I did an inventory. He knew nothing can be removed from the chamber so he took pictures of three pages from our sacred text. And before you ask, no you cannot read it. It is still sacred and until the Goddess replaces me, I will do my job." She looked at the three men on the floor. "Are you going to clean that up?" She pointed.

"No. You brought them here." He crossed his arms while processing what she'd said. Someone had romanced her to steal secrets. Chances are it wasn't just one person, probably a group. "Are you familiar with the Liege?" He watched her carefully. Had it been Lord Roderick who set her up? They still hadn't caught him.

"Yes, I am. Why?"

"One of the original members, Lord Roderick, is still on the loose. Is it possible he set this up?"

Her cheeks pinked as her brows furrowed. "I don't think so. Do you have a picture of him? A recent picture?" she clarified.

Angus pulled out his cell, pulled out a file and showed her Roderick.

She released a long sigh and smiled. "No. It wasn't him, thank the Goddess. I cannot imagine what would happen, no, it was not that man."

"Can you tell me his name? Do you have a picture of him?"

She turned from him. "No. I will not. This is not up for discussion. The Goddess is aware of my transgression, feel free to shame me in any way you choose, but I will not give you more information on this matter. It does not concern you."

"The hell it don't," Angus yelled.

She jumped and backed away as he moved toward her.

"None of this would have happened if you hadn't allowed some asshole inside your chamber. What were you doing while he snooped around? Plus, how did he know where to look? There are thousands of books in here. So, you're wrong, this does concern me and my mate. Now you need to tell me who he is so I know what's coming." He didn't walk up on her, but she couldn't avoid him either.

She licked her lips several times as her gaze flicked everywhere around the room. "I can't tell you. The Goddess forbids it. What's done has been done and cannot be undone. I am sorry. Kill me if you must."

Angus's hand shot out and he wrapped it around her neck, shocking her. She lied, he smelled it. Why wouldn't she be honest with him? He squeezed her neck, watching her eyes as she tried to dislodge his hand.

Her fear permeated the air. He waited for whoever watched to come save her. He ducked to the side, avoiding the dart meant for him. Angus dropped to the floor, shifting as he did and ran after whoever had been in the hall. He stopped at the hidden door and pawed at the wall. After a few moments, he returned to the room to finish dealing with the Chancellor.

She was gone.

CHAPTER 9

Jasmine looked at her watch again. Asia hadn't contacted her. Vanessa and Ethan were in their rooms preparing for dinner. Lilly had made an excuse for not coming, only to call 20 minutes later to say they'd be here. Danielle, Tyrese' wife, stopped smiling when she learned Lilly had changed her mind. Victoria, Jasmine's mom, wanted to have dinner earlier so she could put her babies to bed before nine o'clock.

It was a sad indictment of how off the rails the evening was becoming when Jasmine hid, no, she wasn't hiding, she simply didn't want to hear any more complaints from well-meaning adults. Does being nice equal being a dumping ground? Would Lilly have asked Silas what was on the menu before accepting his invitation? Jasmine snorted in disbelief. Victoria had warned her if she allowed the other women to feel too comfortable, they'd take advantage. No one openly disrespected her, and she liked the camaraderie she had with her daughters-in-law. For the most part, Danielle and Rose got along well. But lately, Lilly and Victoria seemed at odds. When she asked her mom what was going on, she acted as if she had no idea what Jasmine meant.

Asia was her closest friend and equalizer. There was never any games or shady quips from the straightforward woman. Jasmine would give Asia fifteen more minutes and then she'd contact her to find out what happened.

Sitting in the back of the nursery, she watched her children dress for dinner. They didn't eat with the adults often and it was always funny to listen to their animated chatter when they got to dress up.

"Is Vanessa going to be there?" Jackie asked, looking over her shoulder at Jasmine while holding a dress in each hand.

"Yes, she is," Jasmine said, wondering if she'd need to step in to stop her daughter from wearing what appeared to be a Cinderella gown she'd worn in a school play. She released a sigh and thanked God her child was developing some sense of fashion as Jackie tossed the long yellow thing across her bed.

"She was so pretty at her wedding." Jackie pulled a nice red and white dress over her head. When it was all in place, she looked in the mirror. "I want to wear a white dress like that. She looked like a princess."

"Wedding gown," Renee said, walking over to her sister. "It's not just a dress, it's special, something you wear when you get married, like Mom and Dad."

"I know that," Jackie said, glaring at Renee, who looked as if she'd just walked off the runway in a navy and teal dress.

"You're right," Renee said, in a placating tone. "She was really pretty. Maybe she'll tell us how she picked it."

"When I get married, I want to look like a princess," Jackie said, taking her sister's outstretched hand. Together they walked to Jackie's area. Renee picked shoes and other accessories for Jackie to wear.

Dressed in jeans and a short-sleeved red shirt, David sat at his desk, his fingertips flying over the keyboard as he worked on an essay for school. David had asked to miss dinner so he could complete a science project due next week. The essay was due in three days.

"How's it coming, David?" Jasmine asked while watching Adam bounce a ball near the door. "Not indoors, Adam."

"Good, I should be finished tonight," David said without looking up.

"Mom, when are we going to eat?" Adam said as he tossed the ball into a large plastic bin filled with all types of balls.

"In about an hour, but we'll head into the living room when you're all dressed. Her gaze lit on each child. "You're all growing so fast, could you slow down a bit?" Her voice caught as she stood and waved them forward.

"You okay, Mom?" David asked, watching her closely as he walked over to her.

Pride and a sense of loss swamped her in equal measures. As four pairs of eyes watched and waited for her response, she inhaled and pulled them all close. "Just thinking how proud I am of all of you." She leaned back and stared down at them. "So smart, kind, sweet, well-behaved."

Adam groaned but didn't move away. David smiled. Jackie wrapped her arms around her mom's waist. Renee took one of Jasmine's hands, Adam grabbed the other.

"Love you too, Mommy," Jackie said, her face pressed tightly against her mom's waist.

Bending, Jasmine kissed the top of Jackie's head, and then kissed each of them.

"You know we love you, right, Mama?" David asked. Eyes so like her own sought answers.

She cupped his chin in her palm." Yes, baby, I know. But it's still good to hear it every now and then."

"Mama tells us she loves us every day," Renee said, leaning on Jasmine's other side.

Adam nodded. "So we gotta tell her we love her every day, right, Mom?" He squeezed her hand to ensure he had her attention.

"When I tell you I love you, it's how I feel." She paused. "When I was younger, around 12 or 13, my cousin Bucky was really sick and wanted me to come see him. I walked into his room, my stomach cramped at the smell, all the equipment, everything. I ran to the bathroom and I was sick."

"You threw up like Renee when she sees those ugly worms?" Adam asked, stealing glances at his sister.

"That was not a worm, it was a snake eating something big. If you've got to say something mean, at least get your story right," Renee snapped as she held Jasmine's hand tighter.

"Adam, be nice. As I said, I got sick and didn't stay long. When we were in the car, Mama asked if I'd told him goodbye. I hadn't but I begged her not to make me go back inside. He died two days later." Even years later, she still felt bad over how she'd reacted and treated Bucky. They were the same age and had been best friends.

"I'm sorry, Mom," David said softly. "You wish you'd told him you love him but never did, right?"

Jasmine read the understanding in her son's eyes and nodded. "I still miss him. He was a great person." The other three chimed in with variations on what David said.

"Anyway, that's why I always tell you and anyone else who means anything to me how I feel." She tapped the tip of David's nose with her fingertip, drew him close and hugged him. Next, she blew a raspberry on the side of his face causing him and the others to laugh. He was too serious, she proceeded to tickle him and anyone she could reach.

Laughing David squirmed out of her grip but continued playing with his siblings, tickling and laughing, as he should.

"*Mistress?*" Asia called.

Finally, Jasmine thought. "Clean up and come to the living area," Jasmine said. They scattered.

"*Asia, one second, I'm taking the children to the living area.*"
"*Yes, Ma'am.*"

Five minutes later, the children were playing a board game with each other on the living room floor.

"*What happened with the breeder?*" Jasmine asked Asia.

"*Hawke is listening too, there may be a problem.*"

Hearing Asia proclaim a problem, Jasmine knew it was big. "*Let me get Silas, you can tell us both.*" Asia's mental connections were limited to her mate, Hawke, her Mam, Amynta, and Jasmine. It made it a little difficult to communicate with the KnightForce agents under her care, but Asia seemed to be coping well.

"*Yes, Ma'am,*" Asia said.

"*Silas, Asia needs to talk to both of us.*"

"*One second, I'm finishing this meeting with security.*"

73

Jasmine watched the cook and his assistant work in the dining area. Tantalizing aromas made her stomach growl. David looked at her and grinned. She winked at him before he turned back to the board.

"Okay, I'm here," Silas said.

"Asia, what's the problem?" Jasmine asked.

"Daria, the breeder, is a part of a group that seeks other breeders for training. Except they use their pheromones on everyone; humans, full-bloods, and half-breeds. Some things aren't clear, but I get the sense they're building an army."

"How many? Where?" Silas asked.

"She's just a small spoke in a large wheel. For the most part, she escorts men, all kinds including humans, to this place in Arizona, not California like she told Shelby. She's scheduled to pick up two more full-bloods on the way."

"What's the name of the group? Leaders? Base location?" Hawke asked.

"None of that. Like I said, she has very limited knowledge," Asia said.

"You have the location where she's headed?" Silas asked.

"Yes, Sir, and the addresses of the two men she's picking up."

"Asia, take custody of the breeder, take her to the plane, to travel here once you're gone. Make sure she's not seen leaving with you. Take her identity and continue to the next point. Gather what information you can from that contact person. If it's another breeder, we need to know," Silas said.

Jasmine opened her mouth and closed it. She couldn't come up with a better idea and they needed to know what was going on.

"If Asia could wait until I arrive, I could replace the full-blood who was taken by Shelby. That way we can infiltrate any information system they have and get to the core of their operations," Hawke said.

Jasmine had a strong impression this was Hawke's way of giving Silas a reason to approve his trip to Texas to go on this mission with his mate. She doubted anyone could stop him.

"Great idea, Hawke, you still have that chameleon bracelet from Angus. Use it. Call transportation and set things up. Asia, I want you to make Daria think she's being released with the full-blood she was transporting. Once outside, change your appearance, so if anyone's watching they'll think she's with him. Drive to a hotel to rest. When Hawke arrives, switch forms with him. You become Daria, he'll be the full-blood we're holding. Later, I'll have Theron put her on the plane back to the compound. Any questions?"

"No, Sir. Please keep Sarita safe until we return," Asia said.

"Of course, that goes without saying. The kids are going to have a sleepover. Maybe some of Lilly's kids will stay as well. Don't worry, I'll watch over her," Jasmine promised.

"Thank you. Have you informed Alpha Theron of your plans, Sir?"

"I'm doing that now."

"Hawke is preparing to fly out. He's bringing scanners, jammers, and other things. The jet is being fueled and the pilot is on the way. It will be at least four hours before we continue the ruse, wouldn't you say?" Asia asked.

"Yes, that's about right. You can rest there if you prefer and leave when Hawke arrives since it'll be dark," Jasmine said.

"I prefer she didn't use the bracelet at Theron's compound," Silas said.

"Oh, sorry. Hotel then," Jasmine said.

"Have Vanessa and Ethan arrived?" Asia asked.

"Asia, I am disconnecting, please let us know when you are on the move and when you arrive at the next pick up point," Silas said.

"Yes, Sir, I will."

"Vanessa and Ethan will be down for dinner soon. It was good seeing her again, she asked about you and was excited when I told her I'd sent you to kick ass and take names," Jasmine said.

"Oh Mistress, I can imagine what she must think."

"She thinks you're one bad-ass sister who handles her business. Seriously, she's a breath of fresh air desperately needed these days. She's agreed to review the school proposals for me. If she didn't seem so excited about it, I'd feel guilty for asking her to work."

Asia chuckled. *"I get the feeling she speaks her mind. If she didn't want to help, she could've easily came up with some sort of excuse, right?"*

"Well, no, not really," Jasmine said.

Asia's laughter came through in her thoughts.

"Well, technically she could've said no, but then Silas would be like 'what does she mean no?'" She imitated his deep voice, unsure if Asia picked up on it through their link.

"Yes, he would. I can hear him say that, probably not that nice though," Asia said.

Jasmine nodded to herself. *"So, I don't ask anyone to do something unless I want them to do it, because my mate won't accept them saying no. Knowing that, I'm really careful. Plus, her taking on the school project was his idea. I let her know that as well."*

Asia snorted. *"All good points. Question."*

"Yes?"

"Lilly has seven kids; you're going to have them all stay tonight?"

"The older ones may not want to stay, they haven't in a while." Jasmine withheld a sigh. *"But the younger ones can. I'll mention it to Lilly so she brings them prepared."*

"Good idea and thanks for taking Sarita, we appreciate it."

"She's family. Plus, I feel better about this job you're on with Hawke by your side. He's good with electronics and he'll make sure you both get home safe. Be careful and contact me if you need me."

"Yes, Mistress. And you're right, Hawke and I work better as a team. I'm glad he's with me on this job, too."

Jasmine disconnected and pulled out her cell to call Lilly. No one picked up, Jasmine left a message about the sleepover.

With the situation in Texas, or Arizona, in the back of Jasmine's mind, she focused on dinner. Her grandsons, Ryan and Ryder, were now walking and getting into everything. Their dark eyes filled with mischief and laughter as they bullied and played with Adam and David. Renee had no problem telling her nephews no and not to touch her digital tablet, which made them want it even more.

Lilly and Cameron came without their kids, which surprised everyone. When Jasmine asked if the girls, Brendell, Nionis, and Amari, were coming later for the sleep-over, Lilly said she hadn't received the message and offered to send for them.

Jasmine didn't want the girls to go through the trouble and promised a special girls' night party for the following week. Lilly's bright smile erased Jasmine' initial concern that something was going on. "They'd love it. Just give me the date and time," Lilly said.

Victoria had returned her four to their nurses to be put to bed and returned with Jacques just as everyone moved from the table to the living area. Danielle sat next to Vanessa, those two bent close talking and laughing. Rose and Lilly sat on a loveseat across from Jasmine and spoke little.

Tyrese placed his hand on Danielle's neck, she looked up and he kissed her. It wasn't that the children never saw their older brothers show affection to their mates, but Tyrese was more private than Tyrone, who couldn't keep his hands off Rose.

"Look at Rone," Jackie whispered to Sarita. The two giggled as they watched. Ryder, the bolder of Tyrone's son, walked over to Jackie and kissed her on the mouth, his tiny hands on her neck mimicking his uncle.

Jackie pushed him away and wiped her mouth with the back of her hand. "Eww, stop that," she said as Jasmine and the other adults laughed.

Undeterred, he turned to Sarita and bent forward.

"Stop," David said, giving Ryder an I'm-not-playing look.

Ryder froze midway to Sarita's lips and stared at David. No one moved or said anything. Ryder looked at Sarita, who smiled at him and then at David, who continued to stare at the boy. Jasmine covered her smile as Ryder walked away and lifted his arms to Tyrone.

"See what happens, little man, when you copy your uncle. He's not the one you should model," Tyrone said, moving quickly out of Tyrese's way.

Rose and Lilly laughed.

"Whatever," Tyrese said, rubbing Danielle's back. "Ethan and I are headed to the gym, want to join us?" he asked Cameron.

Cameron glanced at Lilly and then he smiled. "Been a while, I might be rusty." He stood and stretched. Gold highlights and flecks of rust in his full cap of hair looked as if a hair stylist had spent hours blending several colors to develop the perfect style for him. Tonight, he reminded Jasmine of a beefed-up Brad Pitt.

"Look at him, making excuses already," Tyrone said as he picked up Ryan in his other arm. "Baby, you want me to help you get them down before I go play?"

Rose smiled as she shook her head. "No. We'll hang out here a while longer. Go ahead."

Tyrone placed both boys on their feet and they ran, squealing and laughing, toward the other children.

Cameron looked at Lilly for a few moments and nodded. "I'll meet you there in a bit."

Lilly stood and looked at Jasmine. "Thank you for dinner. Vanessa, it was nice meeting you." She turned to Victoria. "Good seeing you, and you too, Danielle."

Danielle smiled and waved good-night.

"Good seeing you, Lilly. Don't forget to send me that recipe you told me about at dinner," Victoria said.

Lilly's gaze widened and then she offered a tight smile. "Of course. Good night everyone." She waved.

"Be back in a few," Cameron said, placing his hand on his mate's back as they left the room.

"I'm going to go change," Tyrese said.

Danielle crooked her finger. He bent close to her mouth while staring into her eyes. "Don't play all night."

"Not on the court, that's for sure," he said, grinning.

"Don't wear yourself out," she whispered as she brushed her lips against his.

"Again, not on the court." He tapped the tip of her nose, turned, and left the room.

Jasmine wondered why they didn't mind-speak like the others.

"They didn't invite the old men to play," Victoria said, stroking Jacques' cheek with her finger. He captured it in his mouth and grinned. "Well, um, yes, I do think we need to leave as well. Thank you for dinner, Jasmine. Don't forget, we're going shopping one day this week. Let me know what day."

"I'd like to do it when Asia returns," Jasmine said, watching the children play.

"When is she coming back?" Victoria asked as she and Jacques walked toward the door.

"I'll let you know." Jasmine waved goodnight.

Silas placed his arm around her shoulder, pulled her close, and kissed her forehead. "*You want me to put the kids to bed so you can talk with the ladies?*"

"*Oh, would you? That would be great.*" He kissed her lightly, stood, and walked over to the kids.

"Come on everyone, time to get ready for bed."

Tyrone kissed Rose, turned, and left.

Ryan lifted his arms to Silas, who obeyed the silent summons. Rather than wait for Ryder, Silas lifted him as well.

"I'll come get them ready for bed," Rose said, standing.

"Sit back and enjoy your visit. My mate can't wait to get you all to herself." He winked at Jasmine.

Vanessa and Ethan stood to the side looking at each other. He kissed her and left.

Danielle walked over to the table, grabbed a bottle of wine, and some glasses. "Please toast with me, my stubborn mate has finally agreed we can start working on our den!"

Jasmine shrieked, jumped up, and wrapped her arms around her daughter-in-law. "Are you pregnant yet?"

"No, but not because we haven't started trying," Danielle said as she poured four glasses. "To babies."

They all drank. "How many do you want?" Vanessa asked as they all moved closer to talk.

"As many as the Goddess gives us." Danielle burst out laughing at what had to be shock on everyone's faces. "Seriously, two will be fine."

Jasmine relaxed with her glass. "From your lips to the Goddess' ears."

Vanessa turned toward Rose. "What was wrong with your sister? Did I do something to offend her?"

Jasmine choked on her drink.

Rose's face pinked. "The two of you just met, I don't think you did anything." She held out her hand. "Lilly is, well, she has a house full of kids, and it's possible, she never said this, but maybe it's not what she thought it would be."

Jasmine nodded.

"What's a housefull?" Vanessa asked.

"Seven," Danielle said.

Vanessa's eyes widened but she didn't say anything, for which Jasmine was relieved. No need to make Rose uncomfortable because of her sister.

"Have you heard from Asia?" Vanessa asked.

Grateful for the change of subject, Jasmine filled them in on what she knew, but kept information regarding the chameleon bracelet secret.

CHAPTER 10

A single light welcomed Asia, appearing as Daria, from the window as they pulled into the driveway of the address taken from Daria's memories. The two full-bloods they'd picked up on the way sat in the back staring straight ahead. The silence in the vehicle had been creepy. Neither of the men had slept or talked or asked to go to the bathroom during the long drive into Durant, Arizona.

Asia glanced at Hawke, who appeared like the first full-blood captive, and then at the men in the back. "Get out and go inside. You'll receive instructions then."

With robotic-like movements, the men, Hawke included, left the car and walked toward the door. Memories of Daria's last visit rose like a silent movie. This should be a casual encounter with an old male friend, by the name of Humphrey. They'd talk about the drive, food, and cost of gas before going to bed. Should be easy. Asia stepped out, stretched, grabbed her bags and followed the men inside.

"There you are," a small oriental man's dark gaze roved over her from head to toe with a smile. "I was about to send them after you. You've been through enough on this trip."

Asia smiled to hide her surprise that the man knew what happened. Depending on what he knew, they may need to rework a few things. She took his extended hand and allowed herself to be pulled into a tight hug. He smelled of old aftershave and whiskey. She noticed the half-empty bottle on the table and stifled a groan.

"Hi Hump, it was nothing." She stepped back as far as his arm allowed and moved further into the living room.

"Are you okay?"

She waved him down. "Yeah, just slowed me down, got here later than I planned." She looked around. "You put 'em down for the night?"

"Yeah, they're in the basement. Bobby's with them." He pulled her in for another hug, this time he rubbed his semi-hard cock against her. "Missed you. How long can you stay before the hubby misses you?" He handed her a bottle of water. Asia smelled the drugs, which included sodium thiopental, a truth serum, and drank a long healthy dose. After all her surgeries, and her messed up physiology, the only thing she needed to be concerned about was acting the part of helpless victim.

"Couple days. He's been asking more and more questions. Why doesn't my mu-ju work on him?" She kissed his cheek and took his hand. *"Hawke, he's taking me to the bedroom after giving me truth serum. No doubt others will be watching. How's it going down there?"*

"He's got us hooked up to some kind of machine, supposed to help us rest better. Shut down the cameras and get into your lover boy's head so we know what's going on. Heads up, if this guy puts his hand on my cock again, I'm breaking his neck and we'll make new plans."

"I don't know. That would make our lives so much easier, don't you think," Humphrey said, squeezing her shoulder. "Come, let me help you forget all your problems." He kissed the back of her hand and led her down the hall.

"On it." Asia's wolf rose slightly, inhaled, and searched the area to discover the camera location. There were three. One in the hall watching them now. And two in the bedroom.

"I need to wash-up, I'm feeling tired. It was a long drive but I didn't think I'd be this tired." She pouted and tossed her bags on the floor.

Humphrey steadied her and led her to a wingback chair next to the bed. "Have a seat, baby. You had a long day." He turned and walked toward the window and closed the blinds. Asia leaned forward, slipped off her shoe, and activated a jammer in the heel Hawke had created. Humphrey nor his friends wouldn't realize they weren't receiving real transmissions for five minutes. She needed to work fast.

He returned to her and snapped his fingers in front of her face. "Daria, what happened in Texas? The Alpha's Bitch took you someplace, where did you go?"

Her head lolled and she struggled to look at him. "Wait, why are you waving like the ocean?"

He grinned.

She grabbed his arm, and activated the bracelet while pretending to be unsteady.

"You'll be fine in a few minutes, just answer the question, where did they take you?" He frowned and scratched the side of his head as Asia used a gentle touch going through his mind.

"To an office."

"What?" He shook his head as if he could shake Asia's probing away. She remained steady, removing information, changing a few things regarding La Patron they shouldn't know, and seeking more names.

"Hold on, I need to sit down." He dropped to the floor and tried to break their connection, but she continued holding his hand.

"Hawke there are two men monitoring, watching. They're located on this block, a couple houses down. He's expecting them to come any minute. Can you hold off killing Bobby until these guys get here? I want to find out what they know."

"Okay."

She smiled at his grumpy response and released Humphrey's arm. Asia slumped in the chair with her head lolling on the side as the door crashed open. Two men ran in holding semi-automatics. The smaller, younger looking man with a lean, wiry build, shaggy reddish-brown hair, and wintry gray eyes, carried a handheld scanner. He walked to her and ran the scanner across her body, then ran it over Humphrey. He shook his head to his partner and put the scanner away.

"Hey," Humphrey said, trying to stand.

"What the fuck happened?" the older guy said as his gaze flicked from Asia to Humphrey. He was slightly taller and larger than the younger gunman. His bald head gleamed beneath the overhead lights as he moved closer to Humphrey.

"Nothing, just got tired for some reason. I was questioning, her." Humphrey pointed. Asia looked at the men through a few strands of thick brown hair, noting they were mercenaries. It was obvious in the way they stood away from the windows, doors, the manner they handled their weapons. She wasn't sure what Daria and Humphrey thought they were involved in, but these men were just hired muscle, which explained why Humphrey knew just a little more than Daria. Both were bottom feeders. Hopefully, these two knew more.

"Coming up, they have guns, that changes things. Oh, and I got some information from Bobby."

Asia would've smiled at her mate's smug tone but she didn't want to tip off these trigger-happy guys.

"What's wrong with your equipment? It went all static a few minutes ago," the older man said without taking his eyes off her. The other walked to the wall and started working on something.

Asia leaned forward. "I'm tired." She yawned to cover the sound of Hawke's approach.

"Tell us what happened in the Alpha's office?" Humphrey asked.

"Whaat?" she asked, looking up at Humphrey.

The bald man moved close to her, raised his hand, but Humphrey stopped him. "No, we don't do that. Go back to your posts, I have this."

"Go on back and monitor things, I'll stay here." The older man moved back against the wall, his finger on the trigger, and watched them. The smaller one nodded and walked out.

Humphrey gave her the bottle of water again. She polished it off and thanked him with a smile.

He stroked her hair. She wanted to punch the hypocrite. "Tell me what happened."

"We went in the store to buy the, the… um, snacks, like we always do. The cash lady asked the dummy a question and he didn't answer." She blinked a few times and coughed. "He didn't say anything."

The man holding the gun cursed.

Humphrey nodded. "So they questioned you. What did you tell them?"

"Me and my lover were on our way home to Arizona, just like we're supposed to say." She shook her head. "Fuzzy."

"I know. Just a few more questions and you can rest. Did they give you anything to eat or drink while you were inside?"

She snorted. "No. No southern hospitality that's for sure. They tried to get him to talk and took him to another room. Then he came back, they thanked us for shopping at the store, apologized, and we got in the car." Squinting, she touched Humphrey's chest. "I did what I'm supposed to do, what about you?"

The smaller man re-entered the room, raised a pistol, and shot the man holding the gun in the arm and then the leg. *"Cameras are all disabled. Let's get out of here. There's another group on the other side of town. I had Alpha Paxon send a small team to secure the men until we arrive to question them,"* Hawke said. *"By the way, all of the full-bloods they take are rebels, that's why there was no alarm. Bobby is a handler, works for Daria's group to make sure the collars work. Lover boy Hump, works for the client."*

"What the hell are you doing?" Humphrey yelled, moving forward until the gun was pointed at him. The smaller man didn't say anything. He placed his hand on the downed man's shoulder ignoring the rainstorm of profanity and threats.

"Take it easy," Hawke said, channeling the dying guy's former partner. Asia watched Hawke take information from the downed man for a few seconds and then she grabbed Humphrey's arm again. This time she stopped his heart.

"Son of a bitch was going to let them kill me," Asia said.

"Yeah, that's why this one stayed behind, to take care of all the loose ends." He tossed her a pair of gloves. They picked up the men and took them downstairs to the basement.

Asia looked around. *"Where are the full-bloods that were here?"*

"Alpha Paxon has them. That's one way to deal with rebels, collar them."

"Who decides that though? Is there another group targeting and selling full-bloods? Even if they are rebels, they're still pack," Asia said.

"Good question, one I can't answer. They'll finish cleaning up here. I'll fill you in on the way."

"Do I stay in this form or change?"

"Change. La Patron doesn't want anyone knowing about the bracelets." Hawke morphed into his natural skin. *"Alpha Paxon thinks we're wearing costumes. Let's keep it that way."*

Asia nodded and followed him out the door.

CHAPTER 11

Shyla woke slowly, pulling herself from a pitch-dark morass with static cling tendencies. She kept her eyes closed against the light in the room while settling her chaotic thoughts. As they re-aligned into some semblance of order, she recalled the nightmare of being sucked through a wall to this place. A mate in danger. She frowned, it was all too weird. The person in the dark sounded as if all of this was a mistake, something that couldn't be changed.

What was with all the secrecy? Honestly, she was over this cloak and dagger crap. It was beyond time for plain speaking. She just wanted to go home and forget this night ever happened. She froze at the sound of the door opening.

"What have they done to you?" the deep, dark voice rolled over her.

Goosebumps raced across her flesh as he moved closer. Incredible heat buffeted her skin as if she were being cosseted in a large, wool blanket. His palm touched her cheek, marking her, if not forever, definitely for the present.

Curiosity won. She opened her eyes and stared into liquid emerald green pools so tempting, she wanted to dive in and never leave. Black hair cut in some sort of geometrical style flattered his angular face. Her fingers itched to touch his goatee. She swallowed hard at the perfection of his firm lips and wide shoulders, just the right size to lean on. Handsome seemed too tame a label for this man, he was more like an ancient warrior, with high cheeks and a narrow chin. On him it all worked. She wiggled her fingers, eager to touch his shoulder-length hair. Would his lips be soft or hard?

"Good, you're awake. How do you feel? Can you shift?"

She frowned at her scattered wits. "Shift?"

"We need to leave this place. Are you hurt?"

Leave? Of course. She was being held prisoner. But how did he get in and why didn't she sense him? "No, I'm not hurt. Who are you?" She sat up slowly, watching him.

"Angus Blackwolf, and you?" He placed his hand behind her back, offering support. Heat from his touch raced through her body, waking up her beast, who pushed her to shift and submit. Not so fast, Shyla thought.

"Shyla. Shyla Mason. How come I didn't sense you just now?" She edged to the end of the super king-sized bed so she could stand.

He shrugged and even that was sexy. Her brain must have gone to mush.

"Must be some kind of blocker. If I could've sensed you, I would've been here earlier. Now that introductions are out the way, how are you feeling? We need to leave," he said, taking a few steps toward the door.

She stood and stretched arching her back. "That feels good," she said, looking around for her boots. "They took my shoes."

"What?" He looked around the large space but couldn't find them either. "Seems you'll need to shift anyway." He inhaled and shook his head. "Damn."

"What?" Seeing his pained expression, she searched the room for the cause.

"If your beast is anything like mine, if we shift we won't leave this room for days. My beast is pressing me hard to mate with you." He walked to the other side of the room. "Change of plans, no shifting. You can wear my shoes." He bent and started to remove them.

"No. I'll go barefoot." Shyla stole another glance at him and thanked the Goddess. Taller than her, muscular body, and a seriously good aura. She wanted lots of pups with this wolf. Just thinking about little dark-haired pups running around the house made her smile.

"Whatever you're thinking about, please stop. You're releasing pheromones and my beast is about to rip me a new one to get to you.

After we get out of here, we can do anything you want and more, right now let's focus on the problem."

Her cheeks burned. Clearing her throat, she nodded and moved further away. Fortunately, he was thinking with the right head, although it chafed a bit how he could be so clear-headed when all she wanted was to fall back into bed with him inside her. Damn this mating pull.

"How'd you get here?"

Shyla told him about the scroll and what happened after.

"Is that common? For someone to just leave valuable information lying around your home like that?" he asked with genuine curiosity.

"Yes. Mengistia work for higher powers, not pack. Most times the person delivering documents or artifacts has no memories of visiting my home," she said, watching him carefully to see how much he knew of her world.

"Someone used a trick to get you here. Any idea why?" he asked, maintaining his distance.

"I think a mistake was made, whoever is behind this sounded upset." She watched his muscles move beneath his shirt. Goddess, he smelled divine, like earth, honeysuckle, and chocolate. Heat flashed to her core. Her nipples ached for his touch.

"Stop that," Angus snapped. His eyes changed to a dark sea green. "We are somewhere in the middle of the earth with a woman who betrayed the Goddess because she couldn't control herself. I've been told your life is in danger and I need to get you to safety before plunging between your thighs. Now focus on getting out of here."

His words were like ice cold water on her libido. He was right, this was not the time, and if they were to survive whatever waited on the other side of that door, she needed her mind on other things. "Don't yell at me." With that weak rebuttal, she strode to the door and pulled on the handle. It wouldn't open.

"Did you have any problems opening this?" she asked over her shoulder without looking at him.

"No. Let me try."

Stepping aside, she returned to her corner in the room and watched as he tried to open the door without success.

"Shit," he muttered and stopped. "They want us together, why?" he asked softly. "I was told I had to find you to save your life. What did they tell you?"

Curious, she straightened. "That if I didn't do exactly as she said, my mate would die."

"Did she say why?"

"Because a sacred book allowed me to read it. Supposedly, only three people in centuries have ever read it. I didn't understand anything I read, though."

He waved away her comment and rubbed his forehead. "What's read cannot be unread."

"That's what she said," Shyla said. "But she never mentioned betraying the Goddess."

"From what I understand, someone, a male, tricked her. She let him into her chamber and at some point, he took pictures from a sacred text. That set all of this in motion." He raised his hands and dropped them against his side.

Shyla whistled. "No one's supposed to go in the chambers except Mengistia. There are secrets that predate humanity, things between the gods. Let's hope he didn't take anything that'll stop the earth from moving." She smiled at the stricken look on his face. "Just kidding, as far as I know, we don't have that information on earth."

"Right." He paused. "Have you met the Chancellor?"

"No. Was that her chamber I landed in?"

Angus nodded slowly. "I believe so. Which meant she brought you here or knows who did. But why you? You're not the only Mengistia, are you?"

She shook her head. "No, there are several of us across the world. So why did they pick me?" Now that he'd asked the question, she couldn't stop thinking about it. It had to be someone with knowledge of her role as Mengistia, and that was a short list. Her Alpha knew she was pack historian but didn't know her true title.

"They used some kind of key."

"What? The words on the scroll?"

He nodded.

She had already assumed that, but how did he know that?

"That key created an opening and took you to a specific place in the stacks, not far from the sacred text, probably a test to see if you could read it. Still, it comes back to you. Why?" He stared at her as if trying to read the story of her life through her skin. Uneasy pinpricks spread across her neck and back.

She shrugged and wrapped her arms around her waist. "I don't know. Until this happened, I would've said I lived the dull life of a librarian. Things like this don't happen to me." She stared at him for a few seconds. "What about you? Why'd they bring you into this?"

His brow rose. "Mates?"

"Nope, that's not it. Not if they told *you* I would die if you didn't save me. I was told *you* would die. Plus, I had no idea I had a mate." She rubbed her forehead and walked in a tight circle.

"Same here. First I heard of you was when grandfather mentioned it yesterday."

She stopped. "Grandfather? Black wolf about this tall?" She raised her hand to her stomach.

He nodded.

"Green eyes like yours?"

He nodded.

"When did he step out of dreams?" None of this made sense.

"Not sure, but he told me about you. But that raises another question; who told him? I mean, isn't assigning mates something the Goddess does?"

They stared at each other for a few moments as those words settled. If the Goddess was involved, there wasn't a whole lot they could do about it, other than wait and see what happened. "I wish I could reach my Alpha and explain what's going on, this is so confusing," she said.

"You can't reach anyone either?" he asked.

"No, the separation has been hard." She didn't want him to think she was weak, but she'd never been this alone before and it freaked her out.

"You're not alone anymore and never will be again." His gaze caught hers and held it for a few moments. Mesmerized, she didn't look away from the promises, both spoken and unspoken, he made.

"Thank you," she said through a tight throat.

"Our introduction has been unusual, my brother will no doubt give me grief over it for millennium, but we are mates." He shook his head. "I digress. Someone wanted us to be together here. At this time and place. Why?"

She clasped her hands together and walked in a tight circle. "Mates coming together for the first time have little control. Maybe this is a test of sorts, to see if we're strong enough to resist the mating call."

"Possible." His brow rose as he looked at her. "How are you holding up?"

"Not good. My beast wants to meet her mate. It's... it's difficult to keep her contained and think about our problem." She bit her lip and turned her back on him. Maybe if she couldn't see his glorious body she could work through this with him. Then his arousal slammed into her. Her steps faltered as she gasped for breath. No way could she hold out much longer.

"Sorry," he said in a ragged whisper. "I don't think I can stop this."

Shyla gasped as her womb clenched. "Goddess no, not like this."

"Come here." His voice had deepened to a gravelly sound that scraped deliciously against her skin.

Compelled by a need and desire so strong, her legs buckled. Horrified that he'd think her weak, she moved toward him and stopped within an arm's length. He took two steps forward and wrapped her in his embrace.

Without warning, he fisted her hair, forcing her to look at him. Her beast howled in pleasure. Orderly thoughts scattered as she saw her need mirrored in his eyes. Would he take her now and cement their bond? Excitement raced through her as she fought for her next breath. He stepped closer and placed his hand dangerously low on her back. For a moment, they stood like that, inhaling and holding each other.

"I never thought I'd find or have a mate," he said against her hair. "I've walked this earth over 300 years, just never thought there was a you." His arms squeezed her waist.

"I've dreamed of this. Having a mate. Lately, it's all I could think of. I want to be the center of someone, well, not someone anymore." She smiled against his chest. "Your world."

"You are. I left everything to come for you."

Shyla gasped, her brow furrowed. "They knew that." She leaned back and looked into his eyes. "That's what this is about. They want us to mate, to strengthen the bond so they can control us."

"Shift."

She eyed him for a few seconds and flowed into her beast. Seconds later, he also shifted and then stood over her. *"Do you hear me?"*

She yipped as their mental links opened and solidified.

"It's easier to connect in this form. Now we can communicate without being heard. Why do you think they want to control us?" He moved to stand behind her.

Shyla sat on the floor with her head on her paws for a few seconds before inching closer to him. His tantalizing scent permeated her skin as if he were marking her from the inside.

"Because she told me I had to do exactly what she says if I want you to live. I think you're going to pay for me reading the book or something like that. If we bond, there's no separating us. Your life for my life."

94

"I'm there already," he said.

"From what I understand, what we feel now is tame compared to what it's like as bonded mates. Separation is painful, knowing you're in any kind of distress will make me crazy, it's different than this, and this is hard," she said.

"If that's true, then they'll win. I can't hold out much longer." He bent forward and touched the back of her head.

Heat from his words scorched her. She morphed to human and remained on the floor looking up at him.

Angus shifted and eased on top of her. *"I have to taste you."*

"Please touch me." Every inch of her skin burned in anticipation. When his lips brushed against hers, tingles raced across her body broadcasting her excitement.

He placed small kisses across her face and then nibbled on her lips. Lifting slightly, he stared into her eyes and stroked her hair. One second, they undressed each other with their eyes, the next, his lips slammed against her, nearly knocking all the wind from her lungs.

Delicious tingles shot through her body as he pressed his tongue to the seam of her lips and, with a little encouragement from her, delved inside her mouth. Her brain lit on fire. Warmth spread throughout her entire body as she reached up and tangled her arms around his thick, strong neck. Exquisite moments passed as their tongues dueled with one another. They broke apart on a groan because of the separation.

"Thank you, Goddess." He placed a quick kiss on her lips. *"She is more than I ever hoped for."* His fingers massaged her breast as he watched her eyes flutter with pleasure. *"I will treasure her forever and pledge my life to protect hers."*

The potency of his words shattered her lust-filled bubble. *"No, Angus. There are some things we can never do. I think all of this will come to that, you'll have to choose."* She closed her eyes for a few seconds against the concern in his. *"Your life will be required for something and it must be something neither of us would normally do, otherwise, they wouldn't want to use our bond as leverage. I would rather die than betray the Goddess or my Alpha. Please don't say you'll do anything to protect me."* Her tone had gone from seductive siren to begging for their lives.

Angus cupped her chin in his palm and stared into her eyes. She meant it. Fear of what lie ahead and those who would use them for some nefarious purpose ravaged her heart. What she said made sense. He'd die for his mate, but how far would he go? Someone was betting he'd lose all sense of self and become what? A cold-blooded killer? Betray someone? He stiffened.

"La Patron."

Her eyes widened. *"What? What do you mean La Patron?"*

"Betrayal you said."

"Why would they pick you for that?"

He ignored the doubt in her voice. *"He's my brother. I'm his beta. I will never betray him."* He rolled to the side, pulling her with him as his heart broke with certainty that this was an attack against Silas. *"They cut our mental connection."*

"You're his brother?"

"Yes. And guardian for his pups. I pledged my life to him and his den, and cannot break that vow, not even for my mate." His throat tightened as his beast howled in pain with the unfairness of it all. His hand rubbed her soft, silky skin. *"Mine."*

She smiled at him, her own eyes filling with tears as she pulled him into a tight hug. *"I've waited all my life for you and I'm not giving you up without a fight. Together we'll beat whatever they have planned. I don't want to lose you, not like this."*

His eyes closed to block the mind-numbing pain in his chest. *"If we bond, you will die when I give my life for my Alpha. I won't risk you."*

How could this be happening? After three hundred years of walking alone, losing his mate would be his end? He served his Alpha, his people, and the Goddess as best he could, only to come to this moment in time? His chest constricted. Tendrils of her sorrow wrapped around his heart, syncing with his heartbeat.

Words of comfort lodged in his throat. She rolled over and stared into his eyes.

"They aren't going to let us out of here until we bond." She shook her head. Small curls framed her coffee-colored oval face. A couple large curls swung downward, covering her left eye. *"Or at least until they think we've bonded."* She continued to pin him with her gaze. Moss green eyes filled with an age-old need melted his resistance. His mate needed him. Now.

Again, he plunged his hand into her short, dark curls and pulled her down. *"No biting."*

She nodded. *"No biting. But to make it look real, just suck on my neck."* She paused. *"I really like that."*

He smiled. *"Good to know."*

"Just so you know, I'd still have sex with you even if we didn't need to get out of here. Don't think I'm only in it for the greater good." She smiled as she stood and started removing her clothes.

For a moment, he simply stared at his beautiful mate's long, toned legs, full hips and breasts. The Goddess had gifted him with a full-figured woman. Mouth watering, he stood and stripped without taking his eyes off her gorgeous breasts, small waist, and wide, ample hips.

"Same here." He pulled her close, slanted his lips over hers and kissed her. The knowledge she belonged to him made this coupling different. Everything seemed magnified. Her taste exploded in his mouth, instantly becoming his favorite, something he wanted with every fiber of his being. Her scent wrapped around him, binding him forever to her will and needs. When her arms around his neck tightened, he pulled her closer, never wanting to let her go. Gasping, they broke apart.

Cock hard and pulsing wildly, he pushed her backward and they fell onto the bed together. The scent of her arousal slew him. Unable to resist, like two magnets, their mouths re-joined. Moans of pleasure filled the air. His hand squeezed and kneaded her breasts as they kissed passionately, hardly coming up for air. They jerked apart for air. His lips and tongue blazed a trail down her neck to her breast. He sucked on a hardened nipple as his finger worked on its twin, tweaking and pulling it gently.

She arched into his touch, moaning and encouraging him to continue. Her words dropped as a match to gasoline, setting him ablaze with a desperate need to claim her. One hand slid lower and dived deep, splitting her sex with two fingers as he worked her swollen clitoris. She was drenched and gasping for more.

Angus eased one finger inside.

"Yesssss," she hissed at his entry.

"Goddess, you're tight." He hooked his finger and exited, reinserting two fingers. She moved her hips, bucking against his hand, her walls flexed against his fingers. His cock hurt. Need to take her slammed into him. He released her nipple, rolled onto his back, and lifted her above him. Her greedy fingers grabbed his cock.

He groaned and closed his eyes as pleasure rolled through him.

"This looks good," she said, her thumb spreading the pre-cum juices over the head. "Once we slake our hunger, I need to taste you."

Images of his mate taking him in her mouth sent a tremor through him. She rubbed the tip of his dick against her opening and he let her have her way. Inch by incredible inch, she worked her way down on him. He was amazed by how tight she was and how sopping wet she'd been for him. Sweat rolled down his forehead as he remained still until she was fully seated. Their gazes clashed.

"Fuck me," she said, watching him.

His heart soared. This woman was indeed a match for him.

He moved his hips gently, allowing the tight muscles of her pussy to become accustomed to his full girth. A moan of ecstasy escaped when she moved her hips up and down, clenching her pussy tight around his cock. Heaven on earth. The scent of their play filled the air along with sounds of slapping flesh. He thrust his hips to meet her every move; pushing up when she came down onto him. Unable to stop himself, he pulled her shoulders down slowly to meet his lips, kissing her again as her hips bobbed up and down on his cock. Never had he been so consumed. No doubt he was fucking dying, being rearranged into someone new, better, with each thrust.

She screamed his name and bit down deep into his shoulder.

Something wound tight snapped. He grabbed her hips tight and pistoned in and out of her faster and faster. She screamed his name again, this time as she came. On one final thrust, he emptied inside her as her convulsing muscles milked his cock. Tremors raced through his body, but there was more. An indefinable awareness of the luscious woman in his arms that hadn't been there a second ago. As his heartbeat and adrenaline slowed, it hit him.

His mate had bitten him.

CHAPTER 12

Jasmine headed to her office after taking the children to school. Asia's concern regarding Daria was valid and she would press Jacques to get that information as soon as possible. As she turned the corner she wondered again about Lilly's behavior the other night at dinner. The younger woman seemed withdrawn. In retrospect, Jasmine couldn't remember the last time Lilly had laughed or smiled.

Should she talk to Lilly? Was that a part of her duties as La Patroness? She had no idea. As plain old Jasmine, she would wait for Lilly to come to her, share her problem, and ask for advice if she wanted it.

However, as her husband continually reminded her, she was no longer plain Jasmine. Lilly's position as mate of the state Alpha was important to the pack. Which meant Jasmine would need to schedule a conversation and pray that whatever bothered Lilly wasn't something too personal. With that decision made, she walked through the back door into her office, bypassing the small reception area in case someone was there. She turned on her computer and checked her messages.

Nothing regarding Daria. She glanced at the clock. "Almost nine, I'll give him until noon before bugging him." A soft knock on her inner office door interrupted her thoughts.

"Come in."

Vanessa walked in holding stacks of papers. "Are these the reports you want me to go over?" She held them so Jasmine could see.

"They're upside down, but I think that's them."

"Oops, I'm sorry." Vanessa turned them.

"That's okay, I saw them. I'd appreciate if you'd look over them for me, make sure everything's in order and make notes on anything that seems out of place. I'm just doing this as a precaution. Normally these reports are top-notch."

"Yes. Yes, of course." Vanessa paused, turned slowly, and headed to the door.

"Everything okay?" Jasmine asked, wondering if Vanessa didn't want to do the work after all.

"Yes. No." Vanessa shook her head and then dropped it. "I've been calling Shyla since we got here. At first, I thought she was out shopping or something. But she never called back. Then I called again last night, then later, but she never answered." She looked at Jasmine, her eyes filled with worry. "That's not like her."

Jasmine remembered the strong full-blood, the first person she'd ever fully merged with. Shyla was feisty, and strong with a secret. Had that gotten her in trouble? Jasmine hoped not. "Has Ethan sent someone to check on her?"

"Yes, Ma'am. We're waiting to hear from them. But I can't help but think something's wrong. Shyla doesn't go out a lot, she loves cooking or puttering around her house. We had one of our receptions there, mostly people we work with."

Jasmine nodded. "She's a lovely woman, let me know what Ethan finds out."

Vanessa opened the door and stopped. Her mouth dropped open as her eyes widened. A gentle breeze ran through the room as Vanessa closed her eyes and tears trekked down her cheeks.

"Silas, you need to see this, bring Ethan to my office," Jasmine said as she watched the young breeder's powers unfurl. *"Make sure no one else is close by and lock us in when you come."*

"On my way," he said.

Jasmine sat back in the chair and watched as Vanessa sat heavily in an armchair and placed the papers to the side. "Vanessa? What happened?"

"She's... she's not there. Her purse and everything else is there, but they can't find her," she said in a ragged whisper. "What happened to her? Where can she be? Did someone take her? No.

Shyla would kick ass, but why isn't she answering her phone?" The entire time Vanessa asked and answered her questions, she stared at her closed fists, not seeing or feeling the mini-whirlwinds in the air above her head.

Mesmerized, Jasmine remained still as unfamiliar energy brushed against her. Silas and the boys had told her about the times she lost control and her energy spiked, but she'd never seen it. Not until now. It was indeed a thing of beauty.

"We're here," Silas said, just outside her office. *"Are you having an attack? I feel energy but it's different."*

"It's Vanessa. Let Ethan walk in first."

The door opened. Vanessa didn't turn or acknowledge her mate or Silas, instead, she continued asking herself questions about her friend.

"Nessa?" Ethan said in a soft voice while Silas leaned against the wall, watching.

"Is this what it looked like when I first lost control?" Jasmine asked him.

"Similar. What brought this on?"

Jasmine told him what Vanessa shared with her. *"Shyla's the librarian?"*

"Yes, and she's more."

He looked across the room at Jasmine. *"More?"*

"Yes. When I entered her to defeat Brenda, I had access to her memories. She's something called a Mengistia. I can't believe I remembered that. It's a strange name, maybe that's why."

"Do you know what it is?"

He nodded slowly. *"Keeper of secrets. They aren't under pack law. I didn't know there was one on the east coast. I suspected Maheegan, our national pack historian, was Mengistia, but since they are forbidden to disclose their titles or the location of their chambers, I've never been positive."*

"Do you think her disappearance has something to do with Ethan? Could someone have taken her in retribution for taking out

that small group?" She watched as Ethan stooped in front of his mate, forehead to forehead, and held her loosely. The wind funnels decreased and stopped.

"I don't know. It's something to consider. Right now, we need to deal with this. She has to learn control or someone will get hurt," Silas said, straightening and walking toward Jasmine. He sat on the corner of her desk. *"Vanessa?"*

She lifted her head and looked at him with watery, red-rimmed eyes. "Sir?"

"Jasmine tells me it's not normal for your friend to disappear like this. The first thing we should do is contact her Alpha, Jayden. He will send pack to search for her." He looked at Ethan. "Has this been done?"

"Yes, Sir." Ethan stood, his hand remained on his mate's shoulder. "I contacted him as soon as I received the report she wasn't at home. From what I've been told, there is a search for her right now. Her sire and mam have been contacted. They spoke to her recently; I don't have the exact time, but they are en route to the house from Florida where they were on vacation."

"Mengistia are related by blood, always passes through the mother to the daughter. Her mother may be the only person who can enter the chamber and search for clues," he told Jasmine.

"Clues in the chamber?"

He nodded. *"Wherever the chamber is housed, the house becomes a part of the security system. It helps hide secrets."*

"That's so cool. I'd love to see that," Jasmine said, rising and standing next to Silas.

"It would kill you before you entered the room. The house keeps its secrets." He smiled as she pushed his shoulder.

"Something's wrong, this isn't like her," Vanessa said, her hands clasped tightly.

"Calm down, baby," Ethan said, stooping in front of her again. Their eyes met and after a few seconds, Vanessa nodded. Ethan looked up at Silas. "As you can see, my mate has a problem controlling her energy."

"*You think?*" Jasmine said to Silas.

"Yes, I see. What are you doing to help her?" Silas asked Ethan, ignoring Jasmine's comment.

Ethan stood and rubbed the back of his neck. "Nothing. We haven't had time to get to it. The wedding, moving and coming here." He released a stream of air. "This is the second time I've seen it. The first time she was fighting Brenda, and then today. It seems as if it happens when she's mad."

"I'm sitting right here, Ethan," Vanessa snapped. "I can speak for myself."

Ethan looked at her for a few seconds and smiled. "You're right. My bad." He stepped behind her.

Vanessa looked as Silas and then Jasmine. "Basically, what he said. Although I wasn't mad. I'm scared. She's my best friend, we've always looked out for each other. I'm scared something happened to her, that she's hurt and can't get help. The idea of her lying somewhere helpless and maybe even dying." She paused and covered her mouth. One hand pressed against her stomach. For a few seconds, no one spoke. The air stirred but that was the extent of it. "I can't deal with that," she whispered. "All this waiting to file a missing persons report, they take too long."

Jasmine's heart twisted.

"Pack isn't like human cops, Vanessa," Silas said. "Jayden's already getting reports. No track or scent signatures outside. So, she was in the house when she left. There are some places pack can't access and they're waiting for her parents to arrive with keys to open the other areas. She wasn't taken from the house, she may be locked in one of the rooms inside the house, we have to wait and see."

Vanessa's countenance brightened. "That's good, right? Better than being dragged away. Plus, I talked to her a couple days ago, so she wouldn't be locked in the room too long, right?" Her gaze, desperate for good news, flicked from Silas to Jasmine and then to her mate, Ethan.

"It's good," Ethan said.

Vanessa slumped in the chair and closed her eyes.

Ethan's worried gaze slid from Silas to Jasmine and back to his mate.

"*What are you going to do about her energy spikes?*" Jasmine asked Silas.

"*I'll give Ethan some pointers to help him train her. If she needs more, I'll have her make an appointment with La Patroness, who has firsthand knowledge and experience in these matters.*" He straightened and walked toward the door. "Ethan."

Ethan leaned down, kissed Vanessa's brow, and then stepped out the door behind Silas.

"I didn't get him in trouble, did I?" Vanessa asked after a few moments of silence.

"No. You didn't do anything," Jasmine assured her. Silas' words tumbled through her mind. Could she teach someone how to handle their energy? It had been hard in the beginning, but now she recognized and appreciated it for the tool it was. "I didn't know Shyla and I'm upset she's missing. Once her parents arrive, we'll get some answers." She waved to the stack of papers. "You can get to those later, right now why not rest and wait."

"Please let me do this now, it'll keep my mind off what's happening. Believe me, I need a distraction." She tried to smile but failed miserably.

"Sure, whatever helps you." Jasmine paused. "When you were sitting there asking yourself questions, your hands were balled into fists. What did you feel on the inside?"

Vanessa's eyes widened and then she tilted her head. "Hmm, I never thought about it before, but there was this tight ball in my stomach that grew bigger and bigger." She looked at Jasmine as if she'd just discovered chocolate tasted good on ice-cream.

"The more your thought about it, the bigger and tighter the ball grew?"

Vanessa nodded. "Yes. I didn't think about it at the time, it was as if everything was on a loop, with each scene worse than the one before." She shook her head. "It was a train ride and I couldn't get off."

CHAPTER 13

"Looks like you were right, Sir. Having an extra full-blood was just the thing. This last group is four instead of five. But, we still have the 50 you needed. As soon as they arrive, we'll take off and should make your deadline."

"You leave on schedule, with or without them. If they're late, they are of no use to me. Terminate them."

"Yes, Sir. We will leave in one hour."

Scorpio watched the monitor a few more seconds and clicked off. Adrenaline flooded his system like an intravenous drip, any second his heart would explode. It was coming together. All the pieces of the fucking impossible puzzle. He bent from his waist and breathed deeply to slow his heart, to think.

The door behind him opened and he straightened slowly, wiping every bit of emotion from his face. Victory belonged to them. Their belief and hard work brought them to this point.

"Any news?"

"Yes, everything is on track. We go forward." He looked over his shoulder to see the excitement in the eyes of his brother. No one believed this could happen and yet, it was happening, or soon would.

"Finally! Everything is in place, I will place the call to alert the others on our progress. He will be pleased."

"This must work, we cannot fail him. Not after all this time, we cannot fail." They exchanged looks and nodded. "I will recheck everything so that we are prepared for anything. Failure is not an option."

"Not an option," Scorpio muttered as he looked at the computer monitor. Everything had been planned, contingencies reviewed, it was time to make this happen. His heart tightened in sorrow over a devastating part of their plan. Knowing it was for the greater good offered small comfort to his wounded spirit.

CHAPTER 14

Sex during the mating heat couldn't be explained. There were no manuals or lectures on what to expect, it simply had to be experienced. Bizarre colors, weird scents from their mating, and sounds of unrelenting pleasure echoed in her mind, hampering her ability to think clearly. For months, she had wanted this, had been jealous over Vanessa's secret smiles and whimsical expressions. Now she understood. Being mated had serious benefits when it came to sex. Nothing could compare to the level of close intimacy when your souls merged and bathed your body in constant delight. Even now, her skin tingled in remembrance. She ached in places she never ached before.

Rolling to the side, she gazed at his masculine beauty. Brother to La Patron. She hadn't expected that. Now that she really looked at him, she saw the resemblance. His bloodline certainly could complicate things. Chances were, this was an enemy of La Patron using Angus as leverage and her as bait. That's the only thing that made sense.

Angus' arm draped across her chest, he pulled her closer. *"You okay?"*

Heat raced up her cheeks. *"Yeah, I'm good. You?"* she asked with a cheeky smile.

"I think you wore me out, whoever said age is just a number lied. I feel every year right now."

She ran her hand down his side, stopping at his hip. *"Tired?"*

He rolled on top of her and nudged her legs apart. *"Never too tired for you."* His hard cock pulsed against her mound. Leaning down, he captured her mouth with his and everything in the world ceased. He took his time kissing her, deepening the kiss when she wrapped her arms around his neck. He tasted her slowly. Her greedy, battered pussy throbbed for more of this man.

When they broke apart this time, it was with the assurance they would do this again and again. They had taken off the edge, fed the need so they could think.

"I never knew how much I needed you," he said, his voice filled with wonder. *"But I do. For the first time in centuries, I am complete, which is strange because I never thought I was lacking. Now, it's as if I'm more."* He shook his head. *"Does that make sense?"*

"Perfect sense. You are more, we both are because I have parts of you. I relived your childhood, saw La Patron as a pup, your mam and sire. Also, your memories with Ulric and the pack. Those burdens are no longer yours alone. I share those with you just as you have my memories."

He kissed the tip of her nose. *"Yes, your mother is quite formidable. I look forward to meeting both your mam and sire. It's good to know you have a strong relationship with your family. I did enjoy your training and it's given me some ideas on how to fight this, whatever it is."*

Dread mixed with shame filled her. *"I'm so sorry for biting you after we agreed not to bite or bond. I have no excuse other than I've never been mated before and had no idea how strong the urge would be."*

He brushed his lips against hers. *"Shh, what happened, happened. We move forward together as one to defeat the plans of our enemies."* He kissed her again. *"Okay, my precious?"*

Her heart eased. *"Yes. We will win."*

"Good." He slid off her and walked naked to the door. It opened when he turned the knob. He looked at her over his shoulder and shifted.

Shyla scooted off the bed, shifted, and followed him out the door down the hall. When he stopped, she waited behind him a few seconds, then walked to his side. *"What is it?"*

"Not sure, but this looks a lot different than before. That door wasn't visible before, now it's ajar. I get the feeling they want us to

go that way." He looked at her much smaller wolf and trotted in the opposite direction until they came to a wall. Certain they would turn back now, Shyla looked over her shoulder to find the room they'd avoided earlier. A scraping sound in front of them arrested her attention. Angus had morphed to human and done something to the wall and now returned to wolf.

"Wait for my signal to follow."

She sat on her haunches, watching him pick his way through some sort of dusty maze. When she couldn't see him, she trotted to the edge of the wall, but no further. The last thing she wanted was to cause him any kind of grief.

"Come on. Follow my scent, walk slow like I did. I will meet you."

Relief enveloped her as she picked her way over some kind of embedded stones. Dim lights were situated next to a path that wound right and then rose upward. *"This is someone's escape plan."* Her head grazed against the thick rope railings as she met up with him. When he didn't respond, she stopped and waited. *"Why are they allowing us to leave. And when I say leave, we're using their paths, which takes us to a place of their choosing, so we aren't leaving as much as re-positioning."* If they were going to remain prisoners, they could've stayed in bed a little longer.

He trotted back and sat in front of her. *"I agree, but I don't know what else to do other than play their game. Do you remember anything in the books regarding this?"*

His question set her back a bit. *"No. Nothing here is familiar."*

"Not the location, more like this setup? Anything like that?"

"No. I'm sorry." She hated disappointing him, but she'd never read anything close to landing in a library, being rescued by her mate, and escaping by some underground tunnel.

"Since we recognize this as a trap of sorts, I think we should continue forward and deal with whatever comes our way. The only other option is to remain down here with no food or water."

She hadn't been hungry until he mentioned food. Her stomach growled. *"You got a point."* She stood.

He turned and trotted down the path.

Filtering scents as she followed behind, Shyla patted herself on the back. Her mom always said it was just as important to know how a man handled a disagreement. Angus listened and then presented his case. She agreed with him, but if she hadn't, she believed he would have explored different options to address her concerns. They would be partners in every way.

After what could have been an hour or several, Shyla finally saw a sliver of daylight ahead. So far they'd moved at a sedate steady pace, but knowing they were close to being outside this narrow tunnel quickened their steps. When Angus reached the corner, he waited for her. *"Even though I don't sense anything out there, let me look around first. I won't be long, I promise."*

She nodded and sat tiredly on the path. They needed water and food in that order.

"This is good. I know this place, come outside."

Shyla stepped outside into the late day sun. *"You've been here before?"* She looked around at the green and brown forest. Some trees stretched so high they blocked the sun.

"Yes, I was born in this country, not too far from here. But I spent a lot of time exploring the mountains. Come, I know where we can get water and food."

Her stomach growled again as she followed him. The trek down was slow and tricky, but he navigated it like a pro. In less than an hour, she stood over a bubbling brook drinking her fill of cold spring water while Angus stood nearby watching.

When she finished, he shifted, kneeled, cupped his hand and drank while watching the area. Shyla walked into the cave and looked around. *"It's warded. As my mate, you see the entrance and can walk inside, others cannot."*

"You know mystical things?" She tried to keep the surprise out of her voice and failed.

"Yes, I do. Let's gather some fruit and eat. Then we'll decide what to do next."

She shifted. *"Good idea. I'm starving. Mating is hard work."*

"Extremely satisfying work." He took her hand and they walked naked into the woods for a short distance until he stopped and pointed at a tree with low hanging yellow fruit. *"These are like mangoes but they aren't stringy and not as sweet. But they're filling. If you gather some of those berries, I'll grab a few a couple of these and a few other things, and we can eat inside the cave. I have clothes in there."*

"Sounds good." She pulled the berries as she would grapes from a vine. When she couldn't hold anymore she waited as Angus climbed down from the tree with two large fruits tucked into a large leaf he'd made into a sling.

"Obviously, you've done this before." Her brow rose as he pulled a couple roots out of the ground.

He chuckled. *"I planted most of this when I lived here years ago. This is like a homecoming, if we ignore the beginning."* He strode to the stream and rinsed everything.

She rinsed the berries and followed him into the cave. A few seconds later, wall sconces were lit and she got a better look around. The small area where she stood opened into a larger one. A long table with one chair was in the middle of the room. Several books, microscopes, burners, and other scientific equipment lined shelves and wood-hewn cabinetry.

"What did you do here?" She placed the berries on the table where he peeled and cut the fruit into a bowl.

"Work with crystals. Translated old texts. Created stuff. It kept my mind off other things."

Since she'd seen sensed his loneliness for a long stretch, she understood. Moving behind him, she wrapped her arms around his waist and held him close, sharing her warmth and understanding.

"I still do this at the compound. I have a lab there." He turned and held a piece of fruit next to her mouth, waiting for her to open.

She bit into it. Juice squirted on his chin and ran down her mouth. Laughing, she backed away and ate it quickly. *"That's good."* She reached into the bowl and grabbed another piece.

"Glad you like it. I never discovered the name for it, and don't know the nutritional value, but I've eaten it for over a century and never had any problems." He pointed the knife to a small chest in the corner. "T*here's some clothes in there. See if anything will fit you."*

She nodded.

Angus watched as she stooped and opened the chest. He was almost done with this fruit salad. It wasn't meat but he didn't want to chance hunting for game. Too many humans with guns roamed the mountains these days, it wasn't safe and he refused to take any chances with Shyla, his mate.

His chest expanded as he prepared their first meal. A meal he provided. Later, he would take her deeper into the cavern so she could immerse in his private hot water spring. He grabbed a large pitcher from the wood shelf. "Be right back." He held up the pitcher and headed to the spring outside. Just as he reached the entrance he sensed several heartbeats. Immediately, he layered the ward with another and then another. With each layer, the voices dimmed, but he could still hear them.

Humans.

They'd tracked him and Shyla but couldn't find the entrance. He heard the word, explosives, and then a heated argument. No explosives. They had to find another way to flush them out. Fire? Intrigued, he waited to see what they planned to do.

"What's going on?"

He explained what he knew.

Shyla walked up behind him and placed her hand on his shoulder. *"Are we eating on the run?"*

"Maybe." He took her hand and they returned to the table. In the corner, he lifted a lid and pulled out a long cylinder. Opening it,

he poured water into the bowl and finished mixing the fruit. *"Mash it a bit to get all the flavors."*

She took a large spoon from the wall and mashed the fruit while he dressed. Fully clothed, he rejoined her at the table and took the plate of fruit she gave him. *"This is really good,"* she said.

He smiled. Ideas of where they could go from here, and what they needed to do dogged his thoughts. The fruit salad could have been toast and butter for all the attention he paid his meal.

She placed her hand over his, stopping him from moving the fruit from one place to the other on his plate. *"Eat. Feed your beast. We'll need him and you at your peak."*

Her eyes told him she trusted him. In all his life, he'd never felt the heavy hand of responsibility as he did now. He couldn't fail her. Somehow they would return home safely. The next bite fed his spirit. Grandfather said he needed to trust his beast. He ate another spoonful and tested his bracelet. It tingled against his arm. Should he tell her about it? He wasn't sure. Better she not know until all of this was over, no telling what their enemy planned. Letting them leave the country wasn't in their immediate future.

He finished the rest of his food and polished off what was left in the bowl after she claimed to be stuffed. He poured her a glass of water, from which she drank deeply. He drank two glasses and returned the cylinder. *"Could you stand over here, please?"* He needed to cloak this room so that if the men made it through the first series of wards, they wouldn't see this area, they'd go to the open chamber on the other side. Next, he ushered her to the back of the cave.

"Next time I will bathe you in the hot springs. I don't think we'll properly enjoy it today." He pulled her close and pressed his lips against her forehead. She smelled incredible. His cock hardened as her scent raced through him.

"Soon, when this is done we will spend days getting to know each other," she said, turning from his hardness and pulling him past the steaming waters.

Holding her hand, he led her through a series of inter-connected caves and then stopped. Inside was a table, chair, and a bed.

"Angus, we can't," she said, even though he knew she would if he pushed. But he wouldn't.

"We need to talk about what to do next. This area is warded heaviest because it's where I rest." He pointed to the chair. *"Please sit."*

She sat perched on the edge and looked around the room before her gaze settled on his. *"They tracked us here."*

He nodded and leaned against the wall. *"I got the feeling there was a time element involved, did you?"*

"Yes, I think so."

"Grandfather was afraid I'd be too late. They allowed us to leave and sent trackers, why allow us to leave?"

"Maybe they assumed we'd go through the door and not the wall. Maybe you surprised them by not operating according to their plans. This whole hunt them down thing is an unexpected problem." She chuckled. *"Glad we could mess up their day."*

"True. But we can't stay here much longer."

"They don't know that."

"Huh?"

"Think about it. No one knows what's in here. You've kept people out for years and unless they've masked their scents, no one has been inside these caves. They don't know what's in here exactly."

He thought about it for a few seconds. *"Okay. You're right. They don't know, but we can't stay more than a day. No food, very little water. We need to leave."*

"And go where?"

He shook his head. *"We aren't far from Alpha Ulric's lands."* He paused. *"If these are hostile forces, I can't have them follow me there. Too many pups. There could be collateral damage."*

She nodded. *"I agree. So, where does that leave us?"*

Neither spoke for a few moments.

"If I could contact Barticus, he could get us out of here or at least even the odds. But I need to get to a phone."

"Do you think the humans outside have phones? Will you be able to get a signal?" she asked.

"I'm sure one of them does, but it's risky." He could use the chameleon bracelet, take on the characteristics of the human, make the call and wait. But what about his mate? There were no bracelets here. He couldn't share his, which would leave her vulnerable.

"Perhaps it's our best option." She jerked. *"Did you hear that?"*

Angus had been monitoring the area outside this room the entire time. He didn't think anyone could break his wards on the front, but if there was a concerted effort to enter the mountain from various points, someone may have gotten lucky. With handheld thermal heat finders, it wouldn't be long before they found this alcove, entering it was another matter.

"Stay here, let me check on things."

"No. We stay together." She stood.

"Please, let me do this. I'll be back, I promise." Her gaze warred with indecision until she crossed her arms over her chest nodded and sat back down. He leaned forward, kissed her forehead, and let himself out. Outside the room, he strengthened the ward and left the illusion of a solid wall.

Footsteps in the distance. One heartbeat. Angus leaned on the wall, activated the bracelet and blended in. Several moments later, a guard, dusty from head to toe, walked past Angus wearing thermal glasses. He stopped at the wall covering Shyla and stared at it a few moments. Angus sprung off the wall, grabbed him by the neck, covered his mouth and activated the chameleon. Seconds later, Abe Jones dropped dead to the ground. Angus emptied the pockets, found the cell phone, a separate communication device, two Glocks, and ammunition. He placed the headphone in his ear and dragged Abe into an area with a long drop down a ravine.

Confident no one followed him, he returned to Shyla, showed her the phone and the equipment while telling her what happened, leaving out the bracelet. *"Do you know how to use these?"* He showed her the guns.

She picked up the Glock, released the magazine, reloaded and pointed it so fast he held his hands up. *"I guess that's a yes."*

"Most definitely a yes." She put some of the ammunition as well as a knife in her pockets. *"Can you get a signal?"*

He looked at the phone. *"This is different, I've never seen one like this."* While he held it, a text rolled through. "Status update." He pursed his lips and then looked at her. *"Chances are these have locators in them, they may know he lost this device."* He shoved it in his pocket, along with the other Glock and ammunition. *"We need to go. If they are tracking this device, I'll leave it somewhere to buy us some time."*

She stood, rolled up the baggy pant legs to her ankle. He muttered the words that would allow them to leave the alcove and then resealed it. He waved her forward. They crept along a narrow passage until they came to an opening with rocks lining the floor and a low overhang that broke off into three directions. Angus slid the phone in one and waved her forward.

"Take off your clothes, we'll put them in this bag so we can dress when we're outside." He shook out a canvas bag from his pocket and started undressing. She did the same. He tossed the bag into an overhead opening, shifted and jumped up. It took a few seconds to get all of his bulk inside the small cavern. He grabbed the bag with his teeth, backed up and waited for Shyla. When she joined him, they crept slowly forward, avoiding jagged rocks from the side.

"This is tight," Shyla said.

"Yes, as human it would tear off your skin and get bloody. Almost there." He continued forward and stopped. *"Full-bloods are nearby."*

"How'd they track us?"

"I'm not sure. They aren't inside. So maybe they are simply patrolling the mountain." The opening spilled into a small ledge overlooking a larger cave. *"We're at the opening. Shift and then change on the ledge, it's too narrow for our wolves."*

He dropped the bag, shifted, and then opened it. *"Here."* He passed her clothes, dressed, and folded the bag before stuffing it into one of his large pockets. *"Ready?"*

She nodded. They jumped down, landing on tightly packed earth.

"I count four," she said.

"Yes, and humans in the distance." Where could they go? Into the mountains? Maybe find a human and use their phone to call Barticus? Too many variables. Options? Fight? And then what? He refused to take this to Ulric. But Ulric could contact Silas, arrange a pick-up for Shyla at least. What if she was taken again? His heart dropped into his stomach. No. This needed to stop now.

The soft pads of her fingers eased into his hand, drawing his gaze. For several seconds a lifetime of acceptance and commitment passed between them. His throat tightened as fear, an old, nearly forgotten enemy, raised its head. What if he lost her? What if they hurt or stole her again? His beast howled in distress. Her palm cupped his cheek, while her thumb stroked it gently.

"Together. That's how we do this. If we are taken, we do not, under any circumstances, betray our Alpha or pack. I'd rather spend eternity with you on a higher plane than live here with that stain covering our souls. Agreed?"

His mouth opened and closed. Once he would have agreed outright, but that was before. Before she became the sun in his dark world. Life without Shyla? His heart bled. He couldn't conceive such a fate. But could he betray Silas? The pups? Torn, he closed his eyes tight to block her worried gaze.

"Angus?" She shook him. *"Agreed?"*

How could he choose? His mate or his Alpha. Goddess, please don't let it ever come to that because he wasn't sure what he would do.

She shook him again. *"Angus."*

Inhaling deeply, he opened his eyes. Her watery gaze locked on his.

"So precious. So beautiful. So strong." He released a long breath. *"I cannot give you the agreement you want, but I will try to honor your request. That's the best I can do."*

They continued gazing at each other and he wondered what she saw. Did she still see him as a worthy mate? Someone she could be proud of, stand next to? Would she reject him if he didn't do as she requested? How would they manage if that happened? He shook off his maudlin thoughts for another time. The full-bloods, all four of them, were close to the exit, they'd probably scented him and Shyla just as he'd scented them earlier.

"If that is the best you can do, that's all I want." Leaning forward, she brushed her lips against his. *"You're my mate for all eternity, there will never be another. Remember that."*

He crushed her in his arms, deepening the kiss, reaffirming their bond, their relationship, and their pack commitment. She broke first, gasping for air and wiping the tears from her cheek. *"Do we fight or save our energy for whoever they work for?"*

What a remarkable woman. She was afraid but didn't allow it to stop her from going forward. *"What do you want to do?"* Truly it didn't matter to him. Chances are these were modified full-bloods, which meant the bracelet wouldn't work on them. But if their hands were free, and if he got close enough to a human, he could gather information.

"Fight. It's only four of them." She grinned and pulled out her weapons.

"Bloodthirsty bitch, huh?" He grinned.

She winked.

"We'll do whatever you want, just stay close."

She nodded.

CHAPTER 15

Silas strode into the conference room, closed the door, and took a seat. Jasmine, Asia, Hawke, Jacques, Cain, and Abel sat watching him. He placed his fists on the table, inhaled, and released it slowly. "Tell me again what the fuck's going on?"

"When we reached the airfield, the plane had left even though I sent a message we were running behind. There was an accident blocking the highway, we arrived 30 minutes late. No one ever responded, they left without us. We drove to Alpha Theron's, took the jet and came back with the rebels, Passen has them now," Hawke said, leaning forward in his chair.

"Where did the damn plane go in such a hurry? Tell me everything about that flight," Silas growled. None of this made sense. Why not wait a few minutes for their cargo?

"The flight traveled to another private airstrip north of Plias," Jacques said.

Silas frowned. "That sounds familiar." He snapped his fingers. "Angus' flight landed near Plias, right?" He looked at Jacques.

"Yes. Within fifty miles, not far by vehicle," Jacques explained.

"Contact Barticus with the location of this flight and Ulric," Silas said. "I want pack to meet this plane and discover what's going on. If any full-bloods or breeds are on that flight I want them identified and returned. That's a good enough reason for packs to get involved." He sat back in his chair, his mind flying over all the pieces to this riddle. He couldn't shake the feeling his brother was in deep trouble and needed his help.

"On it," Hawke said.

Silas rubbed his forehead and looked at Jasmine. "Here's what I've got so far." His gaze swiped the table but returned to his mate. "Angus has to leave the country, travels to our homeland without telling me, and our connection is severed."

He paused as Asia gasped. Cain and Abel sat forward with similar frowns marring their foreheads and Jacques released a long sigh.

"That in itself is wrong on so many levels," Silas said.

"But that's the thing, right?" Jasmine asked, holding his gaze. "Who has the ability to break mental links between an Alpha and his pack?"

He knew she'd go there. In fact, he suspected everyone at the table silently asked the same question. "As La Patron, I can. All Alphas must petition me to break mental links when they turn-out a pack member. It's not something done lightly."

"You didn't break the connection with Angus or Shyla. Remember, Alpha Jayden can't link with her either," Jasmine said. "Either someone has found a way to usurp the natural order or is there another way links are broken?"

Their gazes meshed for a few seconds. She was going to make him say it. "Yes, the Goddess can break and form mental connections."

"Is it possible she broke the connection between you and Angus?" Jasmine asked, maintaining eye contact.

"Anything is possible, I don't think she did," Silas said, his displeasure with this line of questioning becoming evident. "If we ran with that theory, the Goddess becoming that involved, what about Shyla? Did she break that connection as well?"

Jasmine shrugged as she looked down at her clasped hands. "As you say, it's possible."

"But not probable," he snapped.

"Here is another perspective." She held up her hand stopping him. "Listen. What if Angus and Shyla are mates?"

Silas stared at her until she turned and met his gaze. The idea was so ludicrous, so heinous, so unimaginable, that she was in all probability, right. He cleared his throat. "Then that could create a problem. For Angus that is."

"Damn," Cain whispered.

"What are you thinking," Silas asked Jasmine.

"Daria worked for a group similar to what we've seen before, where breeders band together for a common cause. In this instance, they enslave men for profit. Daria was a delivery person who handled transport on occasion."

"Which explained why she didn't know much," Asia said. "I should've dug deeper and found that out."

"No, she's still alive and you learned what was necessary to complete your mission," Jasmine told her. "The fact they used rebels is a different conversation altogether. Even so, we need to get our pack back on Nation soil as soon as possible."

"Will do," Silas said, nodding. "Continue."

"Something's happening in or near Plias. Whoever is behind it needed Angus. To get him to go along with their plans they took his mate and cut his ties to you so you, I mean we, couldn't help him. Whatever it is, the Goddess knows and to a certain point is allowing it to happen." She wet her lips with her tongue. "It must be big."

No one spoke for several seconds.

Silas replayed her words over and over again. For the most part, they made sense until the Goddess part. How was she involved? Why? Why cut him off from his brother? It didn't make sense.

"What do you all think?" he asked to get the discussion going while he dealt with his demons. Jasmine took his hand and he squeezed hers. When she tried to withdraw, he clasped on tight to her hand, continuing to hold it while everyone discussed possibilities.

"Barticus is in Greece and will make his way to Plias to search for Angus," Hawke said.

"Are his people meeting the plane?" Silas asked.

"Yes, his people and Ulric will be there," Hawke said.

"Good, tell him I will contact him after we are done here," Silas said before turning his attention to Cain and Abel. "Jasmine's scenario makes sense. I never thought of Angus and a mate."

"It's the one reason he'd walk away and not explain what's going on," Jacques said.

"Nothing stands between the mating bond," Hawke added. "Which makes me wonder what plans they have for my friend."

"Nothing good," Jasmine muttered.

"Worse, I can't help him." Silas slammed his fist on the table. The absence of Angus' mental connection festered like a sore. Silas missed him. When had he grown so dependent on their connection, friendship, and brotherly affection? He had no answer for that, not that it mattered, he needed to find his brother.

"Mistress, can you find Shyla?" Asia asked. "There may be a residual connection from when you merged with her before. Perhaps if you find her we can verify if they are mates. If not, we can locate her so Alpha Jayden can bring her home."

"Is that possible?" Jasmine looked at Silas.

"Could be," Silas said, watching her eyes light up with a new challenge.

"Let's try it. You'll need to walk me through it again," she told him.

He nodded. *"When we're done here, I want to hear more ideas."*

"What if this has something to do with the Alpha, Ulric?" Cain asked. "Based on what we've learned, he and Angus didn't get along."

"Does Barticus have jurisdiction in Africa?" Jacques asked. "I thought the European nations were his area."

"Who else do we know in that part of the world?" Abel asked his brother, Cain.

"Is it possible the Liege has a remnant and they're after Angus for his creative abilities?" Asia asked. Her words dropped like miniature bombs. Angus was the sole creator of the chameleon bracelets. In the wrong hands, which meant anyone Silas hadn't approved, those bracelets could change the core of nations.

"Not the Liege, as I said before, this isn't them," Hawke said in a sober tone. "But what you said, Angus taken for his abilities, I hadn't thought of that." Hawke looked across the table. Silas read deep concern mixed with fear in Hawke's gaze.

Cain and Abel looked at each other and then at the others at the table. No one spoke for a few moments.

"That is something to consider," Silas said slowly. The very idea of Angus being hunted for the chameleon chilled Silas to the bone. He stood and paced to bring his anger and fear under control. If they hurt his brother, he would never stop hunting them. It would become his life's goal to track the bastards down and dismember them.

"*Silas. Silas, calm down, your energy is spiking,*" Jasmine said.

With his back to them, he stopped, took several deep breaths, clenched and unclenched his fists.

"*Silas.*"

"*I'm trying, Jasmine,*" he snapped through their link. "*It hurts knowing he's in trouble and I can't help. Hurts more than I expected. I can't control the pain or anger. I want to kill them for taking him.*"

"*Rechannel it. That's what you tell me. Keep the anger but make it productive instead of destroying the room. Think of a way to help Angus and bring him home. Rechannel that energy, Wolfie,*" Jasmine said. "*Breathe with me.*" She took several breaths until he synced with her and his beast calmed.

"*Better?*" she asked when he could see the wall in front of him clearly and his beast settled.

"*Some. We have to find him. If someone's taken him for the chameleon, he'll die before giving it to them and that's not acceptable to me.*"

"*Me neither, so let's figure out what to do.*"

Silas returned to the table, ignoring Cain and Abel's incredulous looks. They hadn't seen him in La Patron mode before, not like this.

"How do we get Angus back here?" Silas asked, looking at Hawke and Asia.

"We can take the next flight, hit Plias hard searching for him," Hawke said.

"No," Jasmine said before Silas commented. "At least not until I've located Shyla and we know if Angus is mated." She took Silas' hand. "Because if my brother is mated, he won't leave her behind, nor is he alone. Mates work together to survive better than anyone we send after them. Shyla is smart and tough. I'm not saying they don't need help, but rescuing Tyrese when he was newly mated almost killed the mission."

Asia nodded.

Jasmine continued. "If Angus is not mated to Shyla then Barticus is our best bet to find Angus quickly. In this situation, jurisdiction won't matter, not to Barticus or Ulric. But here's the real reason I don't want the two of you to leave right now. What if someone has discovered a way to break mental links? For a bonded couple that would be deadly."

Silas' grip tightened. "My Bitch is right, we need to know more before allowing you two to leave again."

Hawke and Asia nodded. "Thank you, Mistress. I hadn't thought of that," Asia said.

"Neither had I. The very thought is catastrophic. It hits at the core of our bond. Let's hope the Goddess is involved rather than the other option, although neither is good," Hawke said.

"When does Barticus arrive in Plias?" Silas asked, eager to redirect the conversation.

"In an hour. He is very concerned," Hawke said.

"Good, so am I," Silas said as he leaned back in his chair. A familiar tingling sensation ran down his back. He looked at Jasmine. *"The Goddess wishes to speak to me. The timing is unusual."* He stood and headed for the door. "Please continue, I must see about an important matter."

"Asia, you guys continue. If you come up with anything, let me know," Jasmine said, following Silas. At the elevator, he looked down at her.

"Did she contact you as well?"

"No." Jasmine crossed her arms and looked at the elevator.

"It may not be a good idea for you to attend this meeting if she hasn't called you." He stepped inside the elevator. She followed and pressed the button to the private floor where his prayer room was located.

"Maybe not, but she'll have to tell me that."

Silas took her hand and kissed the back as the elevator moved upward. *"I'm glad you're with me."*

She leaned into him, hugging him gently. *"I can't take a chance of being separated from you, I don't have good enough control yet."*

He smiled as he stroked her back. *"That's true."*

She pinched his side.

"Hey, I was agreeing with you." The elevator stopped. Holding hands, they stepped out and walked toward the room. Once inside, they washed hands and lit the candles. Silas knelt on the edge of the circle and extended his hand to Jasmine. She sat next to him.

An inexplicable peace rolled over him as he sought the Goddess. Fears, concerns, and responsibilities flitted away as his inner vision brightened with her presence. His heartbeat accelerated and his breaths were spaced further apart.

"Silas, Alpha of the wolves, rise, I have need of you," the Goddess said.

In his mind's eye, he stood but saw nothing other than a glowing white light. "I am always at your service."

"Yes, your loyalty has never been in question."

He frowned when she didn't say more. "How may I serve you?"

"All will be explained in time now that I have your consent. Come." The light flashed. Silas' body moved with lightning speed, he couldn't breathe or discern the status of his form. Strangely enough, his beast didn't seem bothered. One moment he was in his

127

prayer room, the next he was on the floor of a large room. It took a moment to find his balance.

Standing slowly, he staggered a bit and leaned against the wall. "Goddess?"

"One second, Wolf, I am speaking to your mate, she is understandably upset."

"*Jasmine?*" Silas straightened and tried to contact his mate again. "*Jasmine.*" Nothing. His beast searched for his mate as he tried to connect with Jasmine, Hawke, Cain, Able, his Alphas, and then his pack.

Nothing.

Silas fell to his knees with his arms wrapped around his head. "No. Goddess, no. My pack, what happens to my pack? My mate? My pups?"

"Wolf, this is temporary," the Goddess said. "I will explain, you must listen. There has never been as much on the line before."

Despite wanting to yell and scream for his mate, the Goddess had spoken to Jasmine, which meant she was okay for now. "Yes, Ma'am."

"Every thousand years, Nicromja is allowed to challenge me over the right to rule the wolves. He has exercised this right once in five thousand years, not including this year. He has a small group of worshipers who have done everything within their power to make Nicromja relevant even though he shows no interest in resuming his responsibilities."

Aching for his mate, Silas half-listened.

"Drink this, it will help." She passed him a translucent glass with fluid.

He took several sips of the bittersweet beverage. Within seconds the gaping hole in his soul filled with his mate's essence even though he couldn't speak to her. "Thank you. It's hard to focus without her."

She smiled. "I know. Your mate is special. She attacked me when I took you."

Silas wasn't surprised, he would have done the same thing. His mate loved him and was very protective. Even though he could take on the biggest and baddest fighters, his heart warmed knowing she struck out on his behalf. "Is she alright?"

"Oh yes. She's smart, knows her rights as your mate and invoked something I hadn't remembered." She shook her head. "So many forget the power of the mate bond." She looked at Silas. "I need a champion to fight Nicromja's champion. Both must be full-bloods and the fight is to the death. There can only be one God and one champion. Do you understand why I called you?"

Silas nodded. He had no concerns over fighting, his skills were top notch. "After the challenger is defeated, I go home to my den and pack?"

"Yes."

"Until when? Another thousand years pass?"

"Possibly. We shall see. This challenge is different."

"How?"

"I cannot explain more. Rest and when the time comes, I will send for you." She left him alone in the room.

"Nicromja? Where have I heard that name before?" He sat at the table, staring at the wall. "Nicromja... Nicromja." He straightened in his chair. "Barticus was a vessel or something of this god." He tried his mental link to contact the Alpha and couldn't. Goddess, he hoped Barticus wasn't the challenger. The man's pack was huge and would give Nicromja an instant army on the continent. Plus, Silas and Barticus were friends, allies. But if Barticus was Nicromja's vessel, he'd be duty bound to fight, just as Silas was. What a cluster fuck.

He stood, looked around the room. Nothing but a bed, table, and chair. No windows or doors that he could see. The more he thought about it, the more it seemed Barticus would challenge him on behalf of Nicromja. Now he understood the Goddess' reticence and the suggestion he rest. This battle wouldn't be easy but he would win.

Losing his den, his pack, and mate were not an option. With this last thought, he walked over to the bed and lay down. "I will not lose."

CHAPTER 16

It was time to leave the safety of the mountain and meet destiny. Angus jogged to the left, raised his hand and the opening in the rock appeared. He stepped out, turned, assisted Shyla, and closed it. They climbed up the rocky hill until they were above the full-bloods. *"Still just these four. Another four humans nearby, probably in the mountain. If they can get out they'll be directed here. So, don't shoot unless there's no other choice, no need to alert them early."*

She nodded. *"Where's the best place to shoot them? Head? Neck? Between the eyes?"*

"I'm guessing between the eyes, that'll slow them down long enough for me to rip off their heads. Oh, and try not to get close to them, some have fingertips dipped in poison."

"They aren't supposed to kill us, just take us in," she said.

"Still, don't get close to them. Pick them off from a distance." Angus stood and jumped, shifting into his hybrid. He landed behind a modified full-blood, reached out, grabbed his head and twisted like he was opening a jar. The head snapped off, blood squirted everywhere. Angus kicked the body forward into an oncoming fighter and threw the head into the face of another one, knocking them both back a few feet.

He jumped in the air and kicked his oncoming opponent beneath the chin, snapping his head back and breaking his neck. Quick as a rabbit, he jumped on the downed man and finished twisting off his head. He tossed it into the face of the full-blood running toward him. The force of the hit knocked his opponent onto a large boulder. His head split but it didn't kill him.

A roar from the last standing full-blood grabbed his attention. Angus waited until the last moment, jumped aside and slammed his fist into his opponent's gut, robbing him of breath. While winded, Angus snapped his neck, pulled off his head, and tossed it aside. He strode to the final full-blood, who lay on the rock as his head healed.

131

Angus grabbed the head with both hands and twisted until it separated.

"*Come down, we need to go before they send reinforcements.*" He pulled off his bloodied shirt and wiped his face.

"*While you were fighting, two humans climbed the ledge behind me, I didn't want to distract you. One sec.*" The sound of gunfire split the air. The next moment Shyla landed beside him. "*Ready?*"

Angus took off down the side of the mountain, Shyla fast behind him. They needed to hide in the forest where he had spent so much of his time when he was younger. In the woods he'd find food, water, and shelter for his mate. They just needed to make it there. He glanced over his shoulder, Shyla was with him. Just a few more feet and they'd be safe, at least for the moment.

She fell.

His heart stuttered as he looked behind him and saw her lying on the ground. Shifting to his hybrid, he turned, picked her up and continued running. The first prick in his shoulder was more a nuisance than anything. Three pricks slowed him down. Five caused him to stumble and drop his precious mate. He sat next to her, pulled out several darts, and shifted into his beast. Unrelenting pain, mixed with anger and shame at failing her rose up his throat. He threw back his head and released a long howl. In the distance, he heard an answer and then his world went dark.

CHAPTER 17

Angus jerked awake and sat up. "Shyla!" He searched for her through their mental link. She didn't respond, but she was alive. Relief flowed over him like a waterfall. Looking around he noticed a shower head and toilet in the corner of the room.

"Nice." He needed to make use of both. Toilet first. Dried blood flaked off his stomach as he walked naked across the floor. Finished relieving himself, he tested the water for the shower and stepped beneath the spray. At least three people were on the other side of the door. He frowned. One modified full-blood, two humans. Maybe now he'd get some answers.

He grabbed a towel from a nearby shelf, dried off and slipped on a navy and orange jogging suit with strange symbols he didn't recognize. In a cubby beneath the towels were several pairs of large slippers. He grabbed a pair.

While he slid into them, the door opened. A tall figure in a navy-blue monk's robe strode inside.

"Good, you are awake and dressed. Come with me." He turned and walked out the door.

Eager to get some answers and put this whole ordeal behind him, Angus followed. Outside, the full-blood remained near the door and the human took up the rear, his hand on something in his pocket. Angus suspected it was another dart gun. They walked down a long corridor in what appeared to be an old castle. Whitewashed walls with long, spidery cracks showed signs of disrepair. The floor was impacted dirt. No pictures graced the walls. Stingy wall sconces provided just enough light to see a few feet in front of them but no more. When they turned the corner, they faced two, ten-foot feet high or more, gold-trimmed doors. Cobwebs and rat droppings made him wonder if anyone had used this place in a long time. It smelled old and rank.

They stopped.

The doors opened slowly. Everything outside this room bespoke a different day and time. But someone had spent considerable time and money to make this opulent room a shrine of epic proportions. It sparkled. From the highly polished marble floors to the huge crystal chandeliers in the ceiling with a least a hundred burning candles. A large, circular raised dais sat in the middle of the floor, reminding him of a gilded boxing ring. Short gold posts with a similar gold chain marked the edge of the circle.

When the robed guy moved inside, Angus followed. The human security person didn't enter.

"Sit here." He pointed to a large cushion on the floor far from the ring. Intrigued, Angus sat and waited to see what unfolded. It didn't take long. Four more robed figures joined the first in the room as the door closed behind them. They formed a semi-circle around a raised dais and held hands.

Across the room, another cloaked figure entered, his robe slightly different from the others. Instead of kneeling alongside the other monks, he stepped in front of them, held up his hand, and pulled a rolled paper from his other pocket.

"Today is a great day. One we have waited a century to see." Unrolling the scroll, he intoned words Angus didn't understand. He looked across the room and blinked. How had he missed the large statue depicting a tall, muscular male with long curly hair, wide nose, high cheekbones, and a large, long phallus, standing with his hands at the side, looking into the sky.

What the hell? Angus continued staring at the large marbled masterpiece, obviously missing his cue to stand until two full-bloods grabbed him beneath his arms, hoisting him upward.

"Answer the question," the man who'd been reading the scroll said in a low tenorous tone.

"I didn't hear it." Angus jerked from the two full-bloods, turned and showed his incisors, warning them away. While his back was turned, one of the robed monks kicked him in his back, sending him flying into the full-blood, who grabbed him in a bear hug.

"Perhaps now you will pay attention," the robed monk said.

Angus released his claws, dug deep into the side of the full-blood and shifted into his hybrid. He pulled back and punched the full-blood in the jaw, sending him flying across the room. Angus jumped, hit his head on the ceiling, and fell on top of the on-coming full-blood, knocking him to the ground. After clearing his head, he grabbed hold of the full-blood's head, twisted until he heard the break, and jumped up. Turning, he headed for the monk who'd kicked him in the back.

"Stop!"

Following the scent of the asshole who'd kicked him from behind, Angus grabbed him from the line and lifted him high.

"Stop or your mate dies," the man on the dais yelled.

"We're going to die anyway, might as well take all of you with us," Angus said, shaking the man a few times before tossing him across the room. Blood smeared the white wall as the man's head cracked open before he slid down and remained still. Angus picked up another monk and activated the bracelet.

"Stop this madness. You and your mate don't need to die, just be our champion, fight in the games," a monk said with urgency as he moved toward Angus.

"Who are you?" Angus asked, even though he'd just taken the name from the person he held.

"Scorpio. I'm the high priest. Release the boy, he's too young to die."

Angus realized the truth of Scorpio's words. The boy was a relative of the monk's and had no idea what was going on. The teen's love of sports and fighting events reminded Angus of Adam. He released him and turned to the monks. "Bring my mate here. If she is hurt I will make it my life's mission to kill each of you and your families." He inhaled deeply to bring his beast under control. If they didn't move quickly, he would destroy them all and deal with the consequences later.

Scorpio raised his hand.

135

An old stone altar rose up from the floor near the statue. Shyla lay on top, dressed in a long, white gown. A crown of white flowers was around her head. Moving quickly, he ran to her, morphing to human as he did.

His fingertips grazed her cheeks and ran over her lips. Checking for marks and bruises, he released a pent-up breath when he found none. His last memory was of her firing pistols and running behind him. Asleep, she looked so peaceful and beautiful. Although he didn't know her that well, he could imagine her response to this outfit her captors had dressed her in. It wouldn't be good. Cupping her cheeks between his hands, he activated the bracelet.

"Angus?" she asked in a whispery thin voice as he sent energy to her through the bracelet.

Leaning forward, he placed his forehead to hers. *"Yes. They've drugged you with something, I cannot reach you through our mind link."* He stopped short of revealing their connection through the chameleon bracelet. *"Fight this and open your eyes. I need to know you're okay."*

He brushed his lips across hers as he prayed to the Goddess to save his mate.

"If you wish her to wake, and fill your den with pups, you'll fight in the arena as our champion," Scorpio said.

"What have you done to her?" Angus kissed Shyla and sent more energy to help her wake. Her cheeks were lukewarm, something unusual for their hot-blooded people. Using his thumb, he pushed back her eyelids, the pupils looked good. He pinched her nostrils together. A few seconds later, she gasped for air but didn't open her eyes.

"She is asleep." One of the monks said behind him. "Nothing will happen to your mate. She will sleep until the challenge has been met." The words held the scent of truth.

"Win or lose, she wakes?" Angus asked, watching the slow rise and fall of her chest.

"Yes, but if you lose, can she remain awake? Won't death immediately follow?" the monk asked in a smug tone.

Angus continued staring at his beloved mate. They were a good match. He touched her hand, stroked the back of it for a few seconds. "I don't know," Angus lied. Since he never bit Shyla, their bonding was never completed. If he died, she would continue to live, but her quality of life would be that of a grieving woman, constantly wanting her mate. Some claimed living half-bonded was like being half alive with a fractured heart.

His beast growled his displeasure at the dark options for their mate. He could not do that to her. "What kind of games?" he asked without looking at them.

"The games have started, but our master has a separate challenge and needs a champion. He required the strongest, most competent fighter in this hemisphere. That led us to you."

Angus snorted. "Quit the bullshit, I don't live here anymore, haven't for years. Just tell me the rules and rewards of this thing."

"Reward? Your mate is released and the two of you leave here. Rules? You fight to the death and win the challenge for our master. That's it," Scorpio said.

Angus pulled back, crossed his arms, and met Scorpio's obsidian gaze. "No. If I fight, I get paid. Half now and half later. Otherwise, fuck off."

"Seems I was misinformed about you, what is your price?" Scorpio snapped, stepping down from the dais.

Angus crossed his arms. "Three million, my mate watches the battle, and no matter what, I will never fight my Alpha."

"We don't know the challenger, so I assume it's not your Alpha. Understand this, the only person who can wake your mate is our master, and he will only do that if he's pleased with your performance. If those rules seem fair, give me your banking information and I'll have the money deposited." Scorpio whipped out a pad and looked prepared to take dictation.

Angus rattled the number for his offshore account, no doubt surprising the man. "Show me a receipt when it's done."

Scorpio strode forward, thrust the tablet in front of Angus and waited. "Here is the transaction receipt." Angus looked at it but didn't really care one way or the other. He had returned to Shyla's side and continued feeding her energy. The payment thing was just a stall. He wasn't sure about the master being the only one who could release his mate, Silas should be able to do it. Or the Goddess. He refused to place his mate's future in the hands of these assholes.

"Now do we have your agreement to fight for our master, to be his champion?" Scorpio asked.

Angus thought of Grandfather's warnings, Shyla's kidnapping, and being on the run. The idea that these humans were able to capture and put him in this position lit a fuse. The only reason he hadn't broken their necks was because Shyla couldn't break free on her own yet.

"Yes, I will fight as your champion, but my mate is to be set free no matter what, and I will never fight my Alpha, agreed?" He pointed at her.

The monks looked at each other. "Yes, that is fair," Scorpio said. The monks returned to stand in front of the dais. With upraised hands, they looked upward singing. "Mighty Nicromja, we ask that we serve you today as we have in the past."

Nicromja? Shock raced through Angus' body at the mention of that name. Barticus and Hawke had told him and Silas about the god's attempt to coerce them into serving him. Barticus' physiology had been modified so that his seed would produce a superior being as the child of Nicromja. No one had counted on the Liege retrofitting Asia with metal arms and legs, which in Nicromja's mind made her unworthy. From everything he'd heard, this god was egotistical and lazy. Not a good combination for any species.

He looked at the statue again with new eyes. Did Nicromja pose for this? Was he vain as well?

The singing continued into another chorus of worship. A few moments later the singing stopped. Angus looked for the teen he'd grabbed and was relieved to discover the child had left.

Scorpio unrolled the scroll and read. "God Nicromja, according to the ancient texts the time has come for you to regain your property as foretold. Today marks another thousand-year rule of the Goddess over the male wolves. Today, your servants sit as witnesses to the challenge to the Goddess to regain your right. Today, you return to the earth to rule the male wolves and rid the earth of our enemies."

Challenge the Goddess? Not only was Nicromja egotistical, he was a fool as well.

The air cooled.

Above the statue, a floating, hazy outline of a large man hovered. The foundation beneath Angus shook. Every candle in the room was extinguished, leaving the floating image as the only source of light.

No other sound was heard as the image continued forming into a large gray wolf. Angus felt a tugging on his beast and realized the god had tried to force his change. Not happening. After a few moments, the god changed from a wolf to a man with long brown hair, tall and muscular, with eyes blazing like the sun lighting the room completely.

"You have provided a champion to fight in the challenge?" Nicromja asked as he strode across the room and stood in front of the robed men.

"Yes, my lord."

"Has he agreed?"

There was a moment of silence. "Yes, he is a bonded male and will fight to save his mate's life."

Nicromja laughed. The booming sound bounced off the walls and hurt Angus' ears. "Bonded? Where is the mate?"

The monk pointed behind Angus "Right there, my Lord."

Angus tried to block Nicromja's gaze but couldn't.

"She is wolf. Good. I will make my challenge." Nicromja disappeared.

CHAPTER 18

Fire raced through Jasmine's body as she strode into the conference room. Asia stood, pulling Hawke up with her. Cain, Abel, and Jacques were flung from their chairs against the wall as Jasmine paced in a tight circle. "I'm fed up with her. She does this shit all the time, for any damn reason," she told Asia.

"Mistress, what happened?" Asia asked, leaning against the wall next to Hawke as Jasmine's energy whipped around the room.

"She took Silas," Jasmine yelled and looked around. "Sorry, guys." She waved her hand releasing the men.

"Who took Silas?" Jacques asked, sounding as if he'd just run a marathon. "He's not answering me."

Jasmine opened and closed her fist and stretched her arms. When she'd jumped on the Goddess, or rather through the Goddess' energy field, she'd burned her knuckles and her arm. They were both healed.

"Goddess. She said some bullshit story about her needing him to be her champion."

"La Patron *is* her champion," Abel said.

Jasmine whirled on him. "He's my mate, damn it. That trumps everything else and she knows it. At least she does now. I told her this was the last damn time I would allow it."

Jacques gasped.

The men stared at her.

"You are right, Mistress. How can I help?" Asia asked. She placed her palm on Jasmine's shoulder. Jasmine covered Asia's hand with her own.

"He's blind. No outside communication. The Goddess couldn't explain everything except this could be really bad, it could break him. As his mate, no one could stop me from interfering, so I told her to expect me to put a damn stop to this BS once and for all. She wished me well, forgave me for attacking her, and disappeared."

"You attacked the Goddess?" Hawke whispered.

Jasmine waved him down and put her hands on her hips. "How can I help Silas?" she asked Asia. "Even though she didn't come out and say it, I think as his mate I can help. We need to find out how and we don't have a lot of time. She gave me a 12-hour window."

Asia nodded, then went and sat at the keyboard. Hawke sat next to her, working together.

Jasmine paced the small room. She refused to believe she'd lose her man. Not today, not for any reason. If he was in hell, she'd make a day trip and bring him home.

"Find out why the Goddess needs a champion, Jacques. Has he done this before?" she looked at him.

"Not that I know of. But he may have before I arrived." He looked at Cain and Abel.

"I don't know of this happening before," Cain said, watching Jasmine.

"Start searching, there's something deep going on here that I'm missing. There's too much on the line to make mistakes," she told Jacques, who pulled up a keyboard and began his search.

"Cain, you and Abel contact the Alphas from Silas' office, they're buzzing in my head trying to contact him. Inform them that Silas is unavailable for the next 18 hours and you and Able are handling communications for him. Take care of what you can, and take good notes. Don't tell them what's going on, Silas will handle that when he returns." Jasmine held both in her gaze.

"Yes, Ma'am." Both men headed out the door.

Jasmine rubbed her chest and closed her eyes for a few seconds. She ached all over missing their connection. Being a breeder, her need was blunted; she couldn't begin to imagine what Silas was going through. Bonded full-bloods needed constant connection with their mates. The door opened and her sons entered in a hurry.

"Ma? What happened?" Tyrone asked, Tyrese behind him.

"I can't reach Silas," Tyrese said. "What's going on? Is he okay?"

She opened her arms. Both boys held onto her while she told them what happened.

"What? You attacked the Goddess?" Tyrone asked, staring down at her.

"Is that all you got out of that?" Jasmine snapped, and hit his arm.

"Ow. No, it's just you're... I love you and I'm glad I'm on your good side," Tyrone said, smiling. He kissed her cheek.

"This is hush-hush right now." She explained what everyone was doing.

"Ethan and I will handle KnightForce, split it in half while Asia works with you. Let me know if you need me or if anything changes," Tyrese said after Jasmine told him to make sure KnightForce's administration was in place. He left the room.

"Wow, she took Silas? I didn't know they could do that," Tyrone said. "And Angus isn't here? That's whack."

"Huh? What did you say?" Jasmine grabbed his arm.

"I didn't know they could just take somebody, if they can do that to him —"

Jasmine held up her finger. "No, Angus. He's not here." She took a step back, thinking of the odds of two brothers being moved from the same area to another area with their mental links broken. It didn't wash.

"Mom?"

She shushed him and moved further away. What if it was all connected? Somehow Angus was lured away, completely cut off from everyone, and now the Goddess takes Silas to be her champion. Jasmine frowned. They were brothers, they couldn't kill each other. What if Silas had to fight Barticus? She rubbed her brow trying to make sense out of this tangle.

"Hawke, where is Barticus?" She asked.

A few moments later, Hawke replied. "Just landing. His people are in position to intercept the plane and his car waits to take him to Plias, where he'll meet Alpha Ulric."

143

Jasmine walked slowly to the table thinking about Angus. "Is it just me or is it strange Angus and Silas are away at the same time and neither have mental links."

Asia and Hawke stared across the table at her. Jacques leaned back in his chair, tapping his chin with the end of his pen.

"Do you think they're related?" Tyrone asked.

"If you're an enemy of La Patron, and could remove him from the compound or country, you'd still need to deal with his beta, who's just as strong," Jacques said. "Especially if you didn't know much about his mate."

"Silas kept a lid on your abilities, Mom. So, it's possible people think they have us at a disadvantage here. Is that what you're thinking?" Tyrone asked.

"I would, except the Goddess took him, and as much as I don't like the way she does things, I know she loves and protects us. Silas is her choice to lead the wolves, not me. She wouldn't handicap us like that." Jasmine picked her way through her scrambled thoughts. "Yet I have a feeling this is all connected somehow, it's just too much of a coincidence not to be."

"On the odd chance there's an enemy lurking about to take advantage of Silas' and Angus' absence, should we alert security?" Jacques asked.

"Depends. What would they do differently with an alert?" She looked at Jacques. "I don't want anyone else to know Silas was taken, is that clear?"

"Yes, Ma'am." Jacques returned to his keyboard.

Jasmine released a breath and placed her hand on her chest again, trying to ease the ache. "I'll talk to Hank and Jarcee later. Right now, I have more questions than answers and the clock is ticking for Silas." She turned to Jacques. "Is it possible Silas and Angus are both in Plias? Search to see if there are any records of any gods having championship fights or whatever they call them in that area."

"Mistress, you don't think Angus and La Patron will fight, do you?" Asia asked, looking up from her monitor.

"Lots of stuff going round in my head right now, just tossing them out to try and make sense of this BS," Jasmine said.

"Who could fight Silas in a challenge and have a shot at winning?" Tyrone asked.

Jasmine met his curious gaze and then looked at Asia. "Barticus?"

Asia shrugged. "I don't know. He's good, but in all honesty, I cannot imagine anyone who can defeat La Patron."

"What if…" Jasmine struggled to get the words right. "If Silas didn't have help from the Goddess? I mean if he were an ordinary wolf without her enhancements."

"From what I understand, she gave him a wolf spirit. It's an Alpha thing but doesn't interfere with his fighting skills, that would be cheating. If the day comes and he cannot defeat a challenger, then he's no longer Alpha," Jacques said.

Everyone stared at him. When his words sunk in, Jacques' cheeks reddened. "But that may not be what's going on here. I haven't… I mean… there's no evidence of a challenge," Jacques stammered.

Certainty hit Jasmine's gut. Someone had challenged Silas for the pack. What did that mean for her and the children? Their Nation? Even the dear people seated in this room? She shook her head to toss the images of a world without Silas aside. Now the Goddess' actions, her remaining behind to speak to Jasmine, made sense. "Just because we don't know of an Alpha challenge doesn't mean there's not one." She met Asia's gaze. "Did we just lead Barticus into a trap or does he know about this?"

"I don't know if he's aware, we can ask," Asia said.

"Ask him." Jasmine sat back, her chaotic thoughts bounced in irregular patterns. When Hawke dropped his forehead into his hand, she sat up. "Get Barticus on the phone right now. I want to talk to him."

"Yes, Mistress." Asia pulled out her phone, tapped in the number and handed it to Jasmine.

It rang once before Barticus answered. "Jasmine, the only thing I know about gods and challenges is what I learned from an old high priest whose name I swore never to repeat. There's something going on between the Goddess and Nicromja, a lesser god who'd been given care over male wolves. He failed and she took over the job. When I saw him, and yes, he's real, he was searching for someone to be his champion. Even tried to take my grandson, Damian. He told the priests not to call him again unless they had someone worthy like Damian." He paused. "The high priest I knew is dead and buried, I saw to that myself. But there are other sects, worshipers around the world, who may be active."

"What about the Goddess? Does she do this kind of thing? Cockfights between men to do what? Prove what? Who's stronger? Smarter? Better? Who does this in this day and age? With the world going to pot in a handbasket this is how gods occupy their time?" Jasmine snapped.

"I have no idea about the Goddess. If she's involved, it makes sense Silas would represent her."

"Is this type thing to the death or just a good beating?" In her heart, she knew the answer but needed to hear it.

"Blood always binds contracts, for gods anyway. If I were betting, I'd say to the death. But don't worry, Silas is the best fighter around. I don't think I could win against him," Barticus said.

"What about Angus?" she asked, and held her breath.

"Angus? What does he have to do with this?"

"He's missing and his link's broken. What if he's Nicromja's champion?" she asked softly, holding her forehead in one hand and the cell phone tight in the other.

Silence met her question. The weight of the eyes of everyone in the room pressed against her. In the pit of her stomach butterflies took flight as it clenched in frustration.

"That would not be a good thing. I think they are evenly matched. Worse, neither would participate in such a battle without a solid reason. Silas has his den, his pack."

Jasmine cleared her throat. "What if Angus found his mate and she was used as leverage." She pulled the phone from her ear as Barticus let loose several expletives.

"They would do that," Barticus snapped. "They did it to me, those bastards. Now that I have a better idea what's going on, I'll send out searches for temples. Damn them! I'll need to get more pack over here to cover as much ground as possible. This is really pissing me off. The goddess needs to get rid of Nicromja's worthless ass."

"As Silas' mate is there anything I can do to protect him?"

"I don't know. My mate refused to serve him and I followed her lead. Maybe that's why he let me go, I'm not sure. At the time, we were both so happy to live through his anger we never checked out the mechanics. Asia was there, maybe she remembers more," Barticus said.

"Thank you and keep us apprised of what's happening," Jasmine said when she couldn't think of anything else to ask.

"Hawke and I are in constant communication, he'll pass everything along." Barticus wished her well and disconnected.

"Well, we know Barticus isn't anyone's champion," Jasmine said, handing Asia the phone.

"Nicromja desperately wants to win against the Goddess," Asia said. "He dislikes women. I can see him using La Patron's brother against him."

"But they cannot kill each other," Jacques said, frowning. "Who would go through all of this trouble and not know that?"

"Someone who doesn't know," Tyrone said.

"Or care," Hawke added. "The priest we met would not have allowed anything to stop him from bringing Asia, her mom or sire, to that temple. They are very determined."

Jasmine straightened in her chair. "So am I." She looked at Asia. "Did we learn anything from Daria's past that could give us some insight on where this challenge takes place?"

"Not really. She worked part time for a group of breeders who paid someone to deliver men so they could enslave them. We have not discovered the name of the group selling rebels. I doubt she or anyone else working this circle of compromising and selling full-bloods knows the real person in charge. It's well organized," Asia answered.

"So are we. Contact the Alpha for that state, I want information, sales records, phone conversations, any correspondence that connects the dots. Get me the names of the supplier. I want to know who's picking off rebels and why? Do I need to add I want that operation shut down and the women involved taken into custody?"

"We're going after humans?" Tyrone asked, sounding surprised.

"If they have knowledge I can use, we hit them hard and deal with the fallout later." She nodded and returned her attention to Hawke. "Have Cain or Abel get that started since they are already in contact with the Alphas."

"Yes, Ma'am." He stood and left the room.

Angus and Silas. *What would Silas do?* Out of habit she reached for him through their link. Nothing. She slammed her fist against the table and stood. "What do we do? If the goddess believes this may break Silas, it will. But what? They can't kill each other. So, what's going to happen?" She placed both fists on her forehead, closed her eyes tight to block out the noise and focused. "What can I do as his mate to stop this?" she thought.

"Jasmine, I can't find anything new about mates," Jacques said. "No one and nothing comes between mates. Mates cannot be blocked by each other. Mates give their lives for each other both figuratively and physically. Basically, a bonded mate has a lot of power to deal with their mates. I don't know if that helps or not."

"Just another piece of a puzzle, although I'm not sure which puzzle. Thanks, Jacques." Jasmine tapped her fingertips on the desk.

"Here's another thought. What if there's more than one rebel group and one group sells members from the opposing group to raise money and get rid of the competition?"

"That's possible," Tyrone said. "But what if rebels aren't selling rebels to the breeders? That leaves a bigger question. First, how are they able to identify and capture these people when our efforts have been semi-successful? Second, if rebels aren't selling their opposition, who is? A rogue wolf? Human? Half-breed? None of those answers are good."

"True. How does the selling of rebels connect to Silas' and Angus' challenge?" Jasmine asked, bringing the conversation back to their current problem.

"I don't know. As soon as we get more information on Daria's group and their clientele, we'll know more," Tyrone said.

"The priests need security and Nicromja will need a small army to deal with the fall-out." Asia raised her hand to stop them from talking. "This is from the priest's perspective. They believe Nicromja will win, which means they must think beyond the challenge. The need for drone-like security fits the bill."

"Why not take full-bloods from the continent?" Jasmine asked.

"Since they aren't as structured as we are here, they don't have the same rebel problem like here. And after the Liege, full-bloods on the continent are harder to catch unawares," Asia said.

"Are there Nicromja worshipers here in the states, do they have temples?" Tyrone asked.

Asia looked at the monitor, tapped a few keys and nodded. "Yes. There is one in Arizona, not far from where we made the drop-off." She smiled. "We can send Alpha Paxon to investigate, he was really pissed that they were in his backyard doing shady business against pack."

Jasmine waved her hand. "Tell Hawke to send an investigative team to the temple. Same thing. I want everything, names, addresses of members, phone and bank records. I want those things as soon as possible."

149

"Yes, Ma'am."

Chest aflame, Jasmine pushed away from the table and walked toward the corner with her hand on her chest. Tyrone placed his arm around her shoulders, pulling her close. The pain of Silas' absence sat in her gut like a slow-burning fire. Closing her eyes, she rested in her son's loving embrace as her brain flooded with pictures of Silas. His arrogant face softening as he looked at her. His eyes twinkling with laughter at something the children did, and his eyes darkening with hunger as he touched her. Silent tears rolled down her cheek onto her lips, salty and cold. Fear that she'd be too late to help Silas seized her stomach and gripped her mind. Her breath caught and she swayed slightly.

"Mom?"

"One minute," she said, pulling strength from her core to assist her. Silas needed her to work this out, she couldn't lose or disappoint him. Energy raced up her spine, jerking her upright. Goosebumps exploded across her skin and tingles chased the butterflies in her stomach away.

Tyrone dropped his arm and stepped aside. "Mom, you're glowing."

She looked at him and smiled. "What?"

He blinked and shook his head. "A second ago you were glowing. What happened?"

She patted his cheek. "Come, we need to find and rescue my mate."

CHAPTER 19

Angus sat next to Shyla, rubbing her arm, infusing her with his energy. Still she lay unresponsive. Despair and pain gripped his chest as he looked at her face. "What if they lied and she never woke? Nicromja didn't mention waking Shyla. An hour or more had passed since the god made his proclamation and left. Initially, the monks were so excited that Nicromja actually showed up, they were hugging and wiping tears away. As time passed, there was less conversation and more worried glances.

One of the monks, he identified himself as Cancer, walked over and gave Angus a bottle of water. "You need to remain hydrated." He tried to press the bottle into Angus' hand.

"If my mate cannot hydrate, how can I?" He turned his back on the man.

"She is not the one fighting for her life, you are fighting for both of your lives. If you lose, she will be left at Nicromja's mercy and he cares nothing for females. No telling what he will do."

Anger ripped through Angus. His beast growled at the idea of harm befalling their mate. He stood so fast, Cancer fell backward and hit the ground. "Right now, you, all of you, think you have won. You think I'm alone. But I'm not. Win or lose, my mate will be free or all of you will die. That you can bank on." Somewhere, Silas, Jasmine, Jacques, Asia, Hawke, the twins, they were working on freeing him. He knew that as sure as he knew his name. When they cut the mental connection between him and Silas, he was certain his brother knew something was wrong and started working on a solution.

"If you're dead, that won't help you any, will it?" Scorpio said as Cancer stood. He left the bottled water on the altar and strode away.

"Death is just a different kind of existence. You have no idea what it's about." Angus turned his back on them and ran his fingertip down Shyla's cheek.

"What do you know about it?" Scorpio asked.

"I've already said what I know," Angus said.

"How is it a different existence? Have you died before and resurrected like the Christ?" Scorpio asked in a taunting tone as he looked over his shoulder at the other monks.

Seizing an opportunity to learn more about these men, Angus shrugged. "Crystals."

Scorpio straightened. Cancer moved toward them. "What about crystals?" Scorpio asked.

"Nothing." Angus moved to the other side of the altar, sat on the edge next to Shyla and kept these two in his sight.

"We have read certain crystals have the ability to heal and in some cases, prolong life," Cancer said. "Have you heard such a thing?"

Angus frowned. "Where'd you learn about that?" What they said was true, Angus worked with the crystal they referred to, but it didn't work for humans. Even though the dark hoods covered their faces, Angus sensed their excitement over his reaction.

"Not important, you've answered our question," Scorpio said.

"What's in it for you?" Angus asked, genuinely curious. "Why are you doing all of this?"

"Service to our master, pleasing him, returning him to his proper place. What else can a servant ask for?" Scorpio said in a pious tone.

"Oh, okay then." Angus kissed the back of Shyla's hand and waited. No matter what these men said, their thirst for knowledge of the unknown would get the better of them. He just hoped they'd answer some questions before Nicromja arrived.

When Scorpio gave the other monks chores or sent them on errands, Angus knew their curiosity got the better of them. Cancer approached him first, and then Scorpio.

"This crystal, you've seen it?" Cancer asked.

Angus read the eagerness in his gaze and inhaled. He looked at Scorpio. "You're sick. Cancer?"

Scorpio crossed his arms over his chest and nodded.

"Is that why you're seeking the crystal?" Angus asked Cancer. "For him?"

"Yes."

"Why? What is he to you?" Angus asked, hoping he could use this information to free his mate

"My brother," Cancer said. "Have you seen this crystal?"

"How do you know about it?" Angus asked.

"Does that matter?" Scorpio snapped.

"Yes, it matters to me." Angus placed Shyla's hand on his thigh and covered it with his hand while the two conferred. Had they forgotten he could hear their terse discussion? Apparently, someone in their family was dying from an advanced stage of cancer. Scorpio's cancer was in remission. All of this was for someone at home.

"We found the information in a book," Cancer said.

"Which one of you romanced the Chancellor?" Angus asked, watching them closely.

"Chancellor?"

"This is not the time for games. One of you played on a lonely woman's emotions, and took pictures of pages from a book you were not supposed to access," Angus said.

Neither said anything and he couldn't see their faces clearly, but he smelled guilt.

Angus shrugged and looked at Nicromja's statue. "You could ask your god about the crystals or for a healing potion. That's one of the perks they give for good service, right?" He glanced at them.

"What do you know about the crystal?" Scorpio asked. "There were a lot of crystals in the caves. Is that where you saw it? In the caves?"

"How long have you served Nicromja?" Angus asked. These men didn't seem too committed to him.

"Ten years."

"Five years." They said at the same time.

Angus' brow rose at the contradiction. "Not that long. Didn't the book tell you where to find the crystal?"

"Are you going to tell us anything or not?" Scorpio snapped. His brother touched his arm but continued staring at Angus.

"What if we swapped information?" Cancer asked.

"Interesting. Go on." Angus crossed his arms over his chest and watched them.

"We served Nicromja five years, I lied to make it sound better," Cancer admitted. "Where have you seen the crystal?"

"In a cave when I was younger," Angus said honestly. "What are you getting out of this whole deal? It must have been expensive, so why do it?"

The two looked at each other for a few seconds and then faced Angus. "Family obligations. Our forebearers owe the priesthood for a lot of stuff that happened a long time ago. One of the things is the responsibility of the temple." He waved toward the statue. "We have to keep it going."

Scorpio inhaled. "Which cave did you find the crystal?"

"I don't remember," Angus said, once again answering honestly. At that moment, he couldn't recall which cave, although he was sure he could find it if he tried hard. "What did you give my mate?"

"I don't remember," Scorpio snapped and jerked his arm from Cancer. "No. This asshole is dicking with us. He's not going to tell us where to find anything." He stomped to the dais and out the room.

Cancer dug into his pocket and held out a small vial to Angus. "This is what we gave her. I don't know what's inside, we were just told to put a half teaspoon in water and force her to drink it or give it to her in an IV drip."

Angus opened the vial and inhaled. He identified most of the ingredients, but two eluded him. Those two were the most damaging since the others lacked the potency to knock out a shifter. He placed the vial in his pocket and waited for the next question.

Licking his lips, Cancer leaned inward. "What part of the country is the cave located? What I mean is it near your cave or another area?"

Angus' brow furrowed as he tried to remember. "It was in an area similar to the Chancellor's, hard to identify without special knowledge. Definitely in a mountainous area with dragon trees."

"On this continent?"

"Of course, this is the mother of all," Angus said, surprised by the question. "How do I wake her?"

Cancer's shoulders slumped. "I don't know. Nicromja will need to wake her, otherwise, she will sleep. But she will not die, she's in stasis, everything's frozen and as long as it remains that way, she lives."

Fear shot through Angus. Had he made things worse by trying to wake her with energy spikes? Goddess, he hoped not.

"Thank you, for this information. I just want to help my brother." Cancer walked out and left Angus alone. He tried to remove Shyla from the altar and couldn't. They'd placed some sort of ward around her. They couldn't leave. Out of options, he sat next to her holding her hand. *"Silas?"* He reached out to his Alpha. The absence of their link was a constant ache in his chest.

He threw back his head and howled.

The sound bounced around the large room. No pack nearby. He looked at Shyla, then ran to the door, prepared to fight his way out. No one stood in the halls. Surprised but emboldened, he ran down the long corridor searching for a way out. When he found nothing, he ran in the other direction and came to another dead end. Frustrated he touched the wall and activated the bracelet. Solid stone.

"Shit." He returned to the room and breathed a sigh of relief upon seeing his mate, they hadn't moved her in his absence. Sitting next to her, he waited and contemplated his fate.

Minutes later, Nicromja reappeared, this time he wasn't alone. The Goddess appeared with him.

Angus dropped to his knees and bowed his head. "Blessed be our Goddess." An energy blast knocked him off his knees and slammed him into the wall.

"You are my champion," Nicromja yelled.

"But he's my servant. You used his mate against him, that's not fair," the Goddess said. A cool, refreshing wave of energy ran through Angus, reviving him quickly. He stood and returned to Shyla's side, listening to the two argue.

"Makes no difference why he agreed, he has agreed to this battle and you will not interfere. You've done enough coddling of them over the years, damaged them beyond anything I could ever do," Nicromja said.

"Don't forget who you're talking to," the Goddess snapped.

"I am merely reinforcing our agreement, that's all. What's written, signed and sealed governs this day, not your feelings." Nicromja looked at Angus. "Tell her."

"What?" Angus asked, confused.

"Tell her you agreed to be my champion."

"Will you release my mate if I refuse to fight as your champion?"

Nicromja scoffed. "Of course not."

Angus looked at the Goddess, hoping she would help. She gazed at him for a few seconds and then looked over his head. His heart and confidence plummeted to the floor. Gut twisting, he couldn't believe she hadn't stood up for him. "Who severed my mind links?" Angus asked.

"Tell her you agreed to be my champion," Nicromja yelled. The force of his demand shook the room.

"It's okay to say the words, Angus. I understand the circumstances," the Goddess said.

"I agreed to be his champion." He watched the Goddess the entire time he spoke. Her serene expression never changed. "Part of the agreement was I would never fight my Alpha."

"What?" Nicromja said in a whiplash thin voice. "You put your Alpha before your mate?"

"No one is before my mate. The agreement to fight as your champion was to your representatives and they agreed on the terms."

"I, Nicromja, did not agree to those terms, which mean they are invalid. You fight whoever her champion is and win, or your mate dies," he said in a low voice loaded with venom.

Again, Angus looked at the Goddess and lowered his head. He would not fight his Alpha. The entire wolf nation depended on his brother. Exhaling, Angus returned to the place next to Shyla and held her hand.

Earlier when he spoke of death, he never thought he and his mate would experience it so soon.

CHAPTER 20

"Barticus has pack searching every temple within a hundred miles of Plias. So far they've come up with nothing," Hawke said, sitting at the conference room table.

Jasmine continued staring at the table and didn't respond.

"Mistress, we have some information on the breeder's recent main client. Phone records and bank statements confirm two large payments from Wernher, a prominent family in Memphis." Asia said, walking into the room and taking a seat next to Jasmine. "Research into this family shows they have a long history of idol worship and they've given numerous donations to temples in Africa, the middle east, and here in the states."

"Do they worship Nicromja?" Jasmine asked with a spark of interest. The past two hours had been hell on her nerves. She'd snapped at her mom. Sent Tyrone out the room, twice. Yelled at Jacques for suggesting she lay down. And the kids would be home from school in an hour. She needed to pull it together.

"Here's something interesting. The Wernher's migrated to New York from South Africa over 125 years ago. They moved around a bit, then settled in Tennessee. They stay to themselves, don't socialize much and for the past decade, the entire family has lived on the family estates. There's not a lot of personal information, but it seems they're a large all-American family with ties to the motherland." Asia met her gaze. "One of their companies chartered the plane Barticus met near Plias."

Jasmine slapped the table and leaned back in the chair. "Have Alpha Gilbert round them up and ship them here." Her heart raced, they were finally getting somewhere.

"Mistress, it may be better if I go in alone and perhaps bring Bradford Wernher back for questioning. He's the patriarch of the family and should have the answers you seek. If there are any problems, I can access his memories and find out the location of the temple," Asia said.

"Time is slipping away. Have Gilbert's wife, what's her name?" Jasmine snapped her fingers trying to remember.

"Patsy," Asia said.

"Have Patsy and a few women go with you in case there are breeders there. Don't let them engage, just stand in the background in case. Bring him here, put him in the dungeon, and find out where's the temple where they're holding my mate," Jasmine growled.

Asia's brow rose as she headed for the door. "Yes, Ma'am."

Hawke stood.

"Sit, Hawke. You can't go this trip, there may be breeders in the house or someone may try to break your links. I have not forgotten." Jasmine waved him back into his seat. "Contact Mercy, Alpha Preston's wife, she may have more information now." She looked at her watch.

"Mercy and five females from the Georgia pack arrested the breeders an hour ago and took them to the Alpha house. The breeders had no security system and no means of defense. Rounding them up had been quick with no bloodshed. Understandably the breeders were confused. It quickly became evident they never considered female full-bloods in the equation. It was comical watching a few breeders attempt to compel Mercy and the others. It didn't work. Seems involving females to fight breeders who prey on wolf males will become a permanent strategy."

"Yes, Ma'am," Hawke said. If he was upset with Jasmine for clipping his wings, he didn't show it.

Seconds later, Jasmine looked at the monitor and smiled at Mercy. "Have you learned anything new?"

"Yes, there were two rebels in the basement. They hadn't been programmed and when the breeders realized the rebels couldn't protect them against us, they gave up. It's been years since I kicked ass, lots of fun."

"Good. Thank you for your hard work. Did you learn anything else?" Jasmine asked.

"There's a feud of some kind going on amongst rebel leaders. A turf war. These two were in the wrong area and were trussed up and sold to the breeders. Right now, there are five large rebel groups. Preston is working on getting more information on how the rebels operate and will report later." Mercy laughed. "Having bitches involved is a great idea, Mistress. When the women with me realized the power and level of destruction these breeders have used on our males, they were furious. I don't think they realized how important it was to stop these women until they saw the rebels in the basement."

"Not all of us breeders are wicked enemies to the pack. Make sure they see and understand the difference," Jasmine cautioned.

Mercy's mouth dropped as her cheeks reddened. "I'm sorry Mistress if I offended you. It was not my intention. Sometimes I forget, but you are right and I will make sure to reinforce what you said. Just as the rebels are full-bloods who violate the law, there are breeders who do the same. No group is absolute."

Pleased her message was received and that Mercy's investigation had opened the door to find the family involved with Nicromja, at least she hoped they had the information of the fight location, she waved down the woman's apology. "No worries. The last thing I want this group to become is biased or prejudiced against others because of differences. We are eyes and ears, reporting what we see and on occasion, like today, acting on behalf of the Nation."

"Yes, Ma'am, you are right. Thank you," Mercy said. "What do you want us to do with the breeders?"

Jasmine wasn't sure. "Silas and I need to discuss it. For now, detain them, and I'll get back with you."

"Yes, Ma'am, and again I apologize if I offended you in any way. You have my utmost respect and loyalty."

"No worries, you and your pack did a great job today, the Nation thanks you." Jasmine disconnected and looked at Hawke, who wore a slight grin. "What can I say? She was beginning to piss me off."

He held his hands up. "Totally understandable. Asia has left and should arrive in less than an hour. Assuming she steals identities along the way, we should have information within 90 minutes. Would you like the kitchen to send lunch?"

She couldn't eat. Not with her stomach twisted in knots needing her mate. "Order whatever you want."

"Mistress, you must eat to keep up your strength," Hawke said,

"I asked you to order lunch, I can't eat what's not here." She pushed back from the table and paced. "Rebel gangs selling pack members, what are they thinking?" She rubbed her forehead. "Who's marketing for the breeders? Someone's coordinating all of this. Has anyone been paid from the breeders' account on a weekly or monthly basis, like a finder's fee?" she asked Hawke.

"I'll check."

"Different things," she muttered. "Breeders provided a piece of the puzzle, but they have no connection to the challenge. Okay, put them on the back burner for now. Breeders filled an order to provide muscle for Bradford Wernher, he charters a plane and leaves before muscle arrives. Has he contacted the person he placed the order with? The breeders have not been contacted, so we don't know." She paused going over the information in her mind again. "Is this isolated?" She looked at Hawke. "This is the only order from Wernher and its within the past six months. So, did he order the muscle for the challenge and that's the extent of his involvement with the breeders?"

Hawke nodded slowly. "That could be the case. When Asia arrives, she should target the patriarch and search his memory thoroughly. The payments came from his account, he should have answers."

"Yes, but will we get those answers in time?" Jasmine said, looking at the clock on the wall.

CHAPTER 21

"How dare you kneel for her and not for me without force?" Dressed in a purple robe that opened in the front and matching baggy trousers, Nicromja strode toward Angus and stopped short of walking on top of him. Laying prostrate on the floor, Angus closed his eyes against the sting of Nicromja's brutal anger. Fiery needles raced across his skin leaving a trail of incomprehensible pain and the stench of smoking flesh.

"You think I won't leave your mate forever in the condition she is now if you don't fight to win against anyone the Goddess sends forth? Not only will I leave her comatose, I will give her to my faithful to use as they see fit. How does your beast like that?"

Invisible strings pulled Angus from his chin to his crotch, stretching his abdominals as his neck and pelvis were curved backward. The unnatural arch of his spine and neck robbed him of air. His body vibrated with pain. Would his back snap? His neck?

"Know this, your mate will become the house whore, freely given to anyone who crawls on top of her. Perhaps I will allow her to understand what's happening but unable to wake fully." Nicromja laughed. "For a bonded mate, that's worse than death I'm told."

Angus prayed to the Goddess to strengthen him to do what was right. The Wolf Nation needed Silas more than Shyla needed him. Intellectually he knew that, but his beast couldn't, wouldn't, accept the thought of Shyla with another. The conflict between his beast and human nature, in addition to the intolerable pain, threatened to drive him crazy.

A door opened. Angus groaned at the spike of pain as his flesh healed.

"Time for the first challenge," Nicromja said.

Whatever held Angus to the floor pulled him up and he got a look at his challenger. How in the name of the Goddess would he fight this beast which was a cross between a hog with long tusks and a wolf?

Was this beast a product of the experiments that had created Angus' dog, Byte? The Liege had left the dog behind in an abandoned lab Angus and his friend Chacal had searched. The dog decided Angus could keep him and refused to leave. These days Byte watched Silas' pups rather than wait for bits of Angus' time.

"The rules are simple. This fight is to the death for the honor of fighting as my champion," Nicromja said. "As a bonus, the winner receives this lovely full-blood as his bride."

Horror slammed into Angus as a picture of Shyla rose on the wall. He searched the room for the altar where she had lain and didn't see it. His beast growled in anger trying to shift to search for her. Nicromja's glee filled the room as he took a seat on the dais.

The pork filled beast snorted as it looked at Shyla. "Tasty." Its long tongue ran across thin strips which could be its mouth while gazing at the picture. Saliva glistened from its tusks as it turned dark beady eyes that seemed small in its oversized head, toward Angus.

"Die." For a large beast, it moved fast as it ran forward. Inhaling, Angus realized this creature was more animal than human. Angus shifted to his hybrid, which matched the creature's size, side stepped and plowed his fist beneath the chin, sending it flying back toward the statue. Its head slammed into the tip of the statue's oversized penis and cracked open.

"No question that was easy, that's why I allowed it to go first. Can you imagine a pig-wolf as my champion?" Nicromja asked in a mocking tone. "No, that would never do." A door opened and a tall, lumbering, hairy beast with blue mottled skin walked in.

Angus frowned. A bluebird? Here? Where had they found the Liege's creation? Angus thought with the Liege out of commission, they'd seen the last of this nasty beast. They were hyper-fast, difficult to kill, and the tips of the claws were poisoned. Angus glanced at Nicromja. The psychopath wore a welcoming smile as he looked the blue goon up and down. He was enjoying this.

"I will tell you what I told the last challenger." Nicromja pointed to the pig-wolf's carcass on the floor and repeated the rules.

Angus hadn't realized bluebirds thought independently of their masters. The creature looked at Shyla's image, his cock rose and leaked drops onto the floor. The pungent smell of lust rose in the air. Angus had no time to channel his anger, he morphed to his largest size and grabbed the bluebird by the neck as it attacked. Hawke had made it clear there was only one way to kill these beasts.

The bluebird tried to break free and bit Angus. Enraged by the threat to his mate, Angus ignored the scratches against his toughened skin, clawed into the chest of the bluebird and snatched out its heart. He held the darkened organ in the palm of his hand for a few seconds as blood gushed out the cavity of the creature onto the floor.

"What will you do now?" Nicromja mocked, standing near the splattering mess, but not one drop marred his image.

Eyes narrowed, Angus tossed the bluebird into the statue. The sound of impact boomed in the room. Angus tossed the heart at Nicromja's feet, morphed to human, and washed his hands in the water-filled basin.

Nicromja clapped. "Still more human than beast. Good. Past experience says that's important, otherwise, you lose focus and will be easily defeated. Yes, this time I will win." He watched as Angus took a sip of water from the basin and wiped his mouth with the back of his arm. "The poison from the bluebird does not affect you?"

Unwilling to share the fact he'd eaten a root for months that made him immune to the poison, Angus shrugged.

"Hmmm, this is better than I thought. Let's see how you do against this challenger." The door opened. A full-blood female, dressed in black, who looked suspiciously like Melange, strolled in.

"What are you doing here?" she asked, stopping when their gazes met.

"Kidnapped my mate and brought me here. You?"

164

She nodded. "Renee is here somewhere." She paused. "I thought I'd be fighting Silas, that's a no-win situation."

"He's the Goddess' champion," Angus said.

Her face tightened. "Fuck. Fuck. Fuck."

"Yeah, I agree."

"Enough talking," Nicromja yelled. Images of Renee and Shyla rose on the walls as Nicromja repeated the rules.

"Will you take care of her?" Melange asked, twisting her hair into a knot while staring at the pictures.

"I cannot fight my Alpha," Angus said in a low voice. "Take care of Shyla."

"No. If Silas destroys me, it will break my love's heart and damage her relationship with Jasmine. It'll be too much for her. We must end this now. Silas will care for them both."

"Silence!" Nicromja knocked both of them down and pinned them to the floor. "You don't negotiate defeat," he yelled. "My champion will not lose to the Goddess, not this time, not ever again."

Red, yellow and blue flames engulfed Angus and Melange. The stench of burning flesh rose sharply, stinging his nostrils. Unrelenting heat burned the flesh from Angus' skin. Intense pain shot through his body as he roasted without relief.

Hatred, deep like a river, rose like the phoenix as he gazed toward the dais. Calling on his beast to conserve their energy, Angus stopped struggling against the fire and focused on his service to his Alpha and the Goddess. Moments later, peace overtook him and the fire no longer mattered. Live or die, his commitment was absolute.

"No! No! No!" Nicromja lifted Angus and tossed him against the wall. Boom! He bounced off and fell to the floor. Within seconds, Nicromja lifted him and shook him like a rag doll. "You have agreed to be my champion and you shall," he growled.

The glow from Nicromja's eyes momentarily blinded Angus. Closing his eyes, he inhaled and then released his breath slowly. Every inch of his body hurt, the fire had been brutal in that it did not burn anything except the skin. Because his body constantly healed, it made the pain of repeated loss that much worse.

"Rest, both of you. In a few hours, you will both meet the Goddess' champion or your mates will be given to the bluebirds for service."

A growl rose from Angus' lips at the threat.

"Save your anger for the battle. Show me how much or little your mate means to you then." Nicromja disappeared.

Melange lay on the floor. Smoke rose from her skin. "How did you break it?" She whispered, trying to rise but failing.

"I focused on the Goddess and my Alpha. My commitment to them. Purpose, it brought me peace." A few moments later, she stood. He reached out a hand to steady her. "Okay?"

She released a breath and opened her eyes. "What the fuck's going on?"

Angus shared what he knew.

"Jasmine does not know Renee is missing," Melange said slowly. "What do you think will happen when she finds out?"

He shook his head. "She knows I'm missing, if Silas is missing as well, she may be on the verge of a melt-down. When she and Victoria learns Renee's involved... I can't imagine things will ever be the same."

CHAPTER 22

Jasmine left the kids in the nursery with their nurses to finish homework and play. It had been difficult to pretend everything was okay. Every day after school she listened as each child, including Sarita, talked about their day. Today, listening to them laugh and speak happily about little things, or friendships gone bad or good, reminded Jasmine what was at stake. Not just her kids, but every child in the Nation's life could be uprooted or changed if Silas lost the challenge.

But at what cost? Killing his brother? Her heart dropped at the thought. Moving quickly, she returned to the conference room they used as a command center. "I haven't heard from Asia yet, have you?" She pointed at Hawke.

"Not yet, Mistress." Hawke moved the platters from lunch onto the side table clearing a space in front of her.

"I need Wernher to tell me where the temple is," Jasmine said to no one in particular. "I'm not losing my man or my brother. Get me that information," she snapped.

"I've looked into Wernher's bank statements and if he's financing something overseas, he's not doing it from this account. Jacques is using his connections to search for off-shore accounts," Hawke said.

"Good." Stomach tied in knots, she paced in front of the table. "Thanks," she said.

Hawke nodded.

"Mistress?"

Jasmine leaned against the wall in relief. *"Tell me you have a name, address, something we can give Barticus."*

"I have news," Asia said. *"May I connect with Hawke and Amynta as well?"*

Jasmine exhaled and glanced at Hawke typing on a keyboard at the table. *"No. Tell me everything first. Then I'll decide what to share."*

"Yes, Ma'am, of course. I am hiding in the basement of the house, it was well guarded. Bradford Wernher is here, upstairs, dying. He's in an advanced stage of cancer. I went in as his nurse, but I didn't need her memories to see the man is suffering."

At that moment, Jasmine had nothing to give anyone involved with the challenge. She remained silent waiting for Asia to give her the information she needed to bring her man home and stop this crap from happening again.

"His memories are murky from the drugs. His eldest son handles the estate now and he wasn't here. He's out of the country."

"Where?" Jasmine snapped.

"No one knows. I've searched the memories of all five people here and none of them know about Nicromja or the son's trip. But I discovered something else," Asia paused. *"Melange was taken for the challenge."*

Initially, the words meant nothing, until it hit. Jasmine slid down the wall to catch her breath. *"Mistress?"*

"Tell me," Jasmine squeezed out the words.

"The old man knew Melange, or he'd seen her work before and instructed his son to have her picked up. But nothing more than that."

"If they took Melange, do they have Renee?" Jasmine whispered. She sensed the silence in the room, the heavy weight of every gaze on her face. She couldn't have held her head up if she wanted. Not my sister and my brother, her heart cried. Incredible pain threatened to break her mind. Silas? Her heart cried. I need you.

"There's no indication here of that, however given the way this has worked so far, I think it's likely," Asia said. *"What would you like me to do now?"*

Jasmine's head throbbed with horrific scenes of Silas fighting Melange and Renee and Angus. She wanted to scream at the

Goddess and these assholes for playing with other people's lives. Her chest hurt. It hurt to breathe.

"Silas," she called to the echo chamber in her heart, wishing as never before to hear his voice. To lean on his strength and his wisdom.

"The information I need is in that house, somewhere, Asia. Find it."

There was a discernible pause. *"Yes, Ma'am."*

Jasmine disconnected and held her head in her palm. "Renee, I'm so sorry."

Arms wrapped around her shoulders. The comforting scent of vanilla and peaches reached inside her chest and eased her troubled spirit. "Mama."

"It's okay, baby," Victoria whispered as she sat on the floor next to Jasmine and held her in her arms for a few seconds.

"They took Renee," Jasmine said brokenly.

Victoria's hand stopped rubbing Jasmine's back for a fraction of a second before continuing. Victoria gasped and held onto Jasmine. They sat quietly for a few moments.

"Jacques says Renee's not answering and hasn't been to her class in two days. How did I not know that?" Victoria whispered.

"Don't." Jasmine leaned away and stared at Victoria. "Don't do that, it's not healthy." She wiped the tears from her mom's eyes.

"No matter how old my children are, it hurts like fire when they're in trouble." Victoria held up her hand, stopping Jasmine from speaking. "But now isn't the time to think about it, we need to get through this, find Silas, Angus, Renee, and Melange and bring them home."

Jasmine swallowed hard and wiped her tears with the back of her hand.

"If you need my energy to help do whatever you do, take it. Jacques will cover me," Victoria said.

"What?"

Victoria repeated her offer.

A kernel of an idea popped in her thoughts. Asia mentioned earlier that she try and find Shyla through their previous mental link. Silas had promised to help her try, but with everything going on, she forgot. Standing slowly, hope and doubts plagued her like a saint and sinner at an all you can eat buffet. Could she do it? What if she made a mistake and went too fast or too slow? What choice did she have? With Renee and Melange now in the mix, Jasmine's back was against the wall. She refused to lose all of her family like this, not when there might be a chance.

"Mom, I've got to get up, there's something I haven't done yet." She waited for Victoria to lean aside and stood. Wiping her palms against her arms, she tried to recall how she'd found Shyla out of a sea of voices.

"Can I help?" Victoria asked.

Just as Jasmine thought to brush her off she read the need to do something, anything, in her mom's eyes and realized Victoria was hurting the same as Jasmine. "Yeah, come with me." Holding hands, she and her mom left the conference room without answering questions or making any comments. Jasmine couldn't talk about it. Not yet.

They rode the elevator to Jasmine's office. Vanessa stood in the hall as if she was lost. When she saw Jasmine, she smiled and walked toward them.

"Come with me," Jasmine said, without breaking stride. Seconds later, the three women were in her office. Jasmine locked her inner office door and paced in front of her desk for a few seconds. She looked at her mom and then Vanessa.

"I'm going to try something I've only done once." She debated whether to explain how she had taken over Shyla's body to defeat Brenda, an out of control breeder who'd tried to recruit Vanessa against her will a few months ago. The expectant gazes on both women's faces made her decide against it.

"Okay," Victoria said. "How can I help?"

Jasmine smiled at her mom's unwavering support. They didn't always see eye to eye on some things, but in the end, her mom always had her back and that knowledge went a long way in soothing her fears.

"I'll let you know in a bit." Jasmine closed her eyes and thought of Shyla. Unfortunately, images of Renee, Silas, Melange, and Angus interfered with her focus. "Damn," she muttered, realizing this would be harder than she thought. Again, she tried to picture the librarian in her mind and failed. Releasing a long sigh, she rubbed the ache forming in the front of her head.

"What are you trying to do?" Victoria asked.

"Contact Shyla."

"What?" Vanessa said. "Can you do that?"

"If she's trying to do it, she can do it," Victoria said, rubbing Jasmine's back.

"I didn't mean to question." Vanessa said. "How can you contact someone you don't know, is what I meant."

"She's pack."

"But there are so many of them. How can you find her?" Vanessa asked, her tone a mixture of hope and doubt.

"Basically, I focus on the person and call them to me. But right now, I can't get an image of her in my mind." Jasmine rubbed her forehead.

"Wait, I have some pictures of her and a few videos we took on my cell. Will those help?" Vanessa asked as she walked to the door.

"Yes, it should," Jasmine said, eager for any help she could get. "I need to connect with Shyla." Once the words left her mouth, she looked at her mom. "When I said that just now, something clicked. This is it, what I need to do."

"Great, baby. I knew you'd figure it out," Victoria said. "Vanessa can help you. Jacques said her energy is strong. I'll stay out of the way while you do what you need to do. If you need me, I'll be here."

Grateful her mom understood she needed Vanessa's help instead of hers, Jasmine kissed her mom's cheek. "I love you."

Victoria wiped the tear from her eye and nodded. "I know, sweetie. Now get my sons back home before dinner."

Vanessa walked into the room holding a bag. "Didn't know how much you'd need. As you can see, I have a lot of stuff." She held up the bag. Jasmine gestured to Victoria to help go through everything. "Here's the self-videos we took." Vanessa handed Jasmine the cell phone and she watched the beautiful, intelligent full-blood talk, laugh, and enjoy life. If Jasmine had to choose a mate for Angus, Shyla would definitely have been in the running. With each picture and each frame of video she watched, Jasmine's anger over Shyla's situation grew.

"No one should be separated from their mate or used as a remote to make a mate follow instructions," she murmured. "Shyla needs a den." Jasmine continued looking at pictures and forming an idea of Shyla in her mind. With half of the pictures still on the desk, Jasmine closed her eyes. "Shyla come to me." With laser focus, Jasmine searched for the full-blood she'd bonded with before.

When Jasmine sensed a weak response, she zeroed in. *"Shyla?"*
"Who… who…?"
"La Patroness. Are you well?"
"La Patroness?"
"Yes, answer me."
"Tired. Can't break it."
"I am going to merge with you." Jasmine didn't wait for an agreement, she eased in slowly. *"This is different, what happened?"* Jasmine sensed a heavy layer burdening the female that hadn't been there before.

"Bless the Goddess. I feel you. I mean you're here. Wait. You have to help my mate. Please, please, help Angus. They're using me to make him fight, but we agreed he wouldn't fight La Patron. I feel his pain at our separation."

"Hold on," Jasmine said, stopping the rant. *"First I need to break this cocoon you're wrapped in. Then we'll stop the fight and make sure it doesn't happen again. Where's Angus?"*

"We are? I mean we can do that?" Shyla asked.

"I damn sure hope so because I don't ever want to go through this again, do you?" Jasmine asked.

"No, Ma'am. I'll skip the encore." Shyla paused. *"Angus is here but in the other room. I heard him earlier, but it's quieter now. He has been feeding me energy, but I haven't been able to break through the cocoon as you call it."*

"I'm checking it out, it's energy multiplied. With a boost, I should be able to create a hole in it at least. Just enough to work the room. But how do we impact the challenge?"

"Ma'am?"

"Do you know anything about the challenge? This fight between Nicromja and the Goddess?" Jasmine clarified.

"No. I don't think so."

"Shyla, I don't mean to be a bitch, but this is not the time to say you don't think so. At this point, you need to tell me you're a hundred percent sure you don't know. Lives and our way of life are at stake. So, think and think hard on everything you've seen or read. Search your mind and heart for the answer to my question. Time out for uncertainties, understand? There's a reason you were chosen."

"Yes, Ma'am."

Jasmine released a breath and pulled out of the connection. "I found her."

"Oh, thank you, God," Victoria said, and sat in the chair behind her.

"Is she okay?" Vanessa asked, her eyes filling.

"She's in some kind of energy barrier that we'll need to break through, but she sounds good. And yes, she's mated to my brother, Angus. Which makes us sisters." At the mention of sisters, Jasmine's stomach clench. She refused to look at her mom or think of Renee. First, she needed to do this.

173

Vanessa squealed in delight and clapped her hands. "That's awesome, I can't wait to tease her. She gave me a hard time —"

"Right now, I need to go back in with a plan to break through the energy field. And a way to stop the challenge. To break the field, I'll need your help."

Vanessa agreed even though she frowned. "Anything you need."

"Let's do a test run, give me your hand." Jasmine held out her hand. Vanessa took it. There was a tiny spark, nothing too major. "I'm going to pull your energy, kind of braid it with mine. Let's see if we're compatible."

When Jasmine focused on Vanessa, her energy spiked as if it recognized Vanessa's signature. That was something she'd talk to Silas about later. "Easy, easy," Jasmine murmured as warm energy licked up and down her arm like a puppy.

"I can't freaking believe this," Vanessa said. "Whatever you're doing feels strange. But not in a bad way," she added. "What I mean is, I've never done anything like this before."

There was a knock on the door. "Vanessa?" Ethan called.

Victoria stood and walked to the door.

"Don't lose focus," Jasmine instructed Vanessa as she drew more energy from the woman.

"Yes, Ma'am," Vanessa said.

Victoria unlocked the door and slipped outside.

"I'm going to expand our energies; you may feel a breeze or something similar." Jasmine inhaled and went through the steps Silas taught her. Vanessa's energy was so responsive, it was like an extension of Jasmine's. When all of this was over, she wanted a DNA test done on the woman in case they were related in some way. "This is good, I'll pull a little more." Wind whipped around the room as Jasmine cranked things up and then controlled the flow into a perfectly formed tunnel that did no damage. Pleased that she could control both energy sources, Jasmine released Vanessa.

"Wow, that was unbelievable. Will you teach me how to control it?" Vanessa asked, taking a seat in a chair.

"Yes, but I think Silas gave Ethan a few tips already. How do you feel?" Jasmine wanted to return to Shyla, break the cocoon, and get everyone on the next flight home, but not if Vanessa was too tired.

"Great, like I could run a marathon." Vanessa laughed. "Must be whatever you did because I never want to run marathons."

"Good." Jasmine smiled and rubbed her hands together. "I'd like to do this if you're ready."

Vanessa stood. "I'm ready."

"You may want to sit. I need to talk to Shyla first, make sure she's ready. When I'm ready, you'll feel a tug on your energy."

Wide-eyed, Vanessa nodded.

Jasmine found Shyla again quickly and merged. "*Have you heard anything?*"

"*Glad you're back, I was afraid you were angry with me and wouldn't come back,*" Shyla said.

"*No, normally Silas backs me, energy-wise, when I merge with full-bloods. But he's not here, I needed to get some help. Vanessa's with me.*"

"*Vanessa? My friend, Vanessa?*"

"*Yes. Do you have any idea how to break this challenge? We're running out of time,*" Jasmine said while testing the layers wrapped around Shyla. Thick bands of energy ran in a crisscross pattern.

"*There's something.*" She told Jasmine about her abduction, the library, and the person in the shadows. "*In that book, there were strange words.*" She repeated them. "*Do they mean anything to you?*"

Jasmine repeated the words. "*They leave a funny taste in my mouth.*"

"Same here." Shyla said the words again and again, but this time she added a few more. *"Strange thing is, every time I say them, I recall more and more. It's like they're taking root or something."* She said the words again.

"Right now those words are the only thing we have. Keep going, there may be a pot of gold at the end of the rainbow. I'm poking a few holes in this cocoon." Jasmine sent energy zingers through cracks in the cocoon to see if she could weaken it. When she identified five spots to obliterate, she tugged on Vanessa's energy and focused everything on the cocoon. The spots sizzled, and after a few seconds, unraveled, leaving a large opening in the back.

"Can you move now?" Jasmine asked Shyla.

"Yes, but I haven't been able to reach Angus. Our connection is broken."

"So is mine with Silas. I can help you leave this room to find your mate."

"We need a plan, otherwise they'll use me to distract him more," Shyla said, earning Jasmine's respect.

"Even though the Goddess didn't come right out and say it, I think mates can stop this whole challenge thing. Nothing's supposed to come between mates and look what's happening. There's probably some rule somewhere that's been broken or forgotten," Jasmine said frustrated.

"I believe you're right." Shyla paused. *"But it must be done a certain way, at the right time."*

"What are you talking about?" Jasmine asked.

"I wish I knew other than I know I'm right. Maybe it's the words we repeated, but there is a way to fix this once and for all. But we can't let anyone know and timing is crucial. They may have to fight."

"Why?" It went against everything Jasmine wanted, but she needed more information.

"Honestly, I don't know, just my gut and the words unraveling in my mind. It's risky because I don't have a full picture or

understanding of everything I need to do, but I know I have to be the one to do it. Wow, see, I didn't know that until I said it," Shyla said.

"My mate, La Patron is involved. There's no way I'm backing out of this." Although Shyla was Angus' mate, Jasmine was crystal clear about her position in saving Silas and the others.

"Thank the Goddess, I would be scared shitless without your support. Physically, two full-bloods must do whatever needs to be done. That's me and Angus. I see that clearly, but not what we do," Shyla said. *"Continue speaking those words, Mistress, but don't share them. I get the impression they're really special."*

"Will you get in trouble for sharing them?" Jasmine said the words in her mind.

"No, because it's you, my Alpha. At least I don't sense a problem, but the idea of sharing with Vanessa hurts, so I know they can't be shared with anyone else," Shyla said.

The more Jasmine repeated the words, more words flowed naturally until her mind was washed with vibrant colored shapes and symbols. Her heartbeat increased and peace rested on her shoulders. *"You're right."*

"Yes. It's time for me to find my mate and get this done. Stay with me, please."

"Of course," Jasmine said, watching as Shyla slid from beneath the energy layers.

CHAPTER 23

Energized by Jasmine's presence, Shyla slid out the door into the hall. Expecting to be stopped by security, she was surprised by their absence. Knees knocking in fear, she crept around the corner and stared at the double doors just ahead at the end of the corridor. She pressed her back against the wall and inch by inch moved toward the doorway, positive at any moment someone would open it and drag her back to that room or worse, inside to torment her mate. If she didn't believe deep in her heart she needed to be in the room, she would find another place to hide.

"I'm here, Shyla. You're doing great. Do you sense anyone?" Jasmine asked.

Inhaling deeply, Shyla released the air in slow measures. Petrified of being found, she hadn't thought to use her senses to find the guards.

"No, not in the halls anyway."

"Good, see if there's another way inside that room. If you go through that door, everyone will see you and if you're not ready for that, it'll be a problem," Jasmine said.

"Right." Since she didn't see any other doors in this hall, she spun around and searched the area. It didn't take long to find a side door unlocked. Inhaling, she sensed nothing in the area. Had the priests left? She opened the door and walked into the darkened room. Several robes like what the priests had worn were on hooks. Moving quickly, Shyla dressed in a robe and boots. Covering her head, she felt easier about walking into the main room. She stuck her hands in the pockets and touched a piece of paper. Pulling it out she saw a picture of a crystal that may have been torn from a reference book or something similar.

Why would the priests be interested in crystals? She told Jasmine what she found.

"Interesting. Place the paper in another robe and leave them in the exact spot as the one you put on in case they return for the clipping," Jasmine said.

"Yes, Ma'am." Shyla rearranged everything as she found it, even replacing the robe and boots from a trunk in the corner. Done, she closed her eyes and repeated the words over and over until she'd recalled them all.

A tingling sensation started from her toes, rose up her belly to her head. The words tumbled out her mouth on their own accord, using her as a vessel. *"There are a lot of people in the other room."*

"Is Silas there?"

"I can't tell, yet."

Propelled toward the door, she exited the room. The scent of her mate slammed into her. Her beast tried to break free to get to Angus, but a powerful compulsion had taken over. More words poured from her belly, the sound lyrical, clean, pure and powerful. *"Mistress, I can't stop."*

CHAPTER 24

Angus couldn't rest. Shyla filled his mind. His fingers itched to touch her. Inhaling, he picked up her lingering scent and hugged it close. Closing his eyes tight, he recalled the last time he held her, felt her lips, watched her smile. Hoarding those memories close, he wondered what would happen to her after the challenge? Could Silas retrieve her body before Nicromja gave her away? Goddess, how could he allow that of his mate? His heart clenched. He couldn't. Torn between loyalties, once again Angus dropped his head into his hands and prayed to the Goddess for guidance.

Time always fly when you wished it would crawl. Nicromja appeared first. He wore a purple robe with gold and white trim. He stepped from the dais with his hands behind his back and stared at Angus and Melange.

No one spoke.

The next moment the Goddess arrived in a cloud of white. The room glowed and then crystallized on her female form. Dressed in white with long black hair and sparkling green eyes, she floated to the dais next to Nicromja but spared Angus a tiny smile.

When the cloud cleared, Angus' heart leapt with joy. "Silas." His brother turned, saw him and they ran to each other and embraced. "I'm so happy to see you." Angus slapped Silas' back over and over.

"Same here, I've missed you," Silas said, leaning back to look at him. "You're well?"

"Mated to Shyla, Ethan's mate's friend, you may remember her." Angus hoped Silas understood the underlying problem of the challenge.

"My bitch called it, she claimed that's the reason you disappeared." Silas' gaze held a question.

"Please care for her," Angus said.

"Enough," Nicromja said. "I've warned you about your determination to allow your Alpha to win this challenge. Do I need to breed your mate in front of you?"

Silas growled and stood next to Angus. "No one can stand between mates, not even you," Silas said. "To use mates as a lever is illegal."

Nicromja waved away Silas' words. "In certain instances, everything can be waived. This challenge is one of those times. Now, I have two reluctant challengers." He pointed to Angus and Melange.

"Shit," Silas groaned as Melange, his sister-in-law, walked towards Angus.

"Is this your champion?" Nicromja asked the Goddess, pointing at Silas.

"Yes," she said.

"Since I don't oversee a pack, I'll use both fighters as my champion," Nicromja said.

"You continue to break protocols and rules with this challenge, are you sure you wish to continue?" the Goddess asked.

Nicromja waved away her question. "Let's discuss the rules." He repeated the same rules for Silas as he had earlier.

"I cannot kill him," Silas said, frowning.

"Do you forfeit?" Nicromja sounded giddy.

"Forfeit? What are you talking about?" Silas asked, his gaze flew from Nicromja to the Goddess, then back to Nicromja.

"If you do not kill him, you lose," Nicromja said.

"I cannot kill him, nor can he kill me," Silas said slowly. "Den-mates cannot kill the other."

Nicromja looked at both men and then at the Goddess. "You set this up, didn't you?"

"No. I had nothing to do with your choice of champion and you alone know the lengths you went through to get them here," she said.

"But you knew they were den-mates?"

181

"Of course, so would you if you paid attention to the pack. But you don't, instead you —"

"Spare me the lecture," Nicromja said, staring at Angus, Melange, and Silas. "You can kill the woman but not the man. Somehow that doesn't seem fair. I've seen this one fight and I want him in the match." Nicromja snapped his fingers. A jewel encrusted sword fell onto the floor in front of Angus. "Use this, it'll kill him. Now let's get this started. Defeat the female first, and then fight your den-mate. My sword will make things even." He stepped back and crossed his arms.

Silas looked at the Goddess.

Angus watched Silas and placed his hand on his shoulder. "Earlier, I refused to fight my Alpha. I will not use this sword or any other weapon against my brother. Our nation needs you and La Patroness. My commitment to you is as strong today as it was the day I pledged my life and my sword to you, your den, and our pack." Holding Silas' gaze, Angus went down on one knee.

"No!" Nicromja's voice boomed across the room shaking the walls. Angus was lifted and slammed against the back wall. He shifted to his hybrid to heal. Before he could take his next breath, he was thrown against another wall.

"You would break another rule, force a full-blood to champion you, who refuses?" The Goddess asked as Angus slid down the wall.

"He promised to fight for me," Nicromja yelled.

"Yes, but he refused to fight his Alpha. Silas is his Alpha, you cannot disregard the conditions of his acceptance just because you want to," she said, sending healing warmth through Angus.

"You will not rob me of my champion," Nicromja spat. He picked up his sword, and within a flash, he stood in front of Angus. "Take this sword, let me see it in your hand."

Wary of deceit, Angus didn't speak or move.

"Let me see this sword in your hand," Nicromja demanded again, this time with some sort of compulsion.

Against his will, Angus' hand reached for the sword. The moment he grabbed the hilt, Nicromja's energy rushed through him, binding him with the weapon. Angus fought against the anger of losing to someone else for centuries, of being overlooked, under-valued, and taken advantage of. Nicromja's frustrations gripped Angus tight in a stranglehold. His thoughts fled as Nicromja's sense of outrage and justice filled him.

Today, he would fix that. Today, he would win and gain the respect of everyone. Standing slowly, Angus held the sword upward.

"Will you fight as my champion?" Nicromja asked with a smug grin.

"Yes," Angus said, staring at the sword.

"Come, fight the challenge and become Alpha of the pack. His den will be yours." Nicromja appeared on the dais next to the Goddess. She shook her head but remained silent.

"Will you fight as my champion?" she asked Silas.

"I cannot destroy my brother," Silas said, and went down on one knee with a bowed head.

"Silas, get up. If you don't fight, Renee has no chance," Melange said, pulling on his arm. "What about Jasmine? Adam? David? Renee? Jackie? You're going to leave them and the Nation?"

As Melange spoke of pack, each name she called slammed into Angus. Images raced across his mind. The children running in their nursery, or asking his help with a project or to brush her hair. Their small faces crowded his mind. Protect. Honor. Defend. A tremor wracked his body. The hilt of the sword sizzled in his hand. He threw back his head and released a howl.

Silas and Melange joined in.

Angus spun, sword raised with a rallying cry. He shifted to his largest form and sliced the phallus from the statue. The sound of metal contacting stone bounced off the walls, followed by the loud crash of the stone cock hitting the floor. Gasping for air, Angus fell to the ground as his body shook. Incredible heat spread from his palm holding the sword. Desperate to be rid of the weapon, he tried to release it and couldn't. Silas tried to help dislodge the weapon. It wouldn't budge.

Silas wrapped his arms around Angus, sending cooling energy to combat the heat. Melange wrapped her arms around Silas, adding her energies to his. The heat receded for a few seconds. Melange screamed as she was tossed across the room against the wall.

Ignoring the lingering pain, Angus took a deep breath and met Silas' gaze. "Brother."

Silas swallowed hard. "Brother." They stood side by side and faced the goddess.

She smiled at them before looking at Nicromja. "Take your sword, you cannot force the challenge." The sword dropped to the floor. The sound loud in his ear.

"The one in black will fight the challenge," Nicromja said, even though it was apparent he preferred Angus.

"As your champion?" the Goddess asked.

"Yes," Nicromja snapped.

Melange moved slowly in their direction, her gaze on Silas.

A monk entered the room from a side door. Angus heard the muttering but paid little attention until the robed monk was closer. His beast growled.

Shyla.

Angus turned and watched her walk forward with her head covered and bowed. She was speaking. He moved toward her and stopped as she passed him. Her words became louder. Silas met Angus and mouthed, "Jasmine is here."

Angus nodded. The two of them stood silently and waited to see how things would play out.

The longer Shyla said the words in her head the less afraid she became. Soon they strengthened her to the point she knew exactly what she needed to do to correct an error that the Wolf Nation had been victims of for centuries. Prompted to move forward by a force she couldn't name, Shyla left the room and walked into the larger room, past the statue, past her mate and Alpha. Speaking the foreign tasting words, she stopped in front of the gods.

Nicromja frowned. "How do you know our language?"

Shyla couldn't answer if she wanted, instead, she allowed more words to pour forth. Based on the expressions on both the Goddess' and Nicromja's faces, whatever she said surprised them.

"*I wish we knew what you were saying,*" Jasmine said.

"*Me too,*" Shyla said. The next second she understood the Goddess and Nicromja were being held accountable for breaking laws. Neither god could leave the room, others were now being called to judge them. A second later, a short, bald man materialized in front of them. The room shook as he grew larger and larger.

"*Oh shit,*" Jasmine said when Shyla stopped talking.

"*I know, right. You don't think they'll kill me for being the bearer of doom, do you?*"

"*No.*" Jasmine paused. "*They shouldn't, it's not like you knew what you were saying.*"

His dark eyes looked like midnight with specks of white light, reminding her of stars. His gaze brushed against hers and then lit on every person in the room.

The Goddess and Nicromja watched their new guest without speaking.

"*They're trying to read my mind, to find out where he came from,*" Shyla said, panicking.

"*Don't worry, they can't,*" Jasmine said with so much confidence, Shyla didn't question her.

"*Do you know who he is?*" Jasmine asked.

"*No, but I think I just called him from somewhere with those funny tasting words.*" Shyla didn't know what to do now that her part was over. She turned and looked at Angus and Silas, two brothers standing tall, together. Her pussy clenched as she read the hunger in Angus' eyes.

"*Damn that man's fine,*" Shyla said, forgetting the tension in the room as her eyes feasted on him. Girl, pull it together, this is not the time, you've let a bald genie out of the bottle who may fry your ass. Focus, Shyla, Angus needs your help

"*Miss my wolfie,*" Jasmine said. "*He knows I'm with you. I bet he's got a million questions.*" She laughed. "*That felt good. Let's finish this, I need my man.*"

Shyla inhaled hoping the entity would finish whatever they needed to do so they could all leave. Seconds later, she sensed several celestials in the room. Fear skittered up her spine as pure power pulsed in the room. Whatever was happening, was a big deal.

The bald man spoke forcefully in the same language she'd spoken.

As words she understood spewed from his mouth, all conversation stopped. Nobody moved or breathed. He spoke of the game played by the Goddess and Nicromja centuries ago, both were wrong in their actions to the Wolf Nation. There was a collective gasp as a wager between the Goddess and Nicromja was brought into the open and condemned by rules as old as time.

Nicromja's anger was tangible, he pointed at Shyla. "Who gave you permission to read the sacred texts?"

"Shershrine chose her. Do not question us, you have violated our laws, this last time by compelling the full-blood to take his sword to kill his den-mate after learning it was against the rules. And to command a bitch to champion you when you have never had authority over bitches means you have not learned anything in centuries," Shershrine said in a hard tone with a cold edge.

Nicromja opened his mouth and then closed it on a snap with a quick bow.

"I was wrong to allow Nicromja guardianship over male wolves, and made it worse by not reporting his inability to lead," the Goddess said, staring slightly above Shyla's head.

"Inability? I'm just as good as any other," Nicromja yelled.

Shershrine looked at him. "Truly? One of the rules says you must be chosen. Will the wolves choose you?" Shyla sensed Shershrine's anger.

Nicromja glanced at Silas and Angus.

"Speak," Shershrine commanded.

Nicromja shook his head. "No, they will not. But that is because they do not know me. She robbed me of my time with them."

Shyla doubted that was the reason neither Angus nor Silas wanted anything to do with the lazy god, but kept quiet.

Shershrine faced the other three entities spread around the room and spoke in the strange language again. He explained the laws and their purpose. "The idea of two champions fighting for the right of Alpha is not a new one. But this is not what we have here. None of these full-bloods are challenging their Alpha." Shyla looked at Melange and Angus. "They were brought here against their will, their mates threatened, and still they refused to challenge their Alpha. Both would have died to protect the pack, something Nicromja knows nothing about. The Goddess has done well maintaining the spirit of the law, even if she broke it by allowing Nicromja's involvement. There will be no other challenges, the wolves belong to her." His gaze lit on Silas and then Angus.

"Who gave permission for humans to breed full-bloods?" Shershrine asked the gods.

"I was not involved with that decision," Nicromja said, stepping back.

"At the time of great unrest, I permitted such a thing to happen. In my opinion, it was the best option for full-bloods. Mortality rates were low, dens were smaller, and I feared their extinction," the Goddess said.

"And I assisted." Grandfather trotted into the room and onto the dais next to the Goddess.

Shershrine acknowledged the wolf. "Blackwolf, how did you assist?"

"My seed was the first to take root in a human, altering her to accommodate our kind," he said.

"Changed how?" Shershrine demanded. "Did you break more laws?"

187

Blackwolf morphed into human. Shyla couldn't stop staring. There was no doubt Angus was related to this handsome, gray-haired man with such a regal bearing. "Natural laws were broken, humans are not capable of handling full-bloods, so their bodies were altered."

"How has this impacted full-bloods?" Shershrine asked, watching Blackwolf closely.

"The pack thrives. La Patron is an excellent leader and his mate is a human breeder. They have many pups in their den with no problems," Blackwolf said, his voice steady.

"It is the posterity of the full-blood who concerns us," Shershrine said, looking at Shyla and then Angus.

Without thinking, Shyla extended her hand to Angus. He took it and they faced the entities.

Shershrine continued speaking. "Mated full-bloods cannot be separated, nor can they be used against the other." Immediately her mind-link with Angus was restored.

"Silas," Jasmine gasped and left Shyla.

Melange ran out the room.

A female of average height wearing a cream-colored cape covering her from head to toe entered the room.

"Welcome, Chancellor," the Goddess said, watching the female.

Chancellor nodded and stood in front of Angus and Shyla. Chill bumps raced across Shyla's skin.

Unable to believe her role in all this, she pinched her thigh. *"I'm standing in front of the Goddess,"* Shyla said to Angus through their link.

"Yes, I'm so proud of you. Thank you for stopping this madness." He winked.

Warmth curled up Shyla's back as a smile curved her lips.

Shershrine cleared his throat.

Chancellor's gaze flicked down to their joined hands. Shyla saw the longing in the female's eyes before she blinked.

"We will finish this now," Shershrine said, drawing everyone's attention.

Angus squeezed her hand. Shyla straightened and watched the bald man. They stood erect for several moments as a thousand invisible fingers ran over their body. Shyla would swear those nasty buggers slipped past her skin as well. Fortunately, the exam was done almost as soon as it began.

"What do you say about the human breeding? How does it impact full-bloods seeking mates? Is there jealousy? Rebellion?" Shershrine asked her.

Shyla didn't know any human breeders except for Brenda and she had been a crazy, suicidal bitch. "Some breeders have problems controlling pheromones and have somehow used their abilities to weaken full-blood males. There's no impact on the females that I'm aware of, but the men can be enslaved easily. What else?" She turned to Angus.

"Only non-mated full-bloods can be controlled," Angus said quickly.

"Less than half of full-bloods are mated, that leaves a large amount available for these illegal breeders to tamper with." Shershrine crossed his arms and continued looking at him.

"Yes, but the breeders I know are loyal, loving, and more nurturing with pups than bitches have been in the past. La Patroness' den is better adjusted because of the amount of time and care the pups receive. I think our people are stronger because of the diversity," Angus said, making her proud.

"Pups grow weak with this kind of care. Bitches do not need to spend years grooming pups, it has never been so. Is there a good reason for full-bloods to dilute their blood with humans?"

Shyla shivered at the menace in the question and looked at the Goddess, who wore a neutral expression, but Shyla couldn't see her eyes.

Blackwolf stepped forward. "Yes. The nation has grown over the centuries. There are electronic inventions that record our

189

movements and conversations. Drugs that render us helpless. Mutants block Alpha control. It is more difficult to hide in plain sight. Also, humans want to attend our schools, hospitals, and sporting arenas, and work in our companies. When we refused to mix as we are taught to do, humans complained to their courts, claimed discrimination. Living in this generation required an extra layer of protection to remain secret. We determined human breeders to be the best solution to solve two problems."

"Who is we? You had no authority to do this." Shershrine extended his arm.

Chancellor tilted her head to the side, the hood fell back revealing a lovely face with deep purple, glowing eyes and a small birthmark on the side of her neck. She took his hand. For several seconds no one spoke.

Blackwolf cleared his throat. "The ancients spoke with the Goddess, explained our concerns. She agreed as long as La Patron's mate came through my line." The old wolf looked across the room at Silas. "He lost his first mate, the Goddess determined he should have one of my line."

Shyla jerked and looked at La Patron. "*He had another mate? When?*"

"*A long time ago,*" Angus said.

"*Where is she?*"

"*Dead. A long time ago.*"

Shyla hadn't been mated long but she recognized the signs. They wouldn't discuss this subject.

"There is nothing written granting anyone permission to allow this," Shershrine said.

"Not written," the Goddess said quickly. "But implied. I have absolute care of the wolves and to that end allowed the mating to solve several problems. It was within the scope of my authority to allow human breeders."

"But they cause many problems. Several full-bloods, male and female, have died from mis-use of power by these humans. How does that help the nation?" Shershrine asked.

"Some have caused problems, others have not. We are diligent in seeking those who cause problems and stopping them. La Patroness has a nationwide network that deals with that issue, it's under control," Grandfather said.

Shyla noticed the look of surprise on La Patron's face and glanced at Angus. He stared at Grandfather. Tension rolled into the room on a dark cloud.

"What's going on?" she asked Angus.

"Trouble."

Instead of asking more questions, she moved closer to him. Angus squeezed her hand again. That small gesture calmed her.

Chancellor tipped her head back, her eyes now lavender as she stared at the vaulted ceiling.

"Human breeding is not sanctioned." Shershrine started speaking another lyrical language.

La Patron released a blood curdling scream and dropped to the floor holding his head with both hands.

"Stop," Grandfather yelled as he and Angus raced to La Patron, now writhing on the ground.

Shershrine continued speaking as blood rolled down La Patron's cheeks from his eyes.

"What's going on, Shyla?" Jasmine asked, her voice frantic.

"I'm not sure. He's chanting or speaking words that I don't understand. La Patron's in pain." She turned to face him so Jasmine could see.

"He's leaving me," Jasmine yelled. *"How can this happen? Where's the Goddess? She promised me things would work out. Where is she? He's leaving me, damn it!"*

"Leaving you? What does that mean?" Shyla asked as shock ricocheted through her chest. Angus and grandfather wrapped their arms around Silas, holding him tight.

Jasmine merged with Shyla. A whirlwind of hot energy flew around the room. Chancellor looked at Shyla. Their gazes clashed as Jasmine challenged the woman.

Shershrine looked at Shyla with a curious gaze.

"What are you doing to my mate?" Jasmine asked Shershrine. Shyla couldn't see past the red haze covering her eyes. Inside, her gut churned with volcanic fury as Jasmine's energy increased.

When no one answered, raw energy ripped around the room. Nicromja's statue teetered. Dirt and debris created a dust storm around Chancellor as she rose in the air. Shyla wasn't sure who elevated the female and watched in awe as Jasmine walked toward Silas.

"What the fuck have they done to him?" she yelled, pointing at the blood on his face and chest.

Grandfather stood and reached toward her.

"Answer me!" His hand fell as he cleared his throat and explained what happened.

"What do you mean we aren't sanctioned? Never mind, I don't care what you mean. Silas is my mate. If you don't stop trying to separate us, he will die and so will you." She faced Shershrine and Chancellor.

Chancellor dropped to the floor, answering Shyla's question as to whose power sent her in the air. Jasmine stalked forward. "Release him or I swear I will pull energy from every bitch in the nation and fry your ass. Do not test me on this. No one comes between mates, no one."

The white spots in Shershrine's eyes glowed. He patted Chancellor's hand. "You are human. Mating with full-bloods was never sanctioned. It is illegal."

"Too late, this human and that full-blood are mated, so get over it," Jasmine snapped, walking closer to him.

"She is also of my seed," grandfather said, moving to stand behind Jasmine. "I am full-blood, she is a part of me."

"Is that the basis of her power?"

"Some, but she is La Patroness, the Alpha's mate. As such, she can tap into the energies of the nation to protect her Alpha, which is what she is doing now. Only a mate can do this," grandfather stressed with a measure of pride.

"Release him," Jasmine said and shook off grandfather's hand on her shoulder. Nicromja's statue crashed to the ground in a large boom, shaking the room.

"Stop that," Nicromja yelled.

Chancellor was slammed against the wall..

Blackwolf howled. Angus joined him.

Chancellor tried to break away, but couldn't.

"You would destroy the keeper of our records?" Shershrine asked, moving forward and waving his hand. Chancellor lowered to the floor, gasping for air.

"I will destroy anyone who comes after my Alpha or my pack, remember that," Jasmine growled. The low, menacing sound rolled up Shyla's belly.

Silas stopped convulsing.

"You are an interesting mix of human and wolf. I see the potential as well as the danger. If all breeders tap into the power of the full-blood, how do we survive them?" Shershrine asked Grandfather while watching Shyla.

"Just as we always have, we weed out the bad and encourage the good. Today you have seen the best of our people. A full-blood mated couple and a full-blood and human. Both strong, vibrant, and loyal to pack. We can survive with the humans, but we need the human half of our people to combat the way the world has changed. We need the breeders," grandfather said, his voice strong in his commitment to seeing that happen.

The moment Chancellor's feet connected to the ground, Angus left Silas and touched her gently on the arm, activating the bracelet.

Shershrine spoke in that language again.

"Stop this Chancellor," Angus said, seeing the conflict the woman fed the Shershrine. "You blacken your position by poisoning the conversation. The decision of mates is not the same as what happened to you, don't make this personal." He rifled through a few more memories before he was pushed out.

"Humans and full-bloods shouldn't mate," Chancellor yelled and bent forward holding her stomach. "They are treacherous liars who cannot be trusted. They will destroy us all."

"You did this? All of this for revenge?" Angus couldn't contain his shock, which was replaced by anger as he thought of everything that had happened to his mate, his brother, and their pack. "Snatched my mate from her chamber, lied to Grandfather and the Goddess, activated Nicromja's minions? All of this because some asshole tricked you? You engaged the Shershrine to what, punish us?"

"Chancellor," Blackwolf said, moving closer to the woman, who backed up like a cornered animal. "You learned the sacred words, read the books?" He sounded confused.

"I forgave your fall, this is how you repay me? Through lies and deceit?" the Goddess asked. The room brightened to the point it was difficult to see anyone.

Angus stepped back searching for Shyla and took her hand. Out the corner of his eye, he saw Renee and Melange step into the room. They remained near the corner and he wondered why they hadn't left. Renee ran to Silas, who remained on the floor, and hugged him. Melange followed, watching everyone, and stood near Silas and Renee.

"No, they are all evil," Chancellor said. "They trick and use you."

"Cease your tampering," the Goddess snapped. "Now that you have brought the Shershrine, you will allow them to see clearly without your opinion."

Chancellor whimpered but didn't speak as she moved backward away from them all.

"You think she has done wrong?" Shershrine asked the Goddess.

"Yes, she had a love affair with a human and it ended badly," the Goddess said in a softer tone.

"Badly?" Shershrine asked, looking at Chancellor. "I sensed none of this during our connection."

"Because you gave them the ability to block us from reading their thoughts," the Goddess answered, she glanced at Angus.

Chancellor covered her face with her palms and released deep gut-wrenching sobs.

"That is true," Shershrine looked at Chancellor again. "Full-bloods are our only concern, are you willing to represent them?" Shershrine turned and asked Angus.

Surprise zipped through him. Shouldn't Silas represent the pack? "*What do you want me to do?*" he asked Silas.

"*Represent us. No one is better qualified to speak on our behalf,*" Silas said.

Pride swelled in Angus' chest. "*I will always stand with you.*"

"*I know and I am a better wolf because of it,*" Silas answered.

"*Is Renee going to let you breathe?*" Angus asked, smiling as the woman wiped the blood from Silas' neck.

"*My bitch may have something to do with this,*" Silas said. "*She says this is what family does.*" Angus heard the resignation in his Alpha's voice.

"*Really? Well, in my defense, I missed that class,*" Angus said.

Shershrine held up his hand. "Before you answer, understand that my decree will be final, no one and nothing can change it, not even the power of the pack, as impressive as it is. Will you and your mate stand proxy for the nation?"

"Yes, our loyalty is to La Patron and La Patroness, both rule the nation with love, wisdom, and honor. We will stand for them and the nation," Angus said, squeezing Shyla's hand as she agreed through their link.

"So be it." Shershrine placed his fingertips on Angus and Shyla's forehead.

Sizzling tingles shot through Angus' mind. He sent warmth and comfort to Shyla. This time she squeezed his hand, standing silent while Shershrine searched their memories. Seconds later the tingling stopped.

Shershrine stepped back watching Angus. "You are full of surprises and wisdom."

Angus wondered if he would say something about the bracelet or crystals. After Chancellor's breach, Angus didn't want her to know about either.

"We are satisfied," Shershrine said into the silence. "Alphas earn the loyalty and respect of their pack, not through the strength of the challenge but through the manner in which they lead and take care of the people. When one Alpha kneels to the other, and both would die for the other, there is no greater praise. Despite the Goddess' misinterpretation of the law, she had no authority to allow human breeding, all matings will stand. There will be no new breeders. Take care of the ones you now have. La Patroness was right, no one should come between mates, not even the gods."

Turning, Shershrine waved Nicromja forward. "Do you understand our decree?"

"There is no way to regain my right to lead the wolves, is that what you mean?" Nicromja said. His tone sullen.

"That right was never yours. It was a symbolic gesture on the part of the Goddess to help you. That can never happen again, full-bloods pay a high price for your pride. Do not engage your priests in this kind of trickery again, as you see the results are damaging and long lasting."

"So I get nothing?" Nicromja said.

"Have you earned anything?" Shershrine asked.

Nicromja disappeared.

No one spoke.

"Goddess, our trust in you remains. Blackwolf, your line is indeed impressive."

Shershrine disappeared.

CHAPTER 25

Cancer looked at his brother and shook his head. "You have to leave now. Take this to father, see if someone can get the crystal to work for him."

"No, we go together, it's dangerous staying here. Nicromja will know we left the temple early and took security with us to search the caves, he may send someone after us," Scorpio pulled off his robe and tossed it aside.

They'd just returned from a successful search of several caves, now it was time to add insurance for their father. Although Scorpio would never admit it, trekking through the woods and caves wore him out. Cancer wanted to make sure his brother got home safe, this next part of the trip was the deadliest and he needed to be able to focus without thinking about his brother.

"There's one more thing we have to do or all of this was a waste of time," Cancer said, noticing the stubborn tilt of his twin's chin. "We don't have time to argue, get these crystals back home safe. We promised and can't fail in this, the stakes are too high."

"What about…?"

Rage rushed through Cancer, he choked down the bitter words that threatened to pull him under. "Forget her, damn it. She was a job, and will kill you, us, if she ever sees or finds us again." He loved and hated this about his brother, Scorpio got too emotional.

"Doesn't it bother you what we did to her? Taking advantage of her like that, knowing she was lonely? That doesn't bother you that we broke her heart?" Scorpio had walked closer, their gazes clashed.

"Not one bit. She was the key to finding the cure to save Dad. That's it. My heart was never involved, she was a damn job, nothing more or less. Now snap the fuck out of it and get ready to get on the damn plane. I want to finish this and get back home. Fuck this heat." He turned, pulled off his clothes, and stepped into the shower.

Going after the full-blood and his mate was dangerous. If there were other option, he'd gladly take it and get the hell out of this damn country. But no one else knew about the crystals, they'd been seeking information for the past five years. If he didn't do this just right, the full-blood would kill him and perhaps carry out his threat to destroy their family. Cancer snorted. His namesake, cancer, had already wiped out a large portion of his loved ones. If the crystal didn't work, his father would certainly die. How did they unlock the power of the crystal? There were no instructions in that blasted book they'd copied from the Chancellor's collection. The full-blood would know. Cancer and Scorpio agreed on that point.

They disagreed on how to gain the full-blood's help after everything that happened so far. Cancer was certain he would be killed on the spot if he ever crossed the large man's path. Scorpio thought they should use the darts and take the couple again, forgetting full-blood's build resistance to chemicals and drugs relatively quickly, making that option a long shot. His chest still clenched in remembrance of how big the son-of-a-bitch grew when he was pissed. No, he wouldn't ever seek out that wolf without leverage, and they'd never get the mate again.

Scorpio knocked on the door. "I'm heading out, be careful, okay. He'll kill you without a thought."

Cancer turned off the water, stepped out grabbing a towel, and dried off. "I know. I don't plan to get close to him. As we speak I've got things in motion so that I can take him without being anywhere near him." A sliver of unease ran through him. He shook it off and inhaled. They couldn't second guess now, they were too close.

"Good, that makes me feel better. When will you take them?" Scorpio looked at his watch.

"In a few hours after they've fucked themselves tired. Once they entered the hotel, our people went into action, everything's set." He sounded more confident than he felt.

"In that case, I'll head out." Scorpio held up the satchel with the crystals and hugged him. "Bring that bastard to his knees."

Cancer smiled. "You know it." He kept the smile in place until his brother strode out the door.

CHAPTER 26

The tip of Shyla's pert nipple pressed into Angus' chest. Closing his eyes, he inhaled the sweet fragrance from their last round. Just thinking how good and tight her lush sweetness felt caused his cock to rise. Damn, this mating heat was fucking fantastic. Horny excitement raced through him, he counted to a hundred to keep from begging for more.

Her warm fingers wrapped around his hardness. Inhaling, he rode the shudder of lust that ripped through him and pulled her on top. Laughing, she leaned down and bit his lip before taking his mouth with a hunger that roared through him. She gripped his hair as she deepened the kiss. Their tongues battled, dueled for supremacy. Gasping for air, she ran her fingertip over his face while staring into his eyes.

"Mine," she growled, pleasing his beast.

"Say it like I'm inside of you." He nuzzled her neck, inhaling deeply. His cock twitched at the recognition of her smell.

She shuddered in his arms. "When I couldn't feel you, the sun went dark," she said in a soft tone. His seductress bitch switched gears, speaking of her feelings for the first time. "Actually it was dark. No light anywhere." He picked up remnants of her nightmare clinging to her mind, haunting her through their link.

Pulling her down, he wrapped his arms around her and placed a kiss on her forehead. "I'm sorry. So very sorry."

Her head moved against his chest. "No, you saved me. Just knowing you were near kept me hopeful it would all be over soon." She paused. Her fingertips traced his La Patron tattoo. "I was scared," she whispered.

Angus swallowed the knot forming in his throat, bringing a hand to her face.

"I thought I was brave. All that talk about giving our lives for the cause." She wiped her tears on his chest.

"You are brave," he whispered against her hair, rubbing her back.

"No." She swallowed hard and pushed up.

He framed her face with his palms. "Yes. My brave bitch saved the day."

Tears rolled down her cheeks. "I didn't think I could help and didn't try. I keep thinking what would've happened if La Patroness hadn't all but kicked my ass and made me dig for the answers."

He kissed the salty fluid from her face. "You saved us."

"That bitch Chancellor used me like a puppet and I didn't see any of it." She looked at him. "Did you know she orchestrated all of this?"

"No. But I thought she knew more than she let on. Listen, even the Goddess and grandfather didn't realize who set all this into motion. Chancellor fed them bits and pieces of information."

Shyla wiped her face. "How'd that happen? The Goddess shouldn't have been fooled."

"Chancellor's thoughts can't be breached by gods because of the information they handle. It's some kind of checks and balance Shershrine put in place centuries ago."

She tapped his chest. "Why hasn't anyone ever heard of them? Scared me shitless when La Patron was on the floor. Who does that kind of stuff?"

Angus smiled at her sense of outrage and patted her ass. "Shershrine aren't meant to be discussed or have a place in our history books."

Her brow rose.

"Can we finish what you started before we have a serious discussion on pack history?" He didn't think she'd go for it but thought he'd try.

"Librarian." She pointed to her forehead. "I need to know." She wrinkled her nose.

He placed a quick kiss on her lips.

"None of that now, talk." She tried to roll over, but he placed his hand on her high, round globes and squeezed.

"Stay."

She nodded.

"They gave life to full-bloods."

"I knew it. Those words tasted funny."

"Yeah, well, they really are sacred and not meant to be uttered. I can't imagine how Chancellor understood what they meant." He paused, thinking about Chancellor, talking about taking revenge too far. "From what the Goddess told Silas, the sacred texts have been removed from the Chancellor and sent to another unknown location."

"Why doesn't she keep them, seems they'd be safer."

He thought how to explain it the way godfather had explained it to him. "Shershrine created full-bloods and left them for the Goddess to oversee. They are similar but different. Everything must remain on earth for the full-bloods." He shrugged. "Kind of hard to make sense of how they think."

She nodded. "It was really weird though. La Patroness was with me when Shershrine appeared. Having both in my head was different, but I'd choose her any time." She shook her head. "When she dropped that statue, I thought I'd pass out. She was so angry that for the first time in my life I saw red and it wasn't coming from me."

"Jasmine is very protective of those she loves. She taught Silas about family, he taught her about pack, which makes the pack stronger. Believe me, she would've done much worse if Silas hadn't calmed her down. She doesn't have the best control of her powers, and when she pulled from the pack, it would've been bad."

"He calmed her?"

"Yes. Although she almost lost it again when her sister's mate wanted to leave Silas behind." Angus smiled. "Melange wanted to get Renee as far away as possible, but they couldn't find a way out. When Jasmine discovered they planned to leave us behind, let's just say she found Melange and helped her see the error of her ways. My sister is not one to play with."

Shyla snorted. "She scared me. I don't ever want to be on her bad side." She paused. "Do we need to live there? In the compound? I'm still Mengistia and my term isn't over yet. The chambers where the scrolls and artifacts are in the house. It's been in my family for generations."

He frowned. "As Beta, I don't know if I can be that far from Silas. Tomorrow when we get home we'll discuss it with him, okay?"

She brushed her lips against his, refueling his need for her. "Okay. You do know this position is passed down through the women in my family. I'll need to train our daughter to take over one day."

Hearing her speak of their den, his daughter and her place in the pack, filled him with pride. "After 300 years, I never thought I'd have a mate or a daughter. Now my life is full with light and promise of a wee one as beautiful and strong as her mam. The Goddess has indeed blessed me." He kissed her forehead and held her close for a few seconds while he pulled his emotions together.

He moved between her legs. Feeling her wetness, he took a moment to grind his cock against her hot flesh.

Shyla wouldn't release him and held fast around his neck. She stroked and squeezed, testing his limits. He couldn't believe how great she tasted, smelled, and felt beneath him. Her scent held him captive. He craved more.

Reaching down, he kissed her as he stroked her long, toned thighs. She widened her legs to allow his questing hand. Leaning to the side, he looked at her beautiful body and inhaled their combined scents. Her pussy was almost bare except for the thinnest layer of soft curls resting over the small apex between her legs. Her folds were soft and damp and shiny with moisture. Forgetting to breathe, he began a slow downward trek toward her weeping sweet box. Reverently, his fingers touched her nether lips. Moaning encouragement, she allowed him to pay tribute. Drawn to her essence, he explored her with his tongue and reacquainted himself with her passion. He inserted two fingers in her tight, juicy canal. "Mine," he growled.

She pulled his hair and pushed his face forward. "Take it," she growled.

Grabbing her hips, he pulled her closer and fed his beast with her essence. "Home," he breathed inside her as he licked, sucked, and brought her to completion. Lapping up her tasty juices, he listened to her whimpers as the tremors subsided. Hard as stone, he slid up beside her and smiled.

"I'm sorry they took you, made you afraid, and that you doubted yourself," he said between plastering her face and lips with hot kisses. "You are the bravest, strongest, sexiest bitch on the planet and I promise to tell you that every day until you believe it."

"Yes, yes, more," she said, gyrating against his mouth.

"Mine," he said again.

His cock jumped. His eyes felt gritty, his mouth dry. The dark neediness of his voice betrayed him as he inched up and ravaged her mouth. Placing his hands under her hips, he lifted her, and rubbed his rod against her heat.

"I need to be buried deep inside this tight pussy, next time I'll spend more time tasting you." He tried to speak coherently but the damn mating thing kicked his ass. Every cell in his body ached for her.

"Promise?" She pouted as she licked his juices from her fingers, eliciting another groan from him. She was too damned sexy. Unable to wait, he pushed her backward and inserted a finger, then another, testing her readiness for him. Her passage was wet and tight. Rising on his elbow, he lifted her leg and looked at her.

Moving her hips in a circular motion and palming her breasts with her hands, she smiled at him. "Get a move on."

Pulling her leg up, he moved and poised his cock for entry. Feeling her pushing up, he pushed all the way in, balls deep. She wrapped her long legs around him, holding him tight.

"Holy shit," He breathed through clenched teeth as he tried to recapture some semblance of sanity as her tight sheath pulsed around him. Head down, he breathed deeply while taking a tentative stroke.

She slapped his ass. "Fuck me, I am on fire and I need you to put it out."

Her words mirrored his feelings.

He held still as she moved beneath him, her seductive movements drove him slowly insane. Her tight walls welcomed his cock and challenged him to work for every stroke. Long legs around his waist, she demanded more and more of him. The slight creaking of the springs in the bed kept a steady tempo as he pounded inside her.

"Mine." He pulled her legs from his waist and placed them high on his shoulders.

"Yes," she screamed as his cock moved even deeper inside her, hitting her tight walls from another angle. Pressing down, thrusting rapidly, matching her moan for moan. Fuck it, he was flying and it was unlike anything he'd ever experienced. He never wanted to land.

Lost in the intensity of pleasure, he yelled when her muscles tightened, milking him as she yelled her release. Linked, experiencing her orgasm triggered his own. Arching his back, he stiffened as his seed pulsed into her hot channel.

Exhilarated and spent, he dropped his forehead onto hers. "Don't ever leave me, I won't survive a day without you." He bit down on her neck, binding them together.

She arched her back and then sighed as he licked the bite marks. Instead of moving immediately, they stared at each other, her fingers touching his face lightly as she explored him. "Lately, I've placed a part of my life on hold, withdrew from dating and shallow relationships. After seeing what Vanessa had, I wanted that. I wanted my mate, someone who sees me for the nerdy person I am and appreciates me. The way you listen, ask questions and then respond to me, it's like exhilarating. You have no idea how rare it is for a man to listen to a librarian." She laughed.

Her laughter was infectious. "I like librarians, didn't you know that. My favorite date is with a sexy librarian."

She kissed him. "Thank you for that. I like nerdy betas too. Something really sexy about them. Seeing you standing tall next to La Patron, ready to take on the world for him, for us. I admitted I needed you as much as my next breath. I won't ever leave you, you have become my world, Angus Blackwolf."

He brushed his lips across her forehead and silently thanked the Goddess for this phenomenal bitch. Silas tried to warn him how things would be when he found his mate. At the time, Angus had no idea this gut-level connection between two people existed, now he would never be whole without his mate.

"Get some rest, I'll be waking you again in a few hours before our flight leaves." He yawned and pulled her close, enjoying the way she curled next to him with her hand on his chest.

"If I don't wake you first, you're like a drug…" She yawned. "In my system. Need more of you."

Angus rubbed his chin over her head and fell into the darkness.

CHAPTER 27

Jasmine sat in their living area with four of her pups and Silas. Gratitude choked her each time she looked at Silas and thought how close they came to losing each other. She'd never been so scared or angry in her life. In retrospect, she hadn't thought of repercussions or anything other than saving Silas. Would she have carried out her threat to destroy that bitch? Yes.

She closed her eyes. What was happening to her? The red haze of anger had blinded her to everything else. Shyla had been terrified. I'll need to apologize to her for that, Jasmine thought. Sitting on the sofa with her feet tucked to the side, she smiled as Adam and David wrestled with Silas while the girls tried to pin down his legs. How could she have faced her children if the Shershrine had been successful? An unmistakable knot of fear grew in her throat, the same one that had threatened to choke her earlier. She had trouble keeping her vision clear.

"Sweet Bitch, I am fine," Silas said through their link.

"I know, but it was close. Too damn close. I need some time to process what happened. I can't just act like it's okay, that they tried to tear me out of you. It would've killed you, those bastards," she said.

"Okay, do whatever you need to do, I understand." He rolled over, taking the kids with him. Their shrieks of laughter clearly said how much they enjoyed this time with him.

She took another sip of her tea. Her phone vibrated on the table next to the sofa. Jasmine glanced at it. "Renee." Was she ready to talk to her sister? They were going to leave Silas and Angus behind. Rage filled her chest, she ignored the call and took another sip of the cool liquid.

Her phone vibrated again. Jasmine snatched up the phone. "Hello?"

"Jazz, I'm sorry," Renee rushed to say. "I didn't, we didn't —"

"Stop." Jasmine stood and walked into the bedroom, closing the door behind her.

"No, we need to talk about this. Things got crazy. They took me in the parking lot of the store, in front of everybody. I think I shit myself, screaming and fighting until they knocked me out. When I woke they told me Melange would die if I didn't cooperate. Our links didn't work. I had no idea what happened to her. My mind replayed so many scenarios of life without her, I couldn't cope, must've passed out. I don't remember most of it."

"Renee." Jasmine rubbed her forehead.

"Let me finish. I wanted to die, hell, I thought I was dead inside. No one told me it would be like this, that it could be like this. The sense of loss… I have no words. Never again do I want to experience anything like that. Melange says it took her a while to wake me, and when she did." Renee sobbed. "All I could do was thank God, she was alive. Her body hadn't fully healed, Jazz. They beat her bad. Seeing her like that broke me. Instead of doing anything else, she spent time comforting me. It was bad. If I'd had a gun I would've killed every one of those fuckers."

Jasmine nodded in complete understanding. She had been there, standing on the precipice of insanity over the treatment of her man.

"You don't know how to use a gun," Jasmine said to break the dark mood.

"Don't matter, I would've taken them out." Renee sniffed. "I wanted her as far from those assholes as possible and urged her to leave. I cried a bucket of tears, like a damn baby, when she didn't move fast enough."

Anger surged through Jasmine at the reminder. "Melange knew Silas and Angus were in the hall, she asked him to look after you if she died."

"Oh no, my poor baby," Renee said.

"You're missing the point; you were about to leave my mate and brother behind. And would have if I didn't stop Melange," Jasmine snapped.

"Because of me, Jazz. She did it for me. I wasn't thinking rationally," Renee said.

"Did you know Silas was there?"

"No. Not at that moment," Renee admitted. "Melange was hurt and trying to comfort me."

"So, it was all about you and not her Alpha?" Jasmine didn't care what Renee said, what they'd tried to do wasn't right and it would be a long time before she forgave Melange.

"I'm sorry, Jazz. We messed up. Melange said you grabbed her wolf, made her turn around, that's when she told me about Silas. She had forgotten," Renee said.

Jasmine rolled her eyes. Love was indeed blind if Renee believed that... wait. Mates can't lie to each other. Had Melange forgotten? It was something to consider later, right now everything was too fresh.

"Silas almost died. They tried to separate him from me, which would've killed him," Jasmine said, still overwhelmed by the close call.

"No. Oh my God, I didn't know. No wonder he was so out of it." Renee paused. "Can they do that? I thought this was a solid deal."

"Now it is. A lot of stuff went down and had to be sorted out." Thinking about everything that happened earlier made her head hurt. She didn't want to talk about it anymore.

"Jasmine, I am so sorry about leaving Silas and Angus behind. Please forgive me."

"I'll let you know. Right now, I'm still shaky over what happened, I'm not at my best right now. I'll call you later in the week, we'll talk then."

"Is Silas going to discipline Melange?" Renee asked in a hard tone that set Jasmine off.

"Silas is not the one she needs to be concerned about. I could kick her ass all over this country for what she did today."

"I see," Renee said softly.

Damn. Jasmine inhaled to calm down. "I told you I'm still wired, don't push."

"Sorry."

"She will need to pledge to her loyalty to us or the two of you can move somewhere else. What happened today was a breach of the highest order and can never be repeated," Jasmine said.

"God, I hope not, we may not make it," Renee said.

Jasmine shook her head at her sister's tunnel vision. "There are no Lone Rangers in the pack. As a nation, we never leave anyone behind. That's what I meant when I said it could never be repeated."

"Oh, yes, I can understand that. You know I love you and would never do anything to hurt you or your family. Today was a misunderstanding. We'll do whatever we need to so this can be right. When you're ready, just let us know."

"Alright, Silas is taking the kids to their rooms. They didn't know what happened, just that he was gone when they came home. We needed to spend time with them and the twins. Things could've been so much different." She cleared her throat and walked into the bathroom.

"But he's home safe now, that's what's important. The Goddess got him back to you right after that bald-headed man disappeared."

"Yes, she did." Jasmine and the Goddess were meeting tomorrow to discuss what happened and what it all means going forward. She appreciated the Goddess' patience with her, but she had to know if any of this would impact her kids and grandkids.

"Love you and think about forgiving us," Renee said, and disconnected.

Jasmine stripped, took a quick shower, dressed, and returned to the empty living room. She picked up and straightened the room to keep the dark thoughts at bay.

Silas walked in.

Their gazes met. The next second she was in his arms holding him tight, breathing him in. He opened their link. Her knees buckled from the rush of conflicting emotions, love, lust, fear, gratitude, anger and hate. The terror he'd experienced when they tried to separate them sliced through her. Tears ran down her face and onto his chest. Sobs wracked her chest as the pain he endured wrapped around them. His tears mixed with hers as he kissed her with a desperation he'd held in check for the past few hours.

Standing in the middle of the room, they shared the horror of the day, comforting each other. She touched him everywhere needing contact. He obliged and returned the gesture.

"I love you so much," she whispered when they broke for air.

"Sweet Bitch, you are my heart, I cannot live without my heart." He grabbed a fistful of hair, pulled her back and kissed her hard, breathing life back into her again. She clung tighter, needing the connection to dissipate the fear.

He held her until she stopped shaking. Not once did he speak, words weren't necessary. Her pain merged with his, burning brighter until she thought she would pass out, and then it sparked. A small light that sizzled in the air and cooled. His steadfast love and commitment surrounded them in a tight cocoon. Her heart lifted with joy that this amazing man was hers and no one would ever separate them. Peace, contentment, and serious thanksgiving sat on her shoulders.

Jasmine rested her head against his chest. "I don't think I've ever been that scared." She punched his shoulder and then rubbed it. "Don't ever make me turn into that mean person again."

Silas chuckled. "That's a promise I'm happy to make, for both of us." He squeezed her tight.

"What happened to Chancellor? Did she get fired?" Jasmine took his hand and walked to their bedroom.

"The Goddess didn't say, but I'm sure she'll be reprimanded." He closed the bedroom door behind them.

"When are Angus and Shyla getting here?" Watching him, she peeled off her clothes and crawled into the bed.

His eyes blazed blue as he stripped off everything. His cock stood straight out, hard, long and thick.

Jasmine licked her lips needing to taste him again.

"Morning."

"Huh?" She looked up at him as he covered her.

"Barticus' private jet is bringing Angus home in the morning."

She nodded.

"I need you now, this will be fast, hard, and quick," he growled as he lined his cock to her entrance.

"Fast and hard is what I need," she said as he slid home.

CHAPTER 28

Angus rolled over, his arm draped over Shyla's waist. *"Soft."* He pulled her closer, inhaling her precious scent. Frowning, he opened his eyes and looked around. This wasn't their hotel room. Hadn't he been naked when they went to sleep earlier? He glanced down at his jeans and shirt. Who dressed them?

"Shyla?" He touched her shoulder trying to wake her.

"Hmm?"

"Wake up, I don't know where we are."

"What?" She stretched and yawned.

"Somebody moved us from our hotel rooms."

Her eyes flew open and met his gaze. *"How could someone have entered our room?"* She yawned. *"We would've heard them."*

"Right." Which meant they were drugged in some way that bypassed their senses. Closing his eyes, he inhaled and searched for scents. Incredible. *"Must have some kind of blocker, I don't smell anything. That's not good."*

"Why am I so sleepy?" Shyla yawned again.

"I think that's part of how they got us here. Question is, who and what do they want?" He rubbed her shoulder. *"I'm getting tired of this bullshit."*

"Me too." Shyla pulled the covers up to her chin. *"What time is it?"*

Angus glanced at his arm. *"They took my watch."*

"Assholes," she grumbled.

A whirring sound came from the far right corner of the ceiling revealing a large monitor. *"This reminds me of what happened with Brenda, the breeder I was talking about. Next, there'll be some kind of BS about La Patron."*

Angus squeezed her shoulder and waited. When Cancer appeared on the screen, Angus wasn't too surprised. He'd wondered what happened to the monks when Shershrine and Nicromja left.

213

The Goddess had opened the hidden passages that allowed him, Shyla, Melange, and Renee to leave the old temple while she transported Silas to Jasmine. Barticus hadn't been far from the hidden temple and took them to the hotel, promising access to his jet once it arrived, to return home.

"Angus, I'm sorry, but I need your help. My father and brother are plagued with cancer. We found the crystal you spoke of but have not been successful in getting it to work. Can you shed some light on what is needed?" He held up the crystal.

"What did you use to knock us out in our hotel room?" Angus asked. Humans thought the world revolved around them without considering consequences. Before telling the bastard to kiss his ass, and breaking out of this place, Angus needed information.

"I don't know. Something our research team developed," Cancer said.

The inability to smell if this was true or false burned. "Where are we?" Angus looked around the large room. In addition to a mammoth-sized bed, there was a table, two chairs, refrigerator and microwave, sofa, and another door leading to the bathroom. There were no exits to leave the room.

"Apologies. You are guests in my home." Cancer looked over his shoulder and then back at the monitor. "How do we activate the crystal to make it work?"

"Why should I tell you anything?" Angus moved his arm from beneath Shyla's neck and sat up. "What makes you think I'd cooperate after you kidnapped me and my mate, again. Did I make a mistake in allowing you to live the last time?" He kept his tone deceptively low, in contrast to the rage brewing in his chest.

Cancer sighed and pinched the bridge of his nose. "No. You didn't make a mistake. Can't you see, understand we're desperate to save him. My father's dying and if there's a way to save him, I have to try. You'd do the same if it were you or your mate's parents."

Shyla shot up. "What? My parents? What do you mean?" Fear shot through their link as Shyla thought her family was in danger.

"If your father or mother were ill, you would do whatever you could to help them," Cancer said in a sober tone, which made Angus wonder if Shyla's parents were in danger.

"Yes, I would," Shyla said slowly while trying to contact her parents through their link. "Have you done anything to them?"

"I simply answered your mate's question as to my methods and motives for trying to save my father."

"How do we know you're telling the truth," Angus said when Shyla couldn't reach her parents.

"Knowing you'd kill me in a nano-second if you could, I would never take that risk if it weren't for my father. He's running out of time." He paused. "How do we make the crystal work?"

Angus sensed the terror in his mate over the lack of response from her parents. "How do you know the crystal will work on him? It may not."

"Hope that it does," Cancer said. "How do we make it work?"

"Help them," Shyla said. *"If they have my parents I need to make sure they're safe."*

"Show me what you've done," Angus said, drawing his mate close.

Cancer held the crystal in his hand so Angus could see. "We laid it across his chest, his neck, placed it in his hand, everything. What are we doing wrong?"

Angus snorted. "It's not active."

"What do you mean?"

"In your hands you're holding a crystalline solid. Unless you tap into its energy it's just a pretty decoration for the mantle," Angus said.

Cancer looked at the crystal for a few moments, then closed his eyes and chanted.

"Where are my parents? Why isn't she answering me?"

"Does she always answer?" Angus looked down at her.

Shyla released a long stream of air. *"No. Not always."*

215

"When did you talk to her last?" Angus tapped the tip of her upturned nose.

"Right before Chancellor sucked me through the wall. They're in Florida, she invited me to join them at the beach."

"Maybe she's busy and will contact you soon," he said.

"You think so? Honestly, you don't think they have my parents?" Their gazes met, he read her desperate need for him to be right on this matter.

"They have a bargaining chip, otherwise we wouldn't be here. Is it your parents? I'm not sure."

Shyla nodded. *"Mama will be so happy about us, she's wanted this for a long time."*

"This? Or me?"

"Me, mated. She worried about me being alone so much."

"You're not alone anymore," he said, meeting her gaze.

"How do I unlock the crystal?" Cancer said, breaking the mood. "Nothing I've said works."

"Do you understand how to tune crystals?" Angus asked, knowing the answer.

"Maybe not. How is it done?"

"Is there a piece in this room?" Angus made a show of looking around, doubting they'd have thought that far ahead.

"Yes, in the refrigerator," Cancer said.

Angus kept the surprise from his face as he left the bed and opened the refrigerator. Taking the crystal, he enclosed it in his palm, changed its position a few times until it fit correctly. Concentrating, he hummed until hitting the right pitch to connect with the atoms in the crystal. His thoughts focused on the healing properties locked away in the stone. Angus had no idea how long he tuned the crystal, he always lost track of time in these matters. The crystal heated. He opened his eyes and palm.

"Blimey, he did it," Cancer said. Scorpio pushed forward to see the glowing rock in Angus' hand. "We'll give anything for that."

"It still may not work," Angus cautioned.

"We'll take the chance," Scorpio said. Cancer nodded his agreement.

"Give me everything you have on whatever you used to knock me out and you can have this," Angus said.

The two looked at each other. "Where should we send it?"

"I need to see it now if you want this. The formula, everything," Angus said, holding the glowing stone so they didn't lose sight of their goal or prize.

Cancer and Scorpio stepped away from the monitor for a few moments.

"What about my parents?" Shyla asked.

"If they had your parents they would have used them by now. I suspect your parents are someplace safe, enjoying the day or night," he said.

"I hope you're right since you didn't bargain for their safety."

He looked over his shoulder. She sat with her arms wrapped around her knees on the bed. His gaze touched hers. *"I would never put your parents at risk, I'm trying to end this game as quickly as possible that's all. They have something, I prefer to know now what that is. The only way to push for that is to negotiate."*

She nodded, slid off the bed and went into the bathroom.

Their relationship was so new, trust was a luxury. In time, she'd learn his character and heart. He prayed to the Goddess he was right regarding her parents, otherwise, they'd have major problems. The idea of a father-in-law interested him. He'd interacted with Victoria, Silas' mother-in-law, but never this side of the coin.

"There's a laptop in the table, the information was sent there. Also, there are packs of drives in the small compartment next to it," Cancer said, intruding on Angus' thoughts.

He placed the crystal on the table, pressed a button, and opened the laptop that appeared. Sure enough, there was a file with the information.

"Read it on your own time, we need the crystal now," Cancer said.

Entranced by the information in front of him, Angus pointed to the crystal without looking up. "Take it."

Scorpio snorted.

"Can you place it in the tray beneath the monitor please?" Cancer asked.

Angus looked at the monitor, retrieved a flash drive and downloaded the entire file. Before standing, he sent the file to the clouds. "Okay," he said after both transmissions were complete. He placed the crystal in the tray. The monitor rose.

"*Silas?*" Angus continued reading the information.

"*Back already?*" Silas sounded as if he'd been asleep.

Angus told him everything that happened since they saw each other.

"*Damn, this is getting crazy. Are they releasing you once the old man is cured?*" Silas asked.

"*So they say. I don't think they have Shyla's parents, but just in case, I unlocked the crystal. This formula I sent to Hawke needs to be checked. We smelled nothing, not now or in the hotel.*"

"*I'll have him look into it. What's the plan if they prove to be liars?*" Silas asked.

"*We're still leaving, just need to make sure the in-laws are safe.*"

Silas laughed. "*I told you this would happen to you. When you get home we'll have a drink and I'll get my 'told-you-so' out the way.*"

"*Deal. I'll keep you in the loop.*" Angus disconnected and continued reading.

"*You were right, Mama said they were busy,*" Shyla said. "*They're at my place, Alpha contacted them when they couldn't find me. She had a lot to say but basically, she's just glad I'm okay. Oh, and she can't wait to meet you and has all kinds of ideas for our mating ceremony. I'd like to have it in the gardens of my home if that's okay with you.*"

Angus stretched out his hand to her. She left the bathroom door and took it. *"Whatever you want. There are some security issues that need to be cleared because of our position as pack Beta, but it should work fine. Just as long as you're happy, I'm happy."*

She sat on his lap and wrapped her arms around his neck. *"Now that my parents are safe, when are we breaking out of this place?"*

"I was just thinking it may be time to leave." He placed a kiss on her lips while stuffing the flash drive into his pocket.

"Any idea where we are?"

"Nope." He smiled. *"Doesn't matter, pack is everywhere. Soon as we leave this place we'll find someone."*

She frowned. *"What about the darts that got us the last time?"*

"I'll have Silas and Jasmine on stand-by to purge any poisons." Shyla cringed.

"What?" He bit back a smile. Everyone knew Jasmine wasn't that smooth with her mergers.

"Does she need to merge again?"

"Yes, but Silas helps make it smooth, you'll be fine. I promise."

She nodded. *"Okay, I'm ready to be alone with you. Honeymoon before the mating?"* She winked.

He slapped her ass. *"Great idea, we'll start as soon as we get out of here. Move back, I need to go to my largest size to break down the walls."* He looked at the bathroom. *"That might be a safe place."*

The screen lowered just as he stood.

"Angus, we need the other crystal tuned," Cancer said.

Prepared to tell the monk what he could do with his demands, Angus faced the monitor. Instead of seeing Cancer, a familiar face lay prostrate on a bed enclosed in a cell.

"Silas?"

"Yeah, you out?"

"Where's Asia?"

CHAPTER 29

"Asia?" Silas rolled over and left the bedroom. *"What do you mean?"*

"I'm looking at a woman in a cage who looks like Asia. Tell me she's there," Angus said. Silas heard the concern in his voice.

"One sec." Silas reached out to Hawke. He hadn't seen the man since he returned. A mid-day meeting was planned later in the day. *"Hawke?"*

"Sir?"

"Where's Asia?"

"At the Wernher's compound in Memphis. When I talked to her last, she'd found something she wanted to check out. Has Mistress spoken to her?"

"I don't think so." Silas wiped his face and sat on the sofa. *"Tell me about Wernher."* Silas listened half in horror, half in pride over how his bitch stepped up to rescue him and Angus. *"I just heard from Angus."* Silas told him what he was told. *"Tell me how you want to handle this,"* Silas said. The pain of his recent separation from his mate was too close to the surface not to allow Hawke to make the decision. *"The jet is there already waiting for her; Angus will tear the place apart and bring them home. Or I can have the jet return for you. Then you go and get her."*

"Both will take too long. I will take a commercial flight. There's one leaving in an hour, I can be on it."

"I can have the jet here in an hour," Silas said, understanding his friend wasn't thinking logically.

"If Angus can get her out of there before I arrive, he can take the jet and return here. I don't want them to wait for me," Hawke explained.

"What do you want him to do?" Silas pressed.

"Free her immediately. Get her out of that place, put her onto the plane and bring her home," Hawke said.

"*Done,*" Silas said and broke their connection. "*Angus?*"

"*Yes?*"

Silas told Angus what he'd learned.

"*The price to release her is to tune another crystal so their father heals. I'll take care of it.*"

"*Do you trust them to keep their word?*" Silas asked.

"*Not at all. But this lines up with what Asia discovered earlier. And now that I know where we are, have Alpha Gilbert stand by. Once I'm done, I want pack in this place. They have some kind of research facilities where they develop all kinds of drugs. I have no idea where it's located, but Gilbert's team can handle that.*"

"*I'll let him know.*"

"*What did Jasmine say?*"

"*About Asia?*"

"*She doesn't know, damn. Okay, she's going to be pissed. Ask her to give me some time to do this,*" Angus said.

"*I'll ask,*" Silas said, without committing to anything. He hoped he could keep Jasmine in check, but she'd probably feel guilt over this and it would propel her to do something.

"*Yeah, I know. I'll keep you updated.*" Angus disconnected.

Silas sat a few moments thinking of everything that had happened in the past two days. Hard to believe their lives were turned upside down because of some BS. Chancellor. If she ever crossed his path, he'd break her neck. The Goddess never answered his question when he asked if she'd be punished. He'd been so happy to be home he didn't push, but now he wondered if this situation with Asia was somehow connected.

Asia.

He exhaled, stood, and headed to their bedroom. His mate lay on her side asleep. If he didn't wake her she would be pissed. "Jasmine."

She didn't respond. He walked to the bed and touched her shoulder.

"Not again, Silas, I need sleep."

He smiled. "I know you need your rest, Sweet Bitch, and would not bother you if I didn't think you'd want me to wake you."

"Huh?" She rubbed her eyes and turned on her back. His gaze latched onto her full breasts. He flicked the nipple. "Stop that." Glaring at him, she pulled the cover up to her neck.

Silas sighed. "You're no fun." He held up his hands to stop her response. "Angus contacted me. Asia's in trouble."

"What?" Alert, she sat up. "What happened? Where is she?"

Silas explained what he knew and that Hawke had left for Memphis.

"I forgot she was still there." She met his gaze. "How could I forget I sent her there and demanded she get information?"

"Jasmine." He reached for her, she slapped his hand away.

"No, Silas, I did this. Where's Shyla?"

"With Angus and no, you are not merging with her again, not for this."

She looked past him as if he hadn't spoken.

"I mean it, Jasmine. They're a newly mated couple and need to work through this together, on their own," Silas said, hoping she'd listen.

"What're you talking about?"

His brow rose. "You weren't thinking of merging with her to help Asia?"

She met his gaze for a few seconds and then slumped against the headboard, rubbing her forehead. "What does being newly mated have to do with this?"

"They're learning each other, she needs to see what he can do and vice versa. Above all, she's his bitch and they need to solve problems together. He needs to see her as she is, what she can do, how she handles problems. This is their bonding time, stay out of her head unless they both ask us for help."

She opened her mouth and then snapped it shut. "Makes sense. She's smart and sassy, I like her. She was scared, shaking, but she pulled it off. If she hadn't, I don't know what would've happened."

"Did you pull energy from Vanessa?" He crawled back in the bed, determined to get a few more hours of rest.

"Changing the subject, not real smooth, but yes. She's strong and steady. Ethan's working with her," Jasmine said, scooting close to him. "Now what?"

He kissed her forehead. "Now we wait."

CHAPTER 30

"Did you hear me?" Cancer said.

Angus had waited until he heard from Silas. Now that Asia's identity was confirmed, Angus faced the monitor. "What are you doing? Trying to start a war? You take our people and think there won't be retaliation, a fall-out?" He pointed at the monitor. "You stepped over a line."

Cancer appeared on the monitor. "I explained all of that."

"The cage," Angus growled.

"That's someone who broke into our compound, interesting stuff on her. Never seen anything like it before." The monitor flicked and various screens showed Asia using the chameleon. "She took over identities and moved through the compound. We stopped her when she got close to the labs, she's there now. Our technicians are super excited to discover how she's able to do the things she does. Have you ever seen anything like it?"

"No."

"Me neither. Do you know her?"

"Yes, I do."

"I told Scorpio she was from La Patron, he didn't agree. Why was she here? You didn't know, so who sent her?"

Angus shook his head. "I was on the other side of the world, I have no idea."

"Silas?"

"Yeah?"

"They have footage of Asia using the chameleon."

"Shit. That changes the game. Under no circumstances can anyone ever get a chameleon. That information needs to be scrubbed, I'll let Hawke know. He can scramble the images if not destroy them. This is a priority."

"Got it," Angus said.

"About the crystal, we need more," Cancer said. There was an underlying sense of gleeful urgency in his voice.

"What are you willing to pay for it?"

"A life for a life? You get the female and give us two tuned crystals."

"You keep changing the game, did the first crystal work?" Angus asked.

"Yes, he's resting much better, but isn't healed. He requested more. Do we have a deal?"

"No."

"No?"

"I need to see the female, make sure she's alive."

"We can't allow you to enter the area where she's resting."

"Move her. I'm not doing a damn thing until I know she's alive and I need to feel her pulse for that. Let me know when you're ready to save the old man's life." Angus walked away from the monitor, took a seat on the sofa, and turned on the TV with the remote.

Shyla joined him. *"That was good. Think they'll go for it?"*

"Either that or they'll all die." He looked at her. *"Asia is mated to Hawke. They're what you call a power couple, second to Silas and Jasmine. Those two can take down this place without breaking a sweat. They must have blocked scents and sound, otherwise they never would've gotten the drop on Asia. Believe me when I tell you she is one of the baddest bitches on the planet and she serves Jasmine."*

Shyla frowned. *"What does that mean? How can she serve La Patroness and not La Patron?"*

Angus shrugged. *"The bond between Asia and Jasmine is unique, hard to explain it, but her loyalty is to her mate and her Mistress, I wish I could say in that order, but I'm not sure. If anything happens to Asia, especially since Jasmine sent her here, Silas will be hard-pressed to leave this building standing. A lot of humans will die. The pack runs the risk of exposure. We can't allow that."*

225

"No, we can't. Tell me what you want me to do."

Her eagerness to help tugged on his heart. *"Once they agree to let me to see Asia, they're going to try to hold you as a hostage."*

"Okay, not excited about that but I understand the logic."

"Put up a fuss, curse, stomp your feet, but in the end, agree."

"That sucks, but whatever you need me to do."

"I'd like to have Jasmine merge with you to make sure they don't poison you again, is that alright?"

She closed her eyes and rubbed her forehead. *"Okay."*

He brushed a kiss against her lips. *"When I leave, act casual but listen to me, follow my instructions. Pack is surrounding this place and will be breaking through soon."*

"Where are we?" she asked, leaning on his shoulder.

"Memphis, Tennessee." He shared the information regarding the family he had received from Silas.

"Wernher. Why does that name sound familiar?"

"It does?"

"Yes. Something in the archives, let me think." She closed her eyes.

"Silas?"

"Yeah?"

Angus shared his latest conversation with Cancer and asked for the merger between Jasmine and Shyla again.

"We're here for whatever you need. About this crystal, can it really heal cancer?"

"It assists in the natural progression of healing, how much it helps humans? That I don't know. He may feel some temporary benefits."

"Can you imagine what happens if it turns out the crystal can do anything, let alone heal permanently? The caves will be decimated, sacred areas destroyed, and possibly a war. How can we minimize those possibilities and get all three of you out of there without alerting human authorities?"

Angus pursed his lips. *"When I tune the crystal, I won't take it to its maximum potential. There should be enough to give him some temporary relief. In a day or two, he'll revert to his present state."*

"Gilbert's pack would've shut down the place by then. Run with that plan."

Angus touched Shyla's arm. *"Silas approved the plan."*

She nodded but remained silent. They sat in silence while the TV played a game show. Angus wondered what Asia had found. Had they examined her? Did they know about her metal limbs? Was Asia really out of it or was this a game she played? Jasmine would've reached out to her, and game or not, Asia would've responded.

"We've moved her to a place where you can check her and tune the crystal," Cancer said several minutes later. "Your mate remains behind."

Shyla jumped up. "Kiss my ass, bitch, where he goes, I go," she yelled, pointing at the monitor.

"Not this time. You stay here in the room until he finishes the job, when he's done, both of you can leave," Cancer said in a firm tone.

She turned to Angus. "Baby, don't trust that one. This is a trick, as soon as you leave, they'll gas me again. I hated that, I don't want to stay here without you." She wrapped her arms around Angus. "You aren't leaving me."

"We're running out of time," Cancer snapped. "Do we have a deal? Yes or no?"

"Don't push me," Angus growled. Concerned by the truth of Shyla's fears, he cupped her cheeks and stared into her eyes. "If you want me to stay, I will."

"No, you won't," Cancer yelled.

"My woman is afraid you'll gas her again or use that shit in the darts and that's your fault. Unless she's calm and believes she's safe, there is no deal." Angus wrapped his arms tight around her. *"I'm sorry, I should've listened to you."*

"I'm really not this weak person, it's just I've never experienced anything like what's happened the past two days. Give me a moment to get into character." She rested her head on his chest.

"We will not do anything to your mate. No one or nothing will enter the room while you are away," Cancer said. "Timing is critical, please let's get this done."

"Do you believe him?" she asked Angus.

"Not at all, so be on guard, merge with Jasmine. Call out to her, the two of you have a connection." He kissed her. "What do you want me to do?" Angus asked aloud so Cancer could hear.

"Hurry back," she whispered.

He kissed her again, stood, and looked at the monitor. "Okay."

The room moved in a circular manner. Angus widened his stance so he didn't fall, and braced his hands on the table.

"What the hell?" Shyla asked as she fell backward.

"This is why we didn't see a door to get out of here before." The room stopped. A large metal door opened. Cancer and Scorpio were on the other side waving him out. Each held guns. Angus wondered what ammunition they used. He walked behind Cancer with Scorpio bringing up the rear. They stopped in front of another door, opened it, and strode inside.

Asia was lying on the bed in the middle of the room. Angus walked over and touched her neck, activating his necklace. Tingles shot down his arm into her. After a second or two, he looked at the men still in their monk garb.

"Where are the crystals?"

"In that refrigerator." Cancer pointed.

Angus opened the door and pulled out two long crystals, ignoring the others. He rolled one of the stones between both palms to get the feel of it. This one was purer than the first and responded to his energy quickly. Closing his eyes, he hummed to find the correct frequency. Warmth from the stone filled his palms and spread throughout his body. He felt lighter, stronger, and at peace.

"Is that one ready?" Cancer asked, interrupting Angus' meditation.

He looked at the nearly translucent crystal and handed it to Scorpio. Cancer watched his brother's eyes widen and then smile as he clasped the stone. Angus picked up the second crystal as Scorpio left the room with the first.

"Thank you," Cancer said in a choked voice.

"Don't thank me, whatever happens probably isn't permanent." He rolled the crystal in his palms.

"I know. But my father wants this and if he only has one day, that's better than nothing." Cancer paused. "Who's the female? Is she someone important?"

Angus' brow rose. "Everyone is someone important."

Cancer waved down his comments. "In the general sense, yes. But is she important to your Alpha?"

"Yes, we are all important to him." Angus glared at the man. "Quiet, I need to focus."

Cancer held up his hand and bowed.

Ignoring him, Angus warmed the crystal in his palm. This one was of lesser quality. It took longer to respond and the energy level wasn't as high. Once it warmed in his palm, he handed the glowing stone to Cancer.

"It's not as bright as the other one." Cancer held it up for inspection.

"No, it's not. Use the first one on your father and this one on your brother. That should work." Angus stepped back and checked on Asia. "How long has she been like this?"

"Before we got back in the country, maybe four hours or so. Thanks for this. Someone will show you back to your room to get your mate." Cancer left.

Angus picked up Asia and turned to reach the door. He engaged his bracelet to check Asia's memories and hit a brick wall. "Good." The door opened and he walked down the hall into the room he shared with Shyla.

229

"Is she alright?" Shyla asked, walking over to him.

"Her heart's beating." Angus went into the bathroom to wash his hands. When he returned, he found Shyla sitting next to Asia, gently touching her face.

"Jasmine?"

Shyla nodded but didn't say anything.

"Let's get out of here." He knocked on the metal door. A guard answered it. "Get Cancer in here." Angus closed the door and paced. Something was off. Cancer should have had someone escort Shyla to him, instead, they're back in this room.

Minutes passed and no one came to release them. *"Silas, Asia is still not responding and the hospitality here sucks. Gilbert and his pack here?"*

"Yes, they are in place."

"Great." Angus morphed to his largest size and punched up into the ceiling. He pulled down several cables and snatched them out. Wires sizzled and popped as he tapped each section of the wall until he came to the area he wanted to kick. Plaster, block, and wood flew outward as he battered down the wall, leaving a huge opening.

"Silas, keep the poison from slowing me down."

"I'm here," Silas said as they merged.

Angus picked up Asia and jumped out the hole onto another level. Turning, he motioned for Shyla to follow his lead.

She jumped and landed next to him. The dim space they landed in was filled with statues of Nicromja and strange writings on the wall. Shyla covered her mouth with her hand and pointed to a wall. Angus couldn't make out the words and morphed to his hybrid.

"You got this?" Silas asked.

"Yeah, thanks."

"That's why his name was so familiar," Shyla said. *"In the records, there's a family who basically sold their lives to two gods. They were released by one but not the other. It was an interesting story of how the family thought they were cursed because men are*

the majority in their line, but they died young. A deal was struck for long life, but they were enslaved or something similar by the god."

"Nicromja?" Angus looked at the altar, the familiar statue, the writings.

"Could be. It was actually a sad story of suffering."

Angus touched the gold candleholder. *"Profitable suffering. Let's go."* They moved toward the door. Shyla threw up her hand.

"Heartbeats in the hall."

He nodded. *"Good looking out."* Gently he placed Asia on the table, and picked up a large statute. Using it as a battering ram, he broke down the door, knocking the guards down like bowling pins. The sting of two darts in his shoulder enraged him and he shifted to his larger form while Silas dispelled the poison. Angus grabbed two men with guns, slammed them together with considerable force, and tossed them aside as he picked up two more. Shyla kicked a guard beneath his chin so hard he flew several feet in the air, then hit the wall so hard the sound of breaking bones filled the air. Angus morphed to his hybrid and picked up Asia.

Shyla grabbed two pistols from the dead guards as she followed. They reached an area that looked like a loft. Angus looked over and saw an emaciated man lying on the bed. Scorpio's hands were tied behind his back and blood ran down his face. Cancer placed the glowing crystal in the old man's hands and closed them around it. With each breath, the older man took, his skin filled, pinked, the stench of death abated. Mesmerized, Angus watched the transformation in shock.

Cancer knelt on one knee and placed his fist on his chest. "Greetings, father."

"Greetings Cancer, Scorpio." He looked at the men holding Scorpio. "Kill him."

Cancer stood. "I beg for mercy on his behalf."

"Mercy? He took the crystal for himself and had to be hunted down to return it. I cannot abide traitors." He snatched a gun out of the waistband of one of the security guards, pointed, and shot

Scorpio in the forehead. With his arm raised, he pointed the gun at Cancer. "There's another bullet in here for you if you want it. Tell me now, are you with me or against me?"

"I've always been with you." Cancer returned to one knee.

"Then bring the woman to me so the exchange can be made."

"Sir?"

"I told Scorpio not to trade the woman. I want her. Bring her to me."

"He told me you said to make the trade."

The old man shot Scorpio again. "Selfish bastard. The woman is able to exchange bodies; I need to rid myself of this one. Find her and bring her to me." He waved Cancer away.

"Yes, Sir."

"Gilbert's men have accessed the basement and will be there soon to take Asia," Silas said.

Angus threw back his head and howled. Shyla joined him. Seconds later, several pack members joined the chorus.

"What is that?" the old man asked, looking around. "Filthy wolves in my home, have security take care of them." He moved slowly toward the wall and then slid behind a panel.

Angus stood in front of Asia and waited for the pack to arrive.

Cancer and his men got there first. "I hoped you'd left the building, why did you hang around?"

Shyla whipped out the two pistols and shot off four rounds that hit their targets before Cancer pulled his weapon. Angus grabbed the two remaining guards, slammed them together like cymbals, and tossed them on the floor.

Cancer took off running out the room.

Angus pulled the dart from his other shoulder and checked his mate.

"I'm good." She exchanged her pistols for an automatic lying in the cold grasp of a fallen guard.

"When did you learn to shoot like that?" His mate was full of surprises.

"As a librarian, I've gone to more self-defense classes with co-workers than I can count. We all bought guns and learned how to shoot." She blew across the nozzle and winked.

"I like that cowgirl thing you got going on," he said, pulling her away from the bodies on the floor.

The building shook, toppling vases, pictures from the wall crashed to the floor. *"An earthquake in Tennessee?"* Shyla asked as she placed her hand on the wall to keep from falling.

"Doubt it. Whatever that is, it's not good." Angus covered Asia with a heavy dark drape that fell from the ceiling and waved Shyla behind him as he ran down the corridor, determined to get his mate and Asia to safety.

There was a large rumbling and a long scream.

Angus moved faster down the steps. They'd reached the outer courtyard when the old man jumped down three stories and landed in front of him holding Nicromja's sword and sliced Angus across the arm.

Angus dropped Asia and morphed to his largest size.

CHAPTER 31

"You denied me in the challenge, but you won't deny me now that I have my own champion," Wernher snarled, looking nothing like the sick man from before. His skin glowed with an eerie light. "I am Nicromja, you should have been honored to serve me, but instead you betrayed me. For that, you will die." Wernher moved so fast, Angus didn't have time to block his move as the blade sliced across his thigh and his head snapped back with an uppercut beneath the chin. Blood spurted from Angus' mouth as he flew backward.

Wernher raised his sword up toward the sky, an arc of lightning struck the tip. His entire body vibrated as he absorbed the shock.

Unbearable pain raced through Angus as he stood slowly while his flesh healed. To his right, Shyla held Asia, who was still unconscious. He'd just taken a step when Wernher flew forward, plowing his fist into his gut, knocking the wind out of him as he flew backward and hit the wall again.

Stars exploded in his skull. For a few seconds, he couldn't see. He tried to stand, but fell, only to get back up again. He heard the sing of the sword and jumped back, keeping his head in the process.

"Coward," Wernher yelled. "Worthless coward. No wonder you didn't want to fight the Goddess' champion, you're a weak, sniveling piece of trash."

Angus inhaled. Every place on him hurt. He morphed to his hybrid to speed the healing.

"What's going on?" Silas demanded.

"Nicromja. Fight. Sword."

Silas merged with Angus. *"Damn it, why didn't you call me?"*

"For a fight?"

"He's a fucking god who hates you," Silas said, sending healing energy through Angus, which helped tremendously.

"Sorry, I gotta do this on my own, my mate is watching," Angus glanced at Shyla. Her eyes were glassy.

"I know. Damn it," Silas yelled and pulled out.

"How's it going?" Shyla asked as he shook his head to stop the ringing.

"Just need to get my second wind, I'll be good." He didn't look at her. He watched Wernher talk to Cancer, who'd joined his father on the other side of the room, and inhaled. He winced at the pain.

A cooling mist flowed through their link, soothing like menthol, easing his bruised places. *"He's not a god, not really,"* Shyla said.

"No?" He didn't mean to sound skeptical, but he refused to believe an old man had kicked his ass without celestial assistance.

"Gods cannot fight humans; it's forbidden and simply cannot happen. They can help or assist on occasion and even that's limited. He's just a man with a sharp toy, Angus. You can take him."

He glanced over his shoulder at her. She winked and blew him a kiss. *"Kick his ass so we can go home, we've got more bonding to do."* Heat rushed through their link, strengthening him as never before. Energized by her faith in him, he morphed into his largest form, threw back his head and released an ear-splitting howl.

Wernher jumped toward him with the sword outstretched. Angus waited, then sidestepped at the last second and elbowed the man in the back, sending him forward into the wall. The old man jumped up and ran screaming at him, his face mottled red with fury as he swung the sword, missing Angus by a hair's breadth. Angus slammed his fist into Wernher's stomach, lifting him off the ground and sending him flying backward into a stone statue that broke into a few jagged pieces.

"I will kill you," Wernher screamed, standing slowly and shaking off debris.

Angus moved back a bit, preparing for the attack, and ducked just in time to miss being skewered by the sword as it came flying past his ear. It hit the wall and fell to the floor. Cancer picked it up and yelled, releasing it. Smoke rose from his palm. He ran from the room.

One second, Wernher was on one side of the room, the next, he picked up the sword and charged Angus again. Jumping up, Angus missed the blade. He kicked out, the side of his foot hit Wernher's head, sending the man flying, and landing on the jagged edge of the broken statue, impaled. The sword fell from his hand and landed on the ground. Seconds later, it disappeared.

Angus morphed to human, strode to his mate, captured her mouth with his, and all the world ceased to exist. Eyes closed, he delighted in the taste of her. He took his time, solidifying his commitment to her, their den, and their future. Gasping, they broke apart. His eyes lingered on her face, so precious, so beautiful, so strong. His beast agreed their future with this woman would banish the cold, lonely memories of his past, they'd be blissfully happy. He swallowed the knot forming in his throat, bringing a hand to her face. "Mine," he whispered.

She leaned up and kissed him. "Mine."

CHAPTER 32

Shyla and Angus sat at the table with Vanessa, Ethan, Asia, Hawke, Silas, and Jasmine, finishing lunch. "Thank you so much, that was good, I'm stuffed," Shyla said, pushing her plate away.

"You're welcome, and again, forgive me for being so pushy the other day," Jasmine said.

Silas snorted.

Asia and Hawke looked away, smiling.

Vanessa bit her lip.

"Pushy is tame compared to what I've heard," Silas said, taking her hand.

Shyla laughed and took Angus' hand. "We got the job done, Ma'am, and that's all that matters." She looked at Angus and traced his lips. "That's the only thing that matters."

"Yes." Jasmine touched Asia's hand. "Feeling better?"

"Much. Based on what Hawke says was in my system, I should've been fine. There's no reason for being unconscious that long. We're still researching the ingredients to understand why it affected me the way it did."

"Good, keep me updated," Silas said.

"Shyla, your mom called me to talk about your bonding ceremony, she's excited," Vanessa said, smiling at her friend.

"She's called me, Angus, Asia, and La Patroness, and we haven't been here a day," Shyla said, throwing up her hands.

"This is her only shot, so she wants it a certain way," Vanessa said.

"But we're the ones mating, not her," Shyla said, cupping Angus' chin. "It's okay if you indulge in in-law jokes, I won't be offended. She's a handful."

He kissed her forehead and wrapped his arm around her neck. "As long as she's not crazy like the Wernhers, we'll be fine."

"No one's like that. What happened to Cancer?" Silas asked Angus.

"Ran away. If Gilbert hadn't found him, we'd probably never see him again. Did they get all the information on Asia?" Angus looked at Hawke.

"I took care of it," Hawke said, picking up his mate's hand.

"Oh, I meant to tell you, Lilly's pregnant. She called this morning with the good news. They'd been trying and she didn't want to get her hopes up again. But the doctor confirmed it," Jasmine said, lifting her coffee cup in a toast.

"Wonderful news," Asia said.

Vanessa frowned. "Is she the one you said had seven already?"

Jasmine cleared her throat and smiled. "Yes, yes, she does."

"Oh," Vanessa looked at Ethan.

Laughing, he stood and pulled her to her feet. "Thanks again for everything. We'll be getting on the road to head back to Maryland." They waved and left the room.

Angus stood and extended his hand to his mate. "Silas, I'm taking a leave of absence to bond with my mate. I'll send you the date of the mating ceremony."

Smiling, Shyla bent to place a kiss on Jasmine's cheek. "Thanks for everything. I appreciate it."

"Thank you," Jasmine said, watching them walk away. "I wasn't pushy, Silas."

"No, you were a tyrant. Cain and Abel are still quaking in their boots."

"Tell him, Hawke."

"You did attack the Goddess," Hawke reminded her. "Few people would even think of doing that."

"Should I call you Sweet Tyrant or Bitch Tyrant?" Silas asked, teasing.

"Neither. Call me yours and we'll call it even." Jasmine leaned forward and kissed him before he could respond.

Chapter 33

Angus stepped into the garden decorated with lavender and cream ribbons and flowers. He looked at the chairs filled with guests, many he knew, some he didn't and nodded greetings.

Silas walked up behind him and slapped him on the back. "Glad to see you're awake. After last night with Cain, Abel and those kegs I thought I'd have to carry you in here today."

Angus chuckled. Last night had been fun, he hadn't seen Silas in a month. Shyla's mother kidnapped him to prepare for the mating ceremony and to assist her in moving back to the house to reclaim her duties as Mengistia until Shyla could return. Based on what Shyla told him about her mom's feelings for the house, he agreed sitting through planning sessions and fittings were a fair trade.

"I woke with the sun. Nothing could've kept me away from this today. I've waited a lifetime for my Shyla." He smiled at Silas. "She's my heart."

Silas grinned. "She's a perfect match for you, I couldn't be happier. Shyla and Jasmine have redone your rooms. Everything will be ready when you return home."

"Shyla told me. She's excited to live in the compound and wants to start our den right away. I never thought I'd have all this." He extended his arms at decorated garden, reception tent and all their guests. "This is beyond anything I could ever imagine."

"Shyla's family did a great job." Silas looked around. "Come on, it's time to take our places for the ceremony."

Angus cleared his throat and walked toward the dais. Grandfather stood on the stand prepared to officiate the ceremony. In the past month, Angus and Silas met with the old man separately to get a better understanding of what happened in Plias. Chancellor had misled them all in a ploy to get back at the men who used her. The Goddess relieved the brokenhearted woman of her duties and sent her away to heal. Now that Shershrine knew all their secrets, grandfather decided to come out of the shadows and made plans to be more involved with his seed.

"Ready?" Grandfather asked Angus.

"Since day one," Angus said eager to finish formalizing his relationship with his mate. Although they'd slept together every night since their return, as far as his in-laws were concerned, today was the day he claimed their daughter as his mate. Since it was important to Shyla, it was important to him.

Standing next to him as witness, Jasmine called it best man, Silas chuckled as the music started.

Jasmine was the first attendant to walk down the aisle, followed by Vanessa. Both wore wide smiles in lavender and cream dresses.

David and Adam, dressed in black suits, walked up the aisle carrying velvet gift boxes containing a gift the mates chose for each other. They stood next to their mom.

Jackie, Sarita and Renee dropped silk flower petals from baskets as they walked up the aisle in lavender dresses.

"Hi Uncle Angus," Jackie said waving at him when they reached the dais.

"Hello, my beauties," Angus said winking at them. The music changed.

Angus' heart clutched as Shyla stood at the end of the aisle wearing a lavender gown that fit her like a glove. She was so beautiful, he couldn't help but stare as her parents walked her toward him. A true gift of love.

Ignoring everyone, he met her halfway, took her in his arms and thoroughly kissed her. Her arms tightened around his neck as he pulled her close, never wanting to let her go. They broke apart gasping for air. He touched her forehead with his own. They stood in the middle of the ceremony, committing their lives to each other through touch.

"Whenever you're ready," Grandfather said.

Angus took her hand and escorted her to the dais. "Let's get this done." The crowd laughed, several howled and within ten minutes this part of the mating ceremony was done. They decided not to have the full pageantry of well-wishing, toasts, and long talks.

When they finished their meals, the music started. Angus pulled Shyla onto the dance floor, held her close and promised to never let her go.

"I love you, Angus Blackwolf," Shyla whispered.

Hearing her say those words never got old and he doubted they ever would. "I love you too, Shyla Mason-Blackwolf."

Hello,

I love paranormal books and characters in general and shifter stories in particular. Throw in the romantic element, strong Alpha characters who bend beneath the power of love and I'm over the moon. Sighs…

Thank you for taking the time to read Angus, La Patron's brother's story. So many people have asked to have his story told and I hope you have enjoyed Shyla and Angus. It's not everyday a goddess is tricked into doing something she knows will have serious repercussions for the wolf nation. But Chancellor pulls some fancy footwork and almost destroys Silas and Jasmine. Good thing Angus and his mate have their Alpha's back.

You're invited to journey with me through all the books in this series. If you like fast paced action, suspense and great love connections like me, you won't be disappointed. Feel free to drop me a line, SydneyAddae@msn.com or join my Facebook group, La Patron's Den, where discussions regarding Silas and the Wolf nation abound. Also you can find me at my website, SydneyAddae.com.

Knight Chronicles is a newsletter for my Readers Group from the characters of the series to keep you informed of what's going on in the Wolf Nation. Each issue has a personal message from Silas Knight, La Patron, or his mate, Jasmine. Character profiles with in-depth interviews and thoughts you won't find anywhere else. Also works in progress, new releases and special give-aways in every issue. If you would like to receive **Knight Chronicles** click this sign up link! Thank you. (http://eepurl.com/bb3csz)

La Patron, the Alpha's Alpha is my first paranormal series and I'd like to ask a favor. When you finish reading, **please leave a review**, whatever your opinion, I assure you I appreciate it.

Thanks again
Sydney

BirthRight
BirthControl
BirthMark
BirthStone
BirthDate
BirthSign
Sword of Inquest
Sword of Mercy
Sword of Justice
La Patron's Christmas
La Patron's 2nd Christmas
La Patron's New Year – Leigh West, Catherine Marsh
KnightForce 1
KnightForce Deuces
KnightForce Tres'
KnightForce Damian
KnightForce Ethan

Angus

Booksets
La Patron Series Books 1-6
La Patron Series Books 4-6
Sword Series Books 1-3

Bear With Me – Bear Mountain Patrol
Jewel's Bear – Bear Mountain Patrol

Last in Line- Vampire Story

Jackie's Journey – La Patron's Den – Book 1
Awakening the Alpha, Adam – La Patron's Den – Book 2